OFF *the* CUFF

USA TODAY BESTSELLING AUTHOR

K.I. LYNN

IBSN: 978-1-948284-31-8

Cover design by T.E. Black Designs
Photo credit: TheCoverLab.com

Editor:
Evident Ink
Marti Lynch
Danielle Leigh

Publication Date: January 11, 2021
Genre: FICTION/Romance/Contemporary
ISBN-13: 978-1948284301

OFF *the* CUFF

Prologue

I rocked the baby in my arms, trying to settle her down. Was she hungry? Did she have a dirty diaper?

My heart sped up as I stared down at her scrunched-up face. What was I thinking?

Panic began to settle in. Only four hours had passed since Social Services called and told me I had a niece. Then, they told me I had to take the baby, or she was going into foster care. Did I let someone else take her? The decision had been a total gut reaction—of course I'd take her.

I wasn't even aware that my little sister, Ryn, was pregnant, but I hadn't seen my sister in six months. Not since her last appearance, when she was strung out and desperate for money.

Was she pregnant then? I did the math and began to shake as anger filled me. For years Ryn had chosen drugs over everything, and it seemed having a baby had done nothing to change that.

She ran. Left the hospital and was gone. Disappearing into another crack den.

"Are you hungry?" I asked the tiny baby in my arms. The baby girl didn't even have a name. My sister couldn't even do that for her.

Once again, because my sister was addicted to drugs, I was left trying to pick up the pieces.

The baby let out another high-pitched cry, deepening the vibrations inside me. What had I gotten myself into? I knew nothing about babies, and in one afternoon, I had one.

Tears filled my eyes as well and I blew out an unsteady breath.

Thankfully, Social Services was able to provide me with some staples to get me by, but I was going to be spending all night on Amazon one-clicking the crap out of the baby section.

It was only Tuesday. What was I going to do about work in the morning? I'd found a job that I loved and had an amazing boss, but how was he going to react when I suddenly had to take time off? Did I even qualify for any type of family leave?

The suddenness of my parenthood was going to be a huge adjustment, and I needed to strategize. That would have to wait until after I talked to my boss.

If I wasn't a hyperventilating mess by then.

The biggest hurdle would be my boyfriend, Pete.

In the four years we'd been together we'd talked about our future, about getting married and having kids, but in all that time he'd never done anything to make it happen.

Every time I brought it up, he came back with some excuse. *"We're still young, Roe. We've got time."*

A vibrating buzz moved through my veins and worry crawled in. I began to second guess myself, but another little grunt from the bundle in my arms tugged at my heart and reminded me that no matter what, she was worth it.

The door lock clicked and I turned toward the entry, my stomach in knots. Pete stopped mid-step, his brown eyes wide.

"What the hell is that crying?" Pete said as he stared at the baby in my arms. "Are you babysitting?"

"Hey, babe."

He glanced around the room, his eyes bouncing to the bags lying on the floor. "Explain," he said as he scowled at the baby in my arms.

I knew that tone. After years together I'd heard all of his intonations, and the hard edge and sharp snap of the word through clenched teeth told me that this conversation was not going to go well.

"This is my niece," I said, turning the baby to show him her face in hopes it would tame him.

"Ryn had a baby?" he asked, then looked at her, his mouth turned down.

"And she's going to live here."

His eyes widened. "Here? With us?"

I swallowed hard. "Yes."

He shook his head. "No. Call Ryn and tell her to come pick her brat up."

"Pete! What the heck?" I knew where he was coming from. Ryn had dumped problems on our doorstep many times over the past few years, but this wasn't the same. This was a baby who needed me. An innocent who needed help.

"Where the hell are we going to put a baby? This apartment is barely big enough for the two of us."

While the Lenox Hill apartment we were living in was larger than our previous apartment, it was still a small one-bedroom—New York City living at its finest.

"I don't know, but we can figure it out."

He shook his head. "No. No, it can't stay here."

"She has nowhere else to go," I said through clenched teeth. There was no discussion—she was staying.

"I don't give a crap. It's not our problem! Let someone else deal with it."

I lifted my chin and shook my head. "She's family. I'm not going to give her to strangers."

His gaze narrowed. "It's not staying."

"Pete, please," I said in an attempt to steer the conversation away from the full-blown explosion it was about to become.

Over the years we'd had it out only a few times, but as we went back and forth now, I noticed how this was the most worked up either of us had become in months.

He shook his head. "No, Roe."

"We can't even talk about it?" I asked.

"What is there to talk about? I don't want a kid right now, especially not your crackhead sister's!"

"What are you saying?" I asked. The crack forming in my heart knew the answer.

Surely the man I'd lived with since college, the first man I'd ever loved, wasn't about to make me decide, make me choose between him and a completely helpless little girl.

"What I'm saying is that it's that thing or me."

And there it was—the ultimatum. The one I knew was coming. Somehow I'd still convinced myself that Pete wasn't going to disappoint me. I needed clarification.

"You're asking me to abandon my two-week-old niece?"

He crossed his arms in front of me and sneered at the baby. "I'm telling you that if you don't give it back, I'm out."

I couldn't believe it. My stomach dropped as I looked at him. Really looked at him. His brown hair was an unkempt as always, brown eyes narrowed, and the sleeves of his dress shirt were rolled up, exposing a string of tattoos. To me he was tall, but he was more than a couple inches shorter than six feet. However, in this stance he seemed larger and more imposing.

Trust didn't come naturally to me. I had reasons, shaped from my life experiences, and I often held a part of myself back. I had one foot out the door at all times. And yet, after years with Pete, I'd silently given him the benefit of the doubt. Believed that our relationship was solid in ways I hadn't before.

A large part of me, deep down, knew the minute the social worker explained my options that somehow this exact situation was coming. Pete's response further hardened my heart.

Internally, I could almost feel our connection severing and the one with the baby in my arms growing stronger. I wasn't letting her go. Not for him or anyone.

"You can't mean that," I said.

"I'm dead serious, Roe. I don't want your sister's problem. She's caused us enough issues over the years, or do you not remember giving her our fucking rent money for rehab, only for her to leave three days later?" He leaned in, his eyes slits. "Besides, you're just not worth all of this."

There it was, the real reason he wasn't okay helping me to care for my sister's child. The words were a punch to the gut, then a deep scrape in my chest as they burned into my heart.

My shoulders dropped, and I unknowingly curled tighter around the innocent child I held.

"Excuse me, what? I'm not *worth* it?" I asked, seething. I was always the good little girlfriend. Went along with just about anything he wanted to do. That was partially due to my desire to be wanted and also because I was normally a pretty easygoing person.

Most of the time.

But he'd just pushed me past acquiescing.

My whole body shook, but when I spoke, it was with a vicious-edged calm. "So if I told you I was pregnant, what then? Would you tell me to get rid of it?"

"That's different, and you fucking know it," he growled.

"Then, if I took her back, I could go off birth control and we could have a baby?" I asked, forcing him to answer honestly.

He froze, his jaw twitching. "I'm not ready for that."

"And I'm not ready for this," I hissed. "But guess what? Life doesn't always make you ready for things."

"I love you, baby, but this—" he waved his hand at the baby in my arms "—isn't happening. Not with me. I'm not staying."

A harsh laugh left me. "You fucking selfish bastard. You love me?" I scoffed and rolled my eyes. We were finally at the pinnacle of what had been building under the surface for a long time. "I'm sure you haven't even kept it in your pants the last four months."

We hadn't had sex in longer than that, which made me wonder—if he wasn't getting it with me, who was he getting it from? By the pink mark on his neck, it was his coworker, Jennifer. I'd watched them flirting at the holiday party his work had the year before. He denied it then, but things had definitely cooled off between us after that.

"I'm selfish? You didn't even talk to me about this. And you don't know what you're talking about as far as my fucking dick is concerned."

"Would it have changed anything?" I asked, my teeth gritted.

"It still would have been fucking no."

Again, there it was. The truth. We'd become too comfortable, and our relationship was stagnant. No longer growing or evolving.

It was still difficult to process that it had come to this. That he wanted to throw our relationship away because of a baby. Though I knew that wasn't true. We'd been building to this, but he was too much of a fucking coward to break up. The baby was an excuse he was taking full advantage of.

"Then I think it's time for you to go," I said through clenched teeth.

"You're making a mistake, picking that over me," he sneered.

Another harsh laugh escaped. "I think my mistake was thinking we ever had a future."

He stood there fuming before he turned and stormed into the bedroom. After quickly packing a suitcase, he hit up the bathroom, then came back into the room and picked up his laptop. I never moved from where I was standing as my relationship crumbled around my feet.

"I'll be back for the rest," he said as he walked to the door and threw on his coat. He turned back and stared at me. "Last chance."

My eyes locked with his. "Get out."

He turned and walked out, the door slamming behind him. As soon as he was gone, I let loose a sob as the silence soaked in.

The baby started to cry with me, and I pulled her close and pressed my lips to her forehead.

"It's okay," I whispered to the tiny baby in my arms as tears slipped down my cheeks. "We don't need him. We'll be okay."

Pete's decision hurt. Badly. Regardless of whether I held part of myself back from him or not, we'd spent so many years together. His response to the precious newborn was the last straw. It forced us both to see our relationship for what it had become.

I should have known I couldn't trust him. Looking back at our relationship, I knew he'd let me down in so many ways—from failing to pick me up after I had my wisdom teeth removed, to small things like using all the towels and not washing them.

None of that mattered now.

Still, I mourned the loss.

It was going to be hard, but once I had her in my arms, I knew I was never letting her go.

One

Roe

10 months later...

"Craaaap," I whined as I glanced at my watch—late again. I was still wiping formula spit-up off my shirt as I stepped onto the elevator. Why did I decide to wear white today? After only three or four hours of inconsistent sleep, I was lucky to be standing.

Thank you, espresso machine.

Kinsey had kept me up half the night—more teething, but hopefully it was the last of it for a while.

When I took on the guardianship of my niece, it was sink or swim. This was a sink kind of day, and to top it off, it was Monday.

It could only get better, right?

Oh, the lies I told myself. Even as I thought about it, I laughed.

It was fifteen minutes after eight when I flew out of the elevator toward my desk. I flashed a glance at Matt's office as I ran by, but he wasn't there.

Shit.

The moment I hit my cube, my bag was on the ground and I was waking my computer up.

"Late again, I see," Matt said from behind me.

I jumped and cursed as I turned to look at my boss. "I'm sorry."

He waved me off. "You know the drill by now."

I nodded and smiled at him. "Short lunch for me today!"

I had an arrangement due to my situation—as long as I got my hours in each day, I was good. However, that often led to working through my lunch breaks.

"Maybe I could use you later to pick up my lunch for me?"

I nodded and let out a sigh of relief. Maybe the day wouldn't be so bad after all.

Picking up Matt's lunch wasn't a punishment like many in the office thought it was. I wasn't reduced to acting assistant or anything. In fact, my boss was one of the few people who knew why I was often late, even if it was only a few minutes most of the time.

By picking up his lunch, it ensured that I would also get a meal, but purchased on company time, not using my extremely limited break for lunch. It was a break I was bound to work through anyway.

"Thanks."

He tapped his hand on the top of my cube wall. "Don't forget to get that new social media pitch in today."

"You'll have it this afternoon."

For two years I'd worked at Donovan Trading and Investment in the marketing department. It was a great company, and I actually loved my job. It helped that the owner happened to be a friend. I'd met James Donovan and his wife, Lizzie, a few years prior in the emergency room—me with my sister and them with their daughter, Bailey.

We'd struck up conversation that turned into a great friendship—one of the few that survived the last ten months.

It was due to our friendship that I'd learned about the opening in the marketing department. While it was my friend's company, the only help I received was the link to submit my resume.

Lizzie was my rock those first few months with Kinsey, as she had a six-month-old at the time. I couldn't thank her enough for helping to keep me sane.

My pitch was ninety-five percent complete, and I spent the next few hours combing over it, fine-tuning my ideas.

At noon, I received a text from Matt with his order, and I saved my work before seeing his assistant, January, for his credit card.

When I stepped into the elevator, I smashed my finger into the wall, misjudging the distance.

"Ouch!" I cried out. I looked down to my middle finger and the cracked nail. Crap.

I shook my hand, hoping that would make the pain fade faster.

It had been nearly a year since I'd gotten a manicure, and I desperately missed them.

After dropping off Matt's lunch, I returned to my desk with my own meal in hand.

I wasted no time stuffing my face with the Cuban sandwich, which smelled delicious, and I was halfway through when a glob of mustard dripped out and onto my shirt.

"Shit," I hissed. Immediately I tried to wipe it away, which only made it smear. A groan of frustration left me, and I threw the napkins down and picked my sandwich back up.

After finishing the last few bites, I headed to the bathroom in hopes that I could get the yellow smear out of my white top. Some cold water, paper towels, and two minutes later, it was still there.

I threw my head back. "For fuck's sake." A half laugh, half cry left me, and I huffed before trying again.

It wasn't coming out. I knew it, the mustard knew it, and so did my shirt.

I gave up and returned to my desk, opening the bottom drawer to pull out my spare shirt, only to find the space empty. A groan left me, and I banged my head against my desk.

A similar disaster had hit last week, and I'd used my backup and apparently forgot to bring another one back.

"Fantastic," I hissed just as my calendar app chimed.

Up popped an event reminder, and I glanced at the clock. There were only fifteen minutes until my one o'clock meeting with Matt and Donte. Thankfully, I just had the re-read of my social media pitch to deal with after that.

I cleaned up my mess before detaching my laptop, grabbing my water, and heading to Matt's office. As soon as I entered, Donte gave me a sad smile.

"Rough day?"

A whimper left me. "Tell me it gets easier."

He patted my arm. "It does, and it will. Teething?"

I nodded. "I think I maybe got two solid hours of sleep and a few cat-naps."

Donte was another of the few people who knew about Kinsey. It wasn't that I was keeping her a secret per se, but I only interacted with a few people in my department. I didn't feel the need to scream out that I suddenly had a baby.

Donte had two kids himself, so he understood.

"Sorry about that," Matt said as he rushed in and got settled back at his desk. "How's everyone's day today?" He looked me up and down, then shook his head at my new stain.

"Yeah, it's that good," I said with a chuckle. Because if I didn't laugh, I might cry from exhaustion.

"Get some sleep tonight," Matt directed.

"Can you tell the ten-month-old that? Because she doesn't seem to agree."

Both men chuckled.

Matt drummed his hands on his desktop. "Okay. The boss wants us to draw up some materials for the initial public announcement of the Worthington Exchange takeover. He wants their customers to be reassured and excited about the changes."

"Print graphics? Commercials? What media are we talking about?" I asked in an attempt to get a handle on the scope while tamping down the excitement buzzing through me.

"All."

My eyes widened. "That is a huge undertaking."

"Which is why I'm giving it to you two. You're going to hand over a lot of your other commitments to Liza and Mateo. This will be your focus."

Donte nodded. "Sounds good."

Matt drummed his hands on his desk again. "All right, get to it. Roe's getting me the social media proposal and Donte's got the editorial in by..."

"Tomorrow afternoon," Donte replied.

"Excellent. Off you go," Matt said, shooing us from the room.

"We should nab some time in one of the conference rooms this week," Donte said as soon as we were out of the door and headed back to our desks.

I nodded in agreement. "Definitely." They always seemed to fill up fast, and we would need a few hours each day to talk things out without disturbing people working around us.

"Now to finish up this social media pitch and figure out what information I need to send with these other projects."

"Want me to go over the pitch for you?"

"Would you mind? I'd really appreciate it." I reattached my laptop to the docking station and woke my computer up. "I've spent the last two weeks on it and could really use another set of eyes."

"No problem. This is just for ads, right?"

I nodded. "Facebook. Twitter. Instagram." My eyes narrowed at the screen. Something wasn't right. I'd enlarged the top font earlier in the day, and it was smaller. I scrolled down, and a few other things I'd changed were also missing.

A prickle of panic shot through me, and my stomach dropped.

"No. No, no, no." My eyes were wide as my breath left me. I saved before I left. I knew I did, but it was back to the point of my arrival that morning. "I saved before lunch, but all those updates are gone!"

"Calm down," Donte said over my shoulder. "We'll find it."

"I will seriously cry if it's gone," I said, on the verge of tears as I sat back to let him get closer. I couldn't even think straight, and I was thankful Donte was there with a clear mind.

He leaned over me, focused on a list of files. It was a few minutes before he clicked on one. "I think I found it," he said.

The file popped open, and I gave a huge sigh when I saw a more recent update. As I scrolled through, I noticed it wasn't to the point it was when I left for lunch, but it was closer.

"Almost, but a lot better than that other one."

"It's a large file. You may have closed it down before it finished saving."

That made sense. I was rushing to get out to pick up lunch. "My fault, then." I looked at him and gave him a strained smile. "Thank you so much."

"Is it too far off from where you were?" he asked, scanning the file along with me.

I shook my head. "No, but it still stings, given the day I've had, and this delays me more."

"It'll be okay," he said as he straightened. "Take a few deep breaths, get some coffee, and maybe put in your earbuds to drown everything out."

"That sounds like a great idea."

He smiled down at me. "About time to recognize."

A laugh left me, and I rolled my eyes. "All right, you've got mad skills."

"That's what I'm talking about."

"Thank you again, Donte. So much."

He grinned at me. "I got you, dog."

After he stepped away, I took a more in-depth look at the proposal. Thankfully, I didn't lose much. The only reprieve to my day.

I made a few alterations, staring at the screen until a yawn rolled through me.

Coffee time.

When I got to the break room, I let out a whine at the empty pot sitting on the burner. Why didn't the person who took the last cup make a new pot? We were all coffee addicts; it wasn't like it was going to go to waste.

As I prepared a new pot, another yawn moved through me. I prayed that sleep would fill my night.

I leaned over the counter of the break room, watching the pot of coffee slowly fill. The smell of the fresh brew lifted my spirits, and it helped me knowing soon I'd have a delicious cup in hand that would help me get through the next few hours.

"Are you okay, Roe?" January asked.

I blew out a breath and turned to her. "It's the worst case of the Mondays. Please tell me it will get better. *Lie* if you have to."

"Oh, sweetie." Her gaze moved down my shirt. "It will get better. Stay here. I'll be right back."

Before I could ask or have her just meet me at my desk, she was gone.

My eyes drooped for a second, heavy as afternoon drowsiness hit and combined with my already tired state. After ten months of caring for my baby niece, you'd think I'd have the perpetual lack of sleep down to an art form, but alas, it wasn't so. There was no such thing as getting used to operating on just a few broken hours of sleep. A quick intake of breath and some blinks shook me awake, at least for a moment.

While I spaced out, the dripping of the coffee subsided and I poured a cup. The smell was divine, and I pulled a container from the fridge. I loved to mix in some premade cold mocha to cool it down faster and make it even yummier. I took a sip of my coffee, a moan leaving me. Perfect.

In my tuned-out state, I wasn't aware there was someone behind me. As I turned, my elbow caught his outstretched arm. The jostle sent a wave of coffee over the lip of the mug. Hot, dark liquid splashed across my hand and the clothing covering the person behind me.

My eyes were wide as my body bowed back to avoid more of it landing on me, my hand stinging from the warmth. Thankfully the mocha had cooled it down some.

"Oh, crap. I am so sorry!" My shit day that was having a brighter moment just got even worse.

"Fucking incompetent twit!" he spat as he grabbed for some paper towels.

My mouth dropped open. "I am so sorry," I apologized again, my brain stuck in blame-taking mode even though his words were grating on me. It could also be partially blamed on the hotness towering over me.

The man before me with his whip of a tongue was just as lashing with his looks. I'd seen him around before. Who wouldn't have noticed that razor line of a jaw, stunning blue eyes, dark hair, or his perfect body in a suit that had to be custom made?

He may have starred in a fantasy or two of mine, but that was to be expected with a man like him.

My gaze caught on the flicker of his black cuff links as they glimmered with each swipe of his hand. They struck me as odd and off brand from what little personality I'd built up in my head.

"Sorry doesn't fix this," he growled at me.

He was pissed, and for some reason, that was funny to me. Of course Mr. Too-Sexy-For-His-Suit had a bad attitude. It was an accident. If he'd done something as simple as alerting me to his presence behind me, it wouldn't have happened.

Past his looks, I knew who he was in name only, but our encounter showed me that it was more than enough.

"It was an accident. If anyone is at fault, it's you for sneaking up on me."

He glared down at me, taking in my stained shirt, and tsked.

"You are incompetent," he sneered as he brushed a wet paper towel against his shirt.

Incompetent?

The word repeated in my mind as I stared at him.

The day had been long, the challenges hard, and I had battle scars in the form of the discoloration of my shirt to prove it.

The vein on my forehead throbbed, and the anger that simmered under my frustration of the day boiled over.

I'd had a shit day, and he was the icing on that cake. Icing I didn't want. I already had formula, mustard, and coffee.

Fuck. Him.

I narrowed my gaze at him before extending my arm and tipping my cup, splashing another dark stain onto the very expensive, fitted suit he filled out so well.

"Oops." I smiled, watching the brown soak into the white of his dress shirt before heading to the doorway where January was standing, a detergent pen in her hand, jaw dropped as she witnessed what just happened.

"Thanks," I said as I snatched the pen from her, ignoring the death glare being burned into the back of my head.

Well, my day didn't get better, but I sure felt better after that.

Two

Roe

His words played out in my mind long after I'd left work for the day. Even though the night went by without a peep, I couldn't move past the feelings he inspired in me. Was I truly inadequate, or was he just a dick?

It seemed maybe Kinsey was just as tired as I was. After dinner, she passed out and so did I.

In the morning, I felt refreshed and was determined to have a better day than the day before. I'd been able to get my social media pitch in, and I was going to start the day out passing off projects before meeting with Donte in the afternoon.

It was a new day, and I was excited for my new assignment.

When I arrived at my desk, there was obviously something wrong—my laptop was missing. Everything else was where I left it, but in place of my company laptop was a simple blank Donovan Trading and Investment business card. Instead of an employee's information, neat handwriting in all capital letters spelled out—YOU'RE MINE.

I stared down at the words, trying to understand their meaning.

First thing I needed to do was to find out where my laptop had run away to. I often took it home, but I knew there was no way I was getting work done after the shit day I'd had.

A knock to my boss's open door drew his attention, and he looked up.

"Morning," he said as he waved me in. "Great job on that pitch."

His compliment did little to settle my nerves, which were strangely on edge. "Where's my computer?"

He froze, then cleared his throat. "Ah, about that. You've been reassigned."

I froze. "Reassigned? What does that mean?" I demanded.

He held up his hands. "It's just temporary."

"Why?"

He let out a sigh and rubbed at the back of his neck. I liked Matt, he was a good guy to work for, but something was off.

"Because you had a bad day yesterday and pissed off an exec, and the whole office heard about it. You know how gossip is."

The simmering anger morphed into a stone sitting in the pit of my stomach, growing larger and denser with each passing second. The asshole was an executive. Figured, with the expensive suit and sexy scowl.

I knew my behavior was wrong, but the man didn't need to respond the way he did. Accidents happened, and he'd hit the right nerve on the wrong day. No regrets or anything, but I knew what was happening was punishment.

"How is this even possible? I'm in Marketing!"

"He's the President of Acquisitions. The Worthington take-over takes precedent. He needs help, and he has decided you are the one to fill that role."

"What about *my* Worthington project?"

"Donte will become lead, and you will assist. I've worked it out that you will still be able to work on it some while helping Carthwright."

Some.

Anger coursed through me. I'd worked so hard to get where I was. The prestige of such a project would greatly help my career—only now the credit I'd hoped to receive might not come, affecting my evaluations and raises for years to come.

All for a couple of drops of coffee.

And then a lot more when that pretty mouth of his started insulting me.

"He's waiting for you."

I shook my head. "I'm not going to be some asshole's gopher as punishment for an accident."

He stared at me, his eyebrow raised, and I rolled my eyes in response.

"Please, Roe. I promise you it's temporary. Everything will be back to normal in no time."

"No," I said as I shook my head.

"There's only one other choice in the matter, and I know with your situation you don't want to take it."

He hit a nerve there. No way was I able to just quit. Taking care of Kinsey had drained a lot of my savings over the last year. While I did get assistance from the state and she was on Medicaid, without Pete paying half the rent, the full amount fell on me.

That, and babies were expensive.

And so were cute baby clothes.

"I can't believe this is happening."

"You'll be back in no time and can jump right back in with Donte."

"This isn't fair."

"You, more than many, know that life is rarely fair."

I nodded. I'd made my bed and I would lie in it, albeit unwillingly.

I returned to my desk and got my bag. If I needed anything

else, I could always come back, but for now, I was going to go meet with the asshole ruining my life.

I blew out a breath to calm myself.

You put yourself in this position, I reminded myself. Only I was to blame for my actions, but I still couldn't believe he'd taken it so far.

I could feel the strain on the muscles of my face from the frown of disgust I was wearing. I'd never really ventured to this side of the building. There just wasn't a need, which probably explained why I'd never really seen him but on occasion. Then again, Donovan Trading and Investment occupied three floors, and I'd only seen two because I was always at my desk.

The laptop was sitting on the desk right outside his office. With it were two monitors, one attached to the desktop for his assistant, I gathered. Maybe I'd have more time than I thought if he had the foresight to set up a second workstation.

Then again, Matt did say he got Carthwright to allow me to also work on my regular work. It would be slow, but at least for some of the day I could forget where I was.

"Come on in," a deep, smooth voice called from the door behind me.

I took a breath in and a breath out before I turned and stepped inside, my fists clenching and unclenching with each step. Steps that faltered when my eyes met his.

I knew he was good looking, but seeing him up close, getting my first real good look at him, I was stunned. He went past the fantasy version I'd built. I didn't remember him to be show-stopping attractive. The glower he was shooting me only intensified his gorgeous eyes and the angles of his face. His dark hair was very short on the sides and longer on top and was perfectly swept back.

"Miss Pierce," Carthwright said as I stopped a few feet from the edge of his desk.

"It's Roe," I said as I crossed my arms in front of me, my hip cocking to the side as I shifted my weight—a movement that didn't go unnoticed by him.

His gaze locked on mine. "I'm well aware. Do you know who I am?"

"The suit I bumped into by *accident* and unfortunately splashed some coffee onto."

"Anything else?"

"Carthwright." *The Assholian*. I snickered internally.

He leaned back, his eyes still studying me. "I'm the President of Acquisitions. Do you know what that means?"

I sighed and shifted my weight again, cocking the other hip. Talking to me like I was stupid was my biggest pet peeve. "You're working the Worthington takeover."

"That was an expensive suit."

"Was?" I quirked a brow. "Did I sully it and you had to put it out of its misery?"

The fuck-me eyes of his glowered at me again, but I caught the uptick of his lip. His full, kissable lips.

Get ahold of yourself, Roe!

"Feisty. Yes, I can work with that."

Feisty?

I wasn't sure what his game was, but I'd never had someone get under my skin so easily or fast. I knew better than to accept people at face value. I also knew I couldn't trust them as far as I could throw them. And Thane Carthwright? Well, I didn't think I could even get that man a centimeter off the ground.

He was easily over a foot taller than my even five feet.

"Why am I here?" I asked in an attempt to steer my thoughts away from the god-like man in front of me.

Why did it have to be him?

He ignored my question and continued on. "You are mine now. You work beneath me, and I'm going to hold you there until I'm satisfied," he said with a smirk, his voice smooth and confident.

His words combined with the way he was looking at me flipped a switch I hadn't felt in a while, and heat flooded my face.

The prickle only grew under his scrutiny. The navy blue suit he was wearing only made his eyes pop more, especially with the added bright blue cuff links.

His face had been clean shaven the day before, but today there was a light sheen of scruff. It did nothing to detract from how handsome he was, and I really needed something to detract from that.

What the hell?

"I'm your boss now. You will listen to me and do as I say." His eyes never left mine, and I swallowed hard. "Your future is in my hands."

I clenched my jaw, pissed that he'd gotten the upper hand. His attitude irked me, and I knew I was going to have to leave friendly Roe at the door in order to deal with the ass in front of me.

"Where is your assistant?" I asked in an attempt to gain back some of the ground I'd lost. He wasn't going to walk all over me.

His mouth turned down. "My assistant decided a baby was more important than her job, and she's out."

I thanked the heavens for that cold splash of water, because with one sentence I was miraculously cured from whatever had a hold of me.

"You're pissy because she's on maternity leave?" I asked for clarification.

"For nine more weeks," he grumbled.

I had trouble with my patience and my tongue. "The woman has to heal and bond with her new baby," I said, unable to hold back all the anger in my tone.

Another thing that didn't go unnoticed by the man, and his

brow quirked at me. He called me feisty, and I was going to show him just how feisty I could be.

"She could have made it three weeks and you wouldn't be standing in front of me."

My eyes widened as his words hit close to home. I'd only had three weeks with Kinsey when I first took her in, and I knew it was not enough time. "Wow, and I wasn't sure I could dislike you more."

"I don't care whether or not you like me—you're mine until she returns, so go do your job."

"And what is that, exactly?"

"First is to stop glaring at me."

A harsh laugh left me. "That's going to be a hard one."

His eyes narrowed, but otherwise he ignored me. "Your job is to make mine run smoothly. And you will start that by answering the phone by the second ring and refilling my coffee when my cup is empty. There is a binder sitting on your desk filled with all the information you need. Since you are already familiar with the company and the programs, there is no learning curve there. Get it right."

Yesterday he had called me incompetent, and today he demonstrated that time hadn't improved his perception of me. I knew it wouldn't matter if it had been twenty-four hours, days, or months, it wouldn't change. Thane Carthwright was a complete jackass.

A jackass who believed I was inept and unqualified for any job.

The decision upon me now was whether I would continue to feed that belief, or was I going to knock him on his fucking ass?

Maybe I could accomplish both.

"Yes, sir," I ground out and turned to leave.

"Oh, and by the way, you'll need to wear a blazer."

I stopped and swirled back around. "Why?"

"Because the position requires it."

"Does that mean if I don't, you'll fire me from this position and I'll go back to my *real* job?"

His jaw ticked and his lips formed a thin line. "No."

"Are you going to buy me these blazers?" I asked.

"No."

I smiled at him. "Then no, I'm not going to wear one." I spun back around and continued my path out the door.

I sighed as I gave the desk a look of disgust, then sat down and opened the binder.

Surely, I was in hell.

It didn't take long before his phone began to ring, but I didn't pay much attention to it. I was still reading the extremely boring binder. It circumvented itself so many times, it was no wonder the temps didn't work out. I was having trouble deciphering it, and I'd worked for the company for years.

"Pick up the phone!" Carthwright yelled.

I huffed in annoyance before picking up the receiver. "Carthwright's office."

"Oh, hi, is Crystal there?" a female voice asked. She sounded a bit older, so I had a feeling it wasn't some strumpet. He probably had a dozen of those in the wings.

"She's out for a while. Can I help you?"

"Sorry, yes, I'm calling for Thane."

"Hold, please."

"Who is it?" Carthwright asked from behind me, making me jump.

I glared up at him. "Some woman."

"Some woman?" His jaw ticked. "First, you need to answer the phone by the second ring. Second, you say 'Thane Carthwright's office, how may I help you?' Third, you find out who is on the phone before sending it back to me."

I gave him the fakest smile I could muster. "Yes, sir." Then rolled my eyes.

We glared at each other for more than a minute before he grumbled something and walked away.

My reprieve from his attitude didn't last but a few pages of the binder when he retaliated.

Copies, coffee, filing, arranging his schedule, getting his lunch. It was midafternoon when I had two seconds to even log on to my laptop to check my company email.

The first was an email that set my blood to boil.

To: Pierce, Roe
From: Carthwright, Thane
Subject: Duties

Miss Pierce,

Perhaps my directions were not clear, so I have wasted my valuable time and spelled them out for you. Please show me you are more competent with following directions than you are with superior interaction.

1. Arrange my schedule. This means that there needs to be breaks for lunch at noon and breathing room between meetings. My day needs to flow with ease.
2. Coffee. All day my cup needs to be filled.
3. Answer the phone in two rings, and, to remind you, you will say "Thane Carthwright's office, how may I help you?" Then, make sure to find out who is on the line and notify me so that I may accept or reject the call.
4. Get my lunch. I will email you my order

so that you can place it and then pick it up. I expect to have my meal at noon every day.

5. Any and all miscellaneous functions I require—copies, filing, etc.

If any of this is unclear or if you have any questions, come to me.

Thane Carthwright
President of Acquisitions
Donovan Trading and Investment

Superior, my ass. Maybe he was my temporary supervisor, but he was not superior.

Anger rolled through me and before I knew it, I'd accidentally torn a sheet from the binder into shreds. *Crap.*

I knew I should have paid closer attention in the break room, but he should have as well. I'd apologized and I was still being punished for it.

The subject of the next email in the list had me smiling.

To: Pierce, Roe
From: Arnold, Donte
Subject: In the arms of Hades

Persephone,

I'll pray for you.

Still here, awaiting the return of spring. Awaiting the end of your imprisonment.

Stay strong.

Donte Arnold
Marketing Associate
Donovan Trading and Investment

I couldn't help but laugh, something I desperately needed. Immediately I responded, thankful for the moment that wasn't filled with animosity and annoyance.

To: Arnold, Donte
From: Pierce, Roe
Subject: Darkness envelops

Donte,

The blackness that holds me knows no end. Freedom from the cold gaze of Hades cannot arrive soon enough.

P.S. He's good looking. Maybe we can put him in some of the promotional materials or the commercial.

P.P.S. Thanks, I needed that levity.

Roe Pierce
Marketing Associate
Donovan Trading and Investment

It was only a moment before another email popped up on my screen.

To: Pierce, Roe
From: Arnold, Donte
Subject: Re: Darkness envelops

I got you, dog.

Donte Arnold
Marketing Associate
Donovan Trading and Investment

"Something amusing?" a voice called from behind me.

I had to bite my tongue from saying, "Your face," because that was beneath me and childish and completely untrue. It burned me with how untrue it was.

My reaction to his face? That tingling between my thighs every time he scowled at me? I wished that was amusing instead of incredibly hot and frustrating.

"What do you need?" I asked, failing to hide my annoyance as well as that stupid tingling he was creating.

His gaze slowly moved down my body, then back up. I was leaned back in the chair, one leg crossed over the other.

By his perusal, I expected more than the static disinterest when our eyes met. Guess he didn't like what he saw. Oh, well.

"I emailed you a contract. I need fifteen copies made, collated and stapled."

"Of course," I said with a grimace.

It didn't take long, especially when you knew how the big machine worked and knew the pathway to it. The beast did it all, and all I had to do was send the file and select how I wanted it printed.

Did Crystal know that? Or did she use it as a buffer from his arrogant ass?

Then again, there was the age-old saying—never let them know how long it really takes, because they'll want it done in half that time.

Maybe it wasn't age old, but I'd heard it from my friends who were assistants.

If I could still call them friends. I think I was the one cut from the group when Pete and I split.

I was able to go through my email and read more from the binder of doom before half an hour passed and I walked over to the copy room that held the beast.

"Hi, Sam," I said as I stepped in.

Sam was the go-to guy for any printing needs. He was a young guy, maybe twenty, shy, but he seemed to love what he did. There were a few guys I'd caught in the office teasing him about his autism, and I went all mama bear on them. Sam was sweet and was great at his job. Some assholes just liked to put people down to make their fragile egos feel better.

"Oh, hey, Roe," he replied as he stood. He walked over to a stack of papers, his brow scrunched. "What are you doing over at Thane Carthwright's office?"

A sigh left me. "Serving time."

He turned back to me, his features twisted in concern. "What?"

I shook my head. "His assistant is out and he needed someone from inside the company. I was the lucky pick."

He smiled and nodded. "You are the best pick." He held out my stack, not catching my sarcasm. "All done."

"Thank you so much," I said with a smile. "Have a good day."

He waved at me on my way out. "Bye, Roe."

I gave my desk a longing look and whimper, waving at some of my cube mates as I walked back to Carthwright's office.

He wasn't on the phone when I got back and I headed straight in.

"Your copies," I said, placing them on his desk.

He barely spared me a glance. "I need you to shred those. There was a mistake. You'll need to redo it with the updated file I sent you. Then you need to go pick up my dry cleaning from downstairs."

His dry cleaning? Was he serious?

I blew out a steadying breath before I said something really bad for my career. "I need to ask you something."

"What?" He still didn't even bother to look up at me, further irritating me.

"All this crap because I spilled coffee on you?" I asked.

He leaned back in his chair, his eyes finally on me. "If that was all, I wouldn't have bothered. I'm not a monster, but I get what I want."

"And what do you want?" I asked as I placed my hands on the top of his desk.

His gaze moved down my body, then back up. It was a subtle move, but I noticed, and unfortunately so did every inch of my skin as it lit up.

"To teach you some respect for your superiors."

"Oh, I have respect, but little for you."

His gaze hardened. "You don't even know me."

"You've shown me well enough the kind of man you are."

I took the stack of now useless papers on his desk and tossed them up into the air. They rained all around us as we continued our stare down. I had my hands flat on his desk, leaning toward him. He stood and leaned over as well, his posture mimicking my own, and our faces ended up only a foot apart.

"This is going to be fun, I see," he said, one corner of his mouth lifting into a smirk.

"Ha! And here I thought you were smart."

A delicious scent hit me when I breathed in. We hadn't been that close since I'd spilled coffee on him. Spice, with a hint of grapefruit and musk. I breathed deeper, nearly moaning at how good it was. My word, the man smelled divine. I couldn't imagine how damaging being closer would be.

My triumph and elation were marred by the heat that was spreading through my body. A little uptick of his lips, and I knew he caught me.

He straightened, and again I was aware of how he towered over me.

I bet he could easily pick me up and—

No.

I had to silence that line of thinking. It had been creeping into my thoughts all day, and his cologne only made it worse. Made him more enticing.

He was just so hot, though, and it'd been well over a year since anyone had touched me. A hate fuck sounded like a really good idea.

Get out all my pent-up anger and frustration, free me from having to think, and just feel. Lose control for an hour and be Roe again.

Up against the wall. One hand lightly choking me, the other squeezing my ass while his hips drilled into me.

"Are you listening to me?"

Huh? I blinked and focused on him again.

Fuck. Me. I'd gotten completely lost in a fantasy with the arrogant devil and ignored him.

"Should I be?" I asked, trying to cover my mistake.

"Did you just space out?" he asked.

"Yes." No sense in lying. I was certain it was obvious my mind had wandered.

His brow furrowed and he cocked his head. "Are you on something?"

I shook my head. Only high on your hotness.

Stop, Roe. Stop before you do or say something you will regret.

"Just working through a fantasy."

"A fantasy?" That perked him up, and a devilish smile crept onto his features. "Care to share with the class?"

"It involves you and a roll of duct tape across that mouth of yours."

"Am I naked?"

"Sounds about right."

A satisfied groan resonated from deep in his chest. "Then the most important question in this fantasy of yours—are you naked?"

Heat flooded my face, and I blinked at him. I looked away, unable to take his scrutinizing stare.

"Interesting."

With one word, my jaw clenched and I glared up at him. "Fuck off. I don't want anything from you. Who knows what diseases you've got."

My behavior was a bit childish, but he unnerved me and I lost the ability to think, degrading me to tactless banter.

"None. Clean bill of health just last month. Can you say the same?" he asked, smirking at me.

Heat flooded my face again and I was probably the same shade as the tomato on the salad I had for lunch. That fantasy was trying to rear its ugly, disgusting…perverted, hot, panty-wetting self again at the thought of him bare inside me.

Where the hell did that come from? I'd only ever had sex with condoms, but there was something about knowing he was clean and that I was on birth control that set something off inside me.

"You don't need to know anything about my health or sexual activity, but don't worry your pretty little head—the only thing I tested positive for is a burning hatred for you."

The only reaction I received to my spitting comment was his tongue wetting his lips. He knew he had affected me in a way I hadn't wanted or expected.

"Were you thinking about being naked with me? Thinking about my cock?"

"Arrogant ass," I grumbled before turning and stomping away.

"Miss Pierce, are you forgetting something?" His tone was light, but still held that edge of authority and assholishness.

"Pick it up yourself."

There was no way I could continue to be that close to him.

Three

Thane

Now that *was a fun sparring match,* I thought as I watched her ass sway with each step.

A groan left me as I sat, the head of my hard cock brushing against the fabric of my slacks. Our encounter had a different effect on me than it did the day before.

She made my blood boil then, but I didn't understand what that meant until just now.

Miss Pierce.

Roe.

"This situation is your own damn fault," I said, trying to calm myself before I did something rash.

She was beautiful and full of fire. Small, but feisty, with perfectly plump, kissable lips that I couldn't help but imagine wrapped around my cock, her small hand unable to fully encircle my shaft, forcing her to use both hands.

Expressive hazel eyes that captured me. I was completely enraptured by her and turned on in ways I hadn't been in years.

Luckily, it seemed I wasn't the only one struggling. The way her face flushed and she looked away told me she was just as attracted to me.

Determination settled inside me. I was hell bent on seeing just how far I could push her, how hot for me I could get her. Would she get so worked up she'd make the first move?

I shook my head in an attempt to clear it. My southern head was trying to take over, and I needed to straighten myself out and focus on my job. I knew nothing about Roe Pierce, and she knew nothing about me, but still, I found my mind wandering throughout the day. It was ending very differently than it began.

Unlike the temp who fled my presence just after lunch on Friday, Roe fought back. I was being an asshole and I knew it, owned it, and she just threw more kindling on the fire.

The day before when she'd spilled coffee on me, I'd tried all night long to get that expression of hers out of my mind. She had seemed so shy and timid as she apologized, and that, for some reason, made me angry. Not so much the stain or the heat of the liquid, but the bumbling idiot routine.

But that look. That simmering anger after I insulted her had ignited something in me. Woke me up from a haze that covered my mind.

And then she went for round two.

Now, every second she was near, I wanted to strip her clothes off and fill her with my cock. Make that smart mouth moan. Fuck this frustration into her.

Then do it again.

She intrigued me, and I knew we were putting on quite the show for the cubes that were near.

I'd made her get copies, coffee, my lunch, answer my calls—just to watch her hips or feel that glare as she stared me down. What confused and amazed me the most was the efficiency in which she completed each task. A position she knew nothing about, and yet she took it in stride, despite her anger.

Except for the phone, which she seemed to take great pleasure in using to annoy the fuck out of me.

I couldn't remember the last time I had felt more alive. We weren't talking like she was an employee and I was an executive. No, our conversations were filled with anger and sexual tension. Definitely not workplace appropriate, but I didn't give a crap that neither of us was being professional.

There was something about her, an excitement that filled me. It wasn't until today that I realized how blasé my life had become.

I enjoyed my worked, thrived on it. Nothing spurred me on like attacking until I had my way. But Roe was a person, not a company. A very beautiful, very sexy woman who had my interest from the second our eyes met.

My senses were so acutely aware of her that I found it hard to concentrate on anything. Or rather, my dick was acutely aware. It took some time for me to calm down, and when I finally got back into focus, the phone rang.

Then it rang again. I expected her to pick it up, but it rang a third time. I clenched my jaw and looked up to the doorway to find her sitting at her desk. It rang a fourth time, and I called out to her. She turned to me and raised an eyebrow.

"Get the phone," I growled out when it rang for a fifth time.

She continued to stare at me, and it rang a sixth time before she slowly picked up the receiver as a seventh ring began.

"Thane Carthwright's office," she said with little intonation.

I flexed my fingers, the frustration rippling through me.

Her attitude needed a serious adjustment. I knew she was doing it just to fuck with me. She was a quick learner, it seemed, and she'd figured out one of my pet peeves early on.

She hung the receiver up, and I waited. A minute passed, my anger climbing with each second.

I'm going to spank the shit out of her.

"Who was it?" I called out, my irritation leaking out in my tone.

"There was nobody there."

For fuck's sake, I actually felt the vein on my forehead throb. "Because you let it ring so many times!"

"Oops."

Cheeky.

She was going to test my patience. She was also going to test my strength of will to not fuck every ounce of my growing frustration and agitation into her sexy-as-fuck body.

That was all I could even think about.

By four-thirty, she was done. Which was surprisingly longer than I anticipated.

That night I stroked my dick to fantasies of her, coming more than once.

Our first day together was a spectacular explosion, and I awoke excited for day two. To see how she'd push back, how she'd test me, and how sexy she was doing anything and everything.

Neither of us were acting like civil adults should in the workplace, and I couldn't care less because it had been years since I was that excited to go to work. To have those light brown and green eyes stare me down, or have her quick wit strike, or to stand next to her and take in just how tiny she was and fantasize about how easy it would be to pick her up and all the fun that would entail.

Only one day had passed with her in the position of my assistant, and already I'd spent more time imagining the numerous positions in which I was going to fuck her. Company policy dictated there would be no fraternization between an employee and their superior, but *technically* she didn't work for me.

It was a temporary fill. I was just borrowing her for a short time while she still maintained her position in the marketing department. A simple technicality, yet one I fully intended to exploit.

One day in her presence and I knew, I *knew*, there was no way I would work with her for the next nine weeks without taking her.

Every cell in my body vibrated when she was near. Anticipation of her sheer force of will amped me up. I couldn't remember the last time I was so excited to see someone.

That alone made my dick hard, but nowhere near as hard as when we went at it with words. Her defiance should have angered me, but instead it was a flame of desire licking at me.

That wasn't my intent when I brought her in. Anger had fueled me when I made that decision, and desire drove me now. I had no idea what I was getting into, and after our first day in close confines I had a better picture, but with her beauty and brains I knew it was just the tip of the iceberg.

Roe Pierce was a firecracker in a tiny package that drove me wild. The hazel of her eyes drew me in, her flawless, tan skin, her round face with full cupid bow lips. There was nothing about her that I found unappealing.

Hell, it was like she'd walked right out of one of my fantasies. One I was desperate to make come to life. At least then I could be rid of my stupid obsession with her body.

As I looped my tie, I found my energy level skyrocketing, the minutes before I saw her again winding down.

Four

Roe

"Come on, Kinsey," I whined as I held the spoonful of yogurt in front of her lips. We'd been in a standoff for five minutes, and I was already running five minutes behind schedule.

Her face scrunched up and she turned away, her little brow furrowed as she pushed at the spoon.

I heaved a sigh and licked the yogurt off the spoon before taking another large bite and tossing the container into the trash, then turned to spill some cereal onto her tray. "Happy now?"

She reached out a chubby little fist and squealed while her uncoordinated fingers grabbed as many little O's as they could.

"I'll be right back," I said before stepping into the bathroom. It wasn't like she understood me anyway, but she was someone to talk to, even if she didn't talk back.

In the bathroom, I kept a watchful ear on the sounds coming from the other room while I whipped on some mascara and eyeliner. A peek out, and I found her happily chasing O's around the plastic tray of her high chair before I dipped back into the bathroom to spin my hair up into a loose bun.

It was my default setting lately. I missed the days of being able to style my hair.

Thirty minutes later, I said goodbye at her daycare with a kiss and a promise to see her later. She waved and gave me that sweet, happy smile I loved seeing every day.

Thirty minutes after that, I was getting off the elevator and turning right. Then I was turning around and going left.

All the calm of my morning routine was knocked out of me by that one twist of my foot on the carpet. With each step, my anger at the situation increased.

It was completely absurd. There was no way Carthwright should have been able to do what he did, and I would have hoped if it hadn't been for the Worthington takeover, Matt would have told him to go pound sand.

Then I remembered I was talking about Matt. Great guy, but men like Carthwright ate men like Matt Rolland for lunch.

My boss was a fantastic manager and great with the entire department, but he was a marketing guy. Carthwright was like James—a shark.

When I entered the area outside of his office, I received a few glances of pity from the nearby cubes. The door to his office was open and I blew out a calming breath, calling on all the positive energy I could draw in.

I would not slap him today.

Nor would I punch him.

Or kick.

Or lick.

Or fuc—

Roe! I yelled at myself.

My visions of kicking the shit out of him morphed into other ways to expel the energy buzzing below the surface every time he was close to me. I knew I was flawed—that I wasn't the type of woman that men sought out for the long haul. I didn't expect Thane to treat me any differently. Realistically I wasn't even remotely interested in a relationship—but sex with Thane? That thought had merit.

"You left early yesterday. I wasn't sure I'd see you today," he said from behind me.

I gave a small start before turning toward him and rolling my eyes. "Do you really think you're so scary that I'd quit? Because trust me, the whole stuck-up, cocky, asshole routine just makes me want to bite back."

His lip quirked. "I'll keep that under advisement. Now tell me why you left early."

"Because I leave at four thirty every day."

"From today on, you stay until five."

"That's nice if you think so," I scoffed. "But it won't change the fact that I will be gone at four thirty." I held up my hand to stop his rebuttal. "It's in my contract. Eight to four thirty with a half-hour lunch break. Trying to change that or going to Matt will only result in wasted time and energy."

The way his eyes narrowed at me lit up every nerve. I liked telling him he couldn't do something. It excited me to see how he'd react.

"What makes you so special?" he asked. The twitch in his jaw confirmed his annoyance.

"That's between me and HR."

He blew out a breath, knowing there was no way past that. My situation was cleared through Matt, and Human Resources agreed.

I wasn't the only one who had to pick up a child from daycare, but my arrangement held some restrictions. Due to my sudden thrust into parenthood, finding an affordable daycare on short notice was difficult. We were on the waitlist for some others, but low on the list. Thanks to the area I lived in, I was competing against people who out-earned me, pushing them to the top of the list.

Stacia ran a small daycare, just a few kids, but there were restrictions, the biggest being all children had to be picked up no later than five thirty. While it was nice that she was only a few blocks from home, that meant she was half an hour from work. I tried to leave at my normal five and get there on time, but after the first week of arriving late, once as late as six, I knew I needed to alter my work schedule.

Thankfully, I worked for a company that was willing to facilitate. Hopefully it wouldn't be needed for too much longer, but as long as I got my forty in at the office, all was good. I often spent another ten at home throughout the week.

"I sent you a file. I need fifty copies, all stapled. But before you do that, I need coffee. Black, splash of cream. Remember it. Every day when you arrive, you will get me one."

I wanted to retort with the fact that he was perfectly capable of getting his own damn coffee but bit my tongue. It would only be a shitty start to the day.

Instead, when I entered the break room, I saw the remainder of the day before's leftover pot sitting on the back burner. I poured some of it into a cup, topped it with some from the freshly made pot, slipped in a cream packet, and set it on his desk with a fake smile.

"Thane Carthwright's office," I said an hour later into the stupid headset I was wearing.

Most of my job was between me and the computer and my coworkers. Never did I ever want to be an assistant or even consider being one. I wasn't made to be subservient in that way.

"Roe, what are you doing?" a voice called, pulling me from my dual task of working Carthwright's schedule and organizing instructions on one of my latent projects so that I could pass it off.

I glared up at the Donovan Trading and Investment king, James Donovan, himself. "I'm being punished by the devil."

"The devil?" His brown eyes widened and he quirked his blond brow. James Donovan was definitely a contender with Carthwright for hottest person in the office. Strong jaw, calculating gaze, and he always looked like he walked out of a fashion catalog.

Unfortunately for me, James lost points because he was a friend, and Carthwright gained points because he was so dangerously sexy.

It shocked me that Carthwright hadn't cleared his master plan with James first. His surprise alone led me to believe he wouldn't have approved. I could work with that.

"Roe!" Carthwright called out, and my head jerked and I pushed my jaw forward.

I snapped my head toward the opening to his office. "What do you want?"

"You really want to use that tone with me?" he asked.

"Yes," I shot back.

"Should I come by later?" James asked as he looked from me to the open door.

I leaned forward, my eyes locked on his. "Get him to release me from this hell, and I will watch Bailey and Oliver all weekend long so you and Lizzie can have a sex-filled vacation with no interruptions."

I could see the gears working in his head as he thought about my offer. I knew how to manipulate the man.

Why didn't I think of it yesterday?

Five

Thane

James walked through my door after spending more time talking to Roe than I liked. She'd probably been bad-mouthing me, but I'd been working for James longer than she had.

He shut the door and closed the distance between us. "I've just been made a lucrative offer, so tell me why she should stay here, waiting on you?" he said as he sat in one of the armchairs across from my desk.

Lucrative? What the hell did that mean?

Honestly, I was surprised he seemed to even care.

"Because the temp agency sends over crap assistants, and there are still two months until Crystal returns."

His dark eyes narrowed on me, which was something I wasn't used to. "Roe works in Marketing, and her talents are best focused there."

"She pissed me off."

James studied me. "It's obvious she did more than that."

Was it that obvious? "She reminds me of a cute little hissing kitten. So small, but so fierce."

A throaty laugh left him, and he glanced back to the door. "I wouldn't let her hear that. You've got her riled up."

"At least I'm not the only one," I grumbled and shifted in my chair.

James's eyebrows shot up. "Oh, I see now," he said with a knowing grin.

"See what?"

He shook his head. "Don't mess with Roe. If you're interested in her, there are better avenues with fewer claw marks to be had."

He was right about the claw marks, but I was enjoying her swats. "It's been a while since I had a good sparring partner."

"I don't think she sees this as fun and games like you do." He cracked his knuckles, a long-standing bad habit.

"You know I like a challenge."

He shook his head. "Challenge or not, Roe isn't a game. And she doesn't have the time or patience for them."

It was my turn to scrutinize him. "You seem to know a lot about her."

"Because she's my friend," he answered.

Shit. "Your friend? How?"

"About three years ago, when Bailey was barely a year old she got a high fever and we took her to the emergency room. While there, Lizzie started to freak out, and suddenly Roe was beside her, calming her. You know Lizzie. Roe was her new best friend after that."

Of course. James's wife was a social butterfly, making friends wherever she went. Someone who helped her would gain that friendship in an instant. "That fits with her personality."

"I'm surprised you got Matt to agree to this trade," he said.

"I threw my weight around and used it."

"That's a bit of abuse of your power."

"It's temporary."

"Still..."

"Are you pissed at me for it?" I asked.

He tilted his head as he considered my question. "No. Curious, though."

"About?"

"How this will play out. Just do one thing for me." He stood and adjusted his tie.

"Anything."

"Don't piss her off so badly she quits." With a wave, he was gone and I was left thinking about his parting words.

Her quitting was something I definitely didn't want.

Besides her obstin ance and refusal to answer the phone correctly just to piss me off, she was actually doing a really good job. The coffee always tasted like shit, but in two days she'd cleaned up my schedule, completed tasks with proficiency, and already had my work life running smoother than it had in weeks. What could she accomplish in a week?

Whatever I threw at her, no matter her dislike of me, she completed the task perfectly.

In all honesty, it was nice. Temps had been fucking things up for weeks, and in a few short days she had fixed everything except her attitude. But I was enjoying that.

When I arrived at the office after lunch, the desk outside my door was empty. For a moment I stood next to it and pondered whether she'd quit when she breezed past me and set a bag on her desk.

"Roe," I said in greeting.

Her fingers clenched into a fist and she blew out a hard breath before turning to face me.

My eyes widened and I froze, unable to stop myself from staring at her chest.

She'd worn a high-collared blouse the day before, and the V-neck she was wearing today was by no means low cut, otherwise I would have noticed earlier in the day. The issue was that we were both standing and there was easily a foot or more difference in our height. Being so close, I had to swallow at the peek of two perfectly plump mounds. It was also impossible not to notice her hard nipples pressed against the fabric.

The view was going to be a test of my will.

"A little chilly in here?" I asked, arching a brow at her.

There it was—a flash in her eyes, a pinking of her cheeks, and then the flame of fire.

Game. On.

"It is quite frosty in here today. Too bad there's nothing around to heat me up."

Not five minutes after lunch, and Roe already had one point.

The phone chose that moment to ring, but our eyes remained locked.

"Two rings. See if you can manage to get that right today, sweetheart."

Excitement roared to life inside me at the flash of anger in her eyes. Yes, the day was going to be very exciting.

We continued our stare down as it rang again and she didn't move. I took a step closer and leaned down. "Are you going to get that?"

"Oh, is the phone ringing?" she asked in a sickly sweet tone.

"Yes," I hissed as it rang a fourth time. "Fucking answer it."

She heaved a sigh, rolled her eyes, and then picked up the receiver. "Thane Carthwright's office," she said.

I narrowed my gaze on her, but she didn't react.

"Just one moment," she said before turning to me. "A Trisha Amberley, who sounds like she has two brain cells that don't rub together, is on the line for you."

"I'll take it in my office," I grumbled. She was all too right about Trisha. One date over a year ago and she was still calling me up on rare occasions. "And where is your blazer? It might help take that chill off."

She didn't miss a beat. "Still hanging up in the department store because you haven't paid for it."

Damn, she was good.

Thane—1

Roe—6

I was badly losing and needed to catch up.

~

On Friday she arrived fifteen minutes late, and I realized I didn't have her number in case of emergency. After she got settled, I walked out to her desk.

"What's your phone number?" I asked, my phone in hand, ready to enter her into my contacts.

"Good morning to you, too. And why do you think you need that?"

I disregarded her pleasantry, as it was a jab anyway. "In case of tardiness, like today, which you have an issue with, or call-offs, or emergency. Why are you always late, anyway? Leave earlier. Catch an earlier train."

Her eyes narrowed at me. "Ah, why didn't I think of that?" she asked in a mocking tone. "Something so simple! If only it worked that way."

"Why do you have such an issue getting to work on time, then?"

"Oh, I think you know the answer to that one."

I ground my teeth together. *It's between me and HR*, my mind mocked in her voice.

"It's unprofessional."

"As is stealing an employee from her job just to work as your gofer."

"I didn't realize you were a rodent."

"Go. For. Not a gopher." She rolled her eyes at me, a trait that I found both annoying and enticing. I wanted to see her eyes roll for a different reason. Rolled back while her lips were parted and moaning my name in pleasure.

"Well then, gofer. Go fetch me your phone number. Now."

The energy between us crackled, and that strange urge to push her against a wall made my hands twitch.

What was she doing to me? Not that it didn't excite me, but fuck, when was I last entranced by any woman?

Through gritted teeth she ground out the numbers. I typed up a text and sent it off to make sure. When her phone buzzed and she picked it up, my message was on her screen for us both to see.

+17045552956: Add my number—Carthwright

With reluctance, she added it to her contacts along with my name.

"Was that so difficult?"

"Will that be all, Mr. Carthwright?" she asked in a saccharine-sweet tone.

Each time she pushed back against me, tried to go toe to toe with me, it excited me more and more.

"For now, Miss Pierce."

I didn't have many friends that I spent time with. Occasionally I got together with James, but that had dwindled in the last few years since Bailey was born. Before then, we used to have a guys' night about once a month, but it had been just Jace and me for a long time.

There were others, but they were more casual friends. Jace was my closest friend. If he ever got married, a laughable thought, I was fucked.

When I was sitting at the bar later drinking a beer, I realized something James had said didn't sit right. Not the words, but what they implied.

Though he was right about one thing—Roe wasn't a game.

"Are you even paying attention?" Jace said with a wave of his hand in front of me.

"Sorry, I was—"

"Thinking about a girl?" he asked, cutting me off.

"That obvious?" I asked.

He tipped his bottle away from us. "The blonde at the end?"

I shook my head. "Nobody here."

His brow rose. "Really? What's with the limp dick lately? I haven't seen you pick anyone up in… fuck, months, maybe even a year."

"How would you know?" I asked.

"Because you're always free on Friday nights for drinks and Sunday for football. You're such a fucking dating recluse lately."

He was right. It'd been many months since I'd even been on a date. Longer since I'd fucked anyone. I spent so many hours at work, the most time consuming being Worthington Exchange, which was the largest acquisition in the company's history, that life outside of work had pretty much stopped.

It'd killed my social life, which was probably why Roe had me so amped up. A fuck-hot woman within arm's reach with a smart mouth?

I knew I was a goner. I just hadn't relented yet.

"She… pisses me off," I ground out. I really didn't want to talk about her. It was bad enough the woman had me thinking about her outside of the office.

"Why?"

"Because she's good at her job."

He narrowed his gaze at me, brow quirked in a "what the fuck" kind of expression. "Explain, because I'm having trouble seeing that as a bad thing."

"It turns me on and makes all sense fly from my brain. All I want to do is bend her over my desk and bury my cock inside her."

He took a long pull of his beer. "Man, I haven't heard you talk about any tail like that since, well, never."

I slammed my bottle down onto the bar top. "Do you see my problem now?"

"What if she's interested in you? You know, for more than your dick?"

"She absolutely hates me." Though I knew we had chemistry and I was pretty certain she was attracted to me, I wasn't about to let Jace in on that information.

"Are you sure about that? Could be one of those clingy types."

A vision of Roe all doe eyed and clingy danced in my mind, and I burst out laughing. That wasn't happening. Ever.

"Not this firecracker. She's a fucking ticking bomb."

"Those are the best. Go get her."

His encouragement in pursuing Roe for sex wasn't a bad idea. The hate fuck vibes certainly circulated every time we were together.

Still, she was my acting assistant, though I was certain that she did everything in her power to disobey some of the rules I'd set for the smooth running of my office. I was also certain she made it her life's work to not answer my damn phone, or get me a decent cup of coffee.

What started off as an idea born of anger had me continuing to act like an asshole, but the game we were playing was as fun as it was arousing. And I wasn't ready to stop.

Six

Roe

That Sunday I gathered up a baby bag, loaded Kinsey into the stroller, then headed toward the park. It was only a mile and a half to Lizzie's house, and while not the quickest way to Midtown, our route moved through Central Park, which was a welcome scenery change over my everyday cityscape.

Kinsey loved looking at the trees, and after about half an hour, we popped out onto Fifty-Ninth Street. I pulled out my phone and found her number before hitting send.

After two rings, the sounds of a toddler screeching hit my ears before her voice came through. "Hey, Roe. As you can hear, Oliver is excited for our play date."

"Kinsey can't wait either. She is enamored with Bailey. We're a block away."

"Come on up. I let the doorman know you were on your way."

James and Lizzie lived in a huge apartment, where a single mortgage payment probably equaled about one year of rent for me. Then again, owning a company the size of Donovan Trading and Investment did come with perks, such as money.

We made our way up and knocked on the door. It swung open, and we were greeted by someone who had become one of my closest friends. Her brunette hair was in perfect, loose curls, her blue eyes as bright as her glowing smile. She always reminded me of an angel, until you pissed her off. Lizzie was one of the few friends that had stayed by me and helped me more than I could thank her for when Kinsey had come into my life.

From friend to Mom friend, she'd talked me down from so many cliffs when things became overwhelming those first few months.

"Everything okay?" she asked as she ushered us inside.

"Not really. Got any wine?"

"We might."

"Where's James and Bailey?" I asked, noticing the silence.

"One of our friends is having a birthday party for their son."

"Oh, no. Did I keep you from going?" I asked as I pulled Kinsey from the stroller and set her down on the floor.

Immediately she crawled over to Oliver.

Lizzie waved her hand. "It's okay, I didn't really want to go anyway. Plus, it'll be good for him to have some daddy-daughter time."

"Sorry."

"Stop it, and turn your mouth to spilling what's wrong."

I blew out a breath. Lizzie had been with James for a decade, so I was pretty sure she knew a lot of his confidants in the company. "What do you know about Thane Carthwright?"

"Thane? Not a lot, honestly. Why?"

"Because I can tell you he is an asshole." Just thinking about him made my blood boil.

"Really?" she asked in surprise. "He's always been nice to me. What did he do?"

"He pulled me from my position to be his assistant, all because I spilled coffee on him."

"He what? I'm going to have to talk to my husband about this," she said as she pulled up her phone. "It was an accident, right?"

I swallowed hard before fessing up to my own sins of the situation. "The first bit. The second one not so much." I held up a finger to stop her. "I'd like to point out I restrained myself from pouring the entire thing over his head."

Her lip twitched. "Too tall, huh?"

"Yesss," I groaned. "Being short really sucks sometimes."

She laughed and set her phone down. "I know Thane has worked for James for years. Possibly his most trusted employee. After all, when we had Bailey, he asked Thane to take over the reins while he took paternity leave, and again with Oliver. At times, Thane has practically run the company for months with James's guidance."

I'd never really thought about that. "Wow. I was still pretty new when Oliver was born and was trying to impress my boss, so I wasn't worried about who was doing James's job."

"You're not getting along with Thane?"

I shook my head. "I want to strangle him, Lizzie."

She chuckled next to me as she picked up Oliver's bottle, which had rolled over for what was probably the umpteenth time. "With a certain part of your anatomy?" she asked with a quirk of her brow.

I rolled my eyes. "Yes, he is *very* easy on the eyes. Speaking of eyes..." Thane had the most alluring blue eyes I'd ever seen.

"What about them?"

"Every time our eyes meet, I get stuck, like I'm hypnotized by them. They are the most beautiful bluish-green. The man should not be so good looking and have those eyes, because then I'm just done."

"You do like him," she said with a smirk. "You know, I once read this article that said seventy percent of relationships start in the workplace. Which I can see. That's how I met James, after all."

Ha! Like that would ever happen.

"No, just no. I hate him," I corrected her. I knew the story of how Lizzie and James worked together at an investment company before he struck out on his own, taking her with him. They were equals, and completely different than me and Thane.

She just smiled at me. I couldn't even convince myself. "You just want to have sex with him, then?"

I let out a sigh and looked over to Kinsey. She and Oliver were happily playing with the toys on the floor, and thankfully they were sharing without incident. "I can't have more than that."

"What are you talking about? Of course you can! Just because you have her doesn't mean anything."

"She is instant guy repellent. I tried to go on a date, and he took one look at her when I opened the door and was out. Guys come up to me at the grocery and see her, and suddenly they're gone. My last relationship completely disintegrated because of her."

"And you even got your nipples pierced for him."

I rolled my eyes. "It was a stupid reason. I never would have done it otherwise, but I'm glad I did it." Lizzie had gone with me for moral support and held my hand. She was about to burst with Oliver at the time, and said she wanted some measure of the pain James was going to feel in a few weeks when she was in labor.

Weeks later she called him a wuss when he complained she was breaking his hand.

"Do you think Thane would like them?" she asked.

Heat rose in my face and I stared down at the sparkles in the granite counter. "I don't care what the Assholian thinks."

"Assholian? Is that what you're calling him? I like it."

"What do I do?" I needed some help, because I was at a loss.

"You want my advice?"

I nodded. "Give it to me."

As sweet as Lizzie was, she could also be brutally honest. And no matter how much I didn't want it, I needed her to tell me everything I knew but didn't want to admit.

"Fuck him. Literally. It's obvious you two have some wild chemistry going by what you've said, and I think you need to explore that. If you still hate him after that, move on and be happy for a good time. But you can't keep using Kinsey as a shield or an excuse. There are men out there that aren't afraid of being with a woman who has kids. All those guys were boys, including that shit of an ex."

"I just..." She was right. I did use Kinsey as an excuse, but at the same time, my life had been completely turned upside down in an instant. My only constant was work. That was the last place I could find any speck of original Roe.

"Kinsey is lucky to have you. The sacrifices you've made for her are incredible. You chose her, so make sure you find a man who chooses you both. Until then, a little office romp sounds like fun."

Maybe she was right about one thing—there was someone out there who would want both me and Kinsey.

The problem was, I knew it wasn't Thane.

His assistant put her baby before him, and the obvious disdain he had told me children weren't his thing.

If he couldn't accept his assistant putting her child first, there was no way he'd be able to accept me putting Kinsey's needs first.

Seven

Thane

The entire weekend passed with me trying to work off the energy vibrating through me. I had to stop myself from looking up Roe's information in HR's database to find out where she lived so I could fuck it all out on her.

I was completely unhinged. In all the years, all the women I'd dated, none had hit me so hard. There hadn't been a steady woman in my life in years. Not that I was a commitment-phobe by any means, but there just was not a connection strong enough to make it past a night or two.

But Roe…

She was distracting me from my job, my routine.

There was so much strength and wit in her, but there was something else. That something else drove my curiosity mad and kept me thinking about her more than I should have been. Something she hid, kept from conversation by omission. The short lunches, leaving early, and her sometimes ruffled appearance.

She didn't have a boyfriend, according to James, who only

laughed when I asked. When I got defensive, shooting off how beautiful she was and why the fuck wouldn't she have one, James only laughed harder.

I needed to find better friends.

Because he knew her secret.

It was there in his words, in his warnings, and in that stupid laughter. Jealousy rose in me, hating that he knew her in ways I didn't.

Jealousy. *Why* was I feeling that emotion?

What the fuck did I have to be jealous about?

Maybe getting to know her better would quench that, and only time could change it. And maybe a date. Maybe then she'd open up to me.

Then open her thighs.

Fuck.

I knew I wasn't the only one feeling the intense attraction. It made me say and do things I would otherwise never do in the workplace.

Those were two things I had always kept separate until my eyes met hers.

All of these thoughts and feelings were unnerving to me.

I arrived at the office at my usual few minutes before eight and she, of course, wasn't there. Tardiness annoyed me almost as much as her refusal to answer the phone correctly. The trains moved on a tight schedule, and every few minutes. Why was it so hard to get out a few minutes earlier?

My jaw ticked in annoyance and after unlocking my office, I moved back to the doorway. There was no sign of her, so I sat in her chair. At six minutes after eight, she rushed around the corner toward me, her eyes on her phone. When she stopped, she jumped, startled to see me sitting at her desk.

"Late again," I said as I looked her over. Her cheeks were flushed and her breath heavy. Black slacks covered her legs, flip-flops on her feet, and a green short-sleeved button-down that made the green in her eyes pop was twisted at the waist.

She must have caught my lingering gaze on her feet because she paid me no attention as she set her bag on her desk and pulled out a pair of black pumps.

"Are you going to explain?" I asked.

She swept a stray lock of hair back and slipped the pumps on. "The reason doesn't matter, because all you're going to do is be an ass about the fact that I'm a few minutes late."

Her small feet were cute in the flip-flops, but the four-inch heels were sexy and made her the perfect height for bending over her desk. Thank fuck she wasn't wearing a skirt like she had on Thursday.

I stood and looked down at her. "Come in when you're settled."

I returned to my desk and went through my email while I waited. Ten minutes passed before she appeared.

"Shut the door," I said. I waited until she was done before asking her to take a seat. "One week down."

"That's it?" she asked with a groan.

"Yes, one week of wondering how big my cock is."

Her eyebrows rose. "Oh, I figured that out on day one."

"Did you?"

"Three and a half, maybe four inches."

"It may be that small flaccid, but you just proved you have been thinking about my size."

Her eyes widened, realizing she fell into my trap. The pink of her skin spread, and I grinned at her.

"What do you want?" she huffed in annoyance.

"To watch your squirm."

She rolled her eyes and shook her head. "Happy?"

"Not until I get you to bend to my will."

"I'm not a horse. You can't break me."

"Oh, I don't want to break you that way. My way is much more pleasurable for us both."

She rolled her eyes again, but I didn't miss her biting down on her plump bottom lip.

"The last man to say that to me was done in thirty seconds. I'm sure you're no different."

A grin spread on my lips. "Don't make me prove you wrong right here, right now."

She cleared her throat and stood. "Is that all you wanted?"

No, but it would do for now.

"To watch you squirm has made my morning. Now all I need is some coffee."

"As you wish," she said with that sweet sarcasm that spurred me on.

"Oh, and Roe?" I stopped her, and she turned back. "You should smile more."

She lifted her arm and flipped me off before continuing on.

I chuckled as I stared after her.

Yes, it was going to be another fun week.

Days later, the stress of my job was weighing on me. I'd had so many meetings that one seemed to bleed into the next. Thankfully Roe was exceptionally good at taking notes, because I was not able to keep everything straight on my own.

Worthington Exchange was almost ours, but a couple of other companies we had interest in were coming to a head at the same time.

A groan left me as I ran my hands over my face. I scratched at the stubble on my jaw and glanced at the clock on my monitor.

When did it get to be noon? The last time I'd looked it was barely after nine. Had I even moved in the last three hours?

By the twinge in my back, I was guessing no.

The phone rang as I stretched my arms above my head and waited for Roe to answer it.

Another ring went by, and still nothing.

"Roe!" I called out as the phone rang again. The sound was grating. Over the last week she'd been better at answering it, but I couldn't even see her.

Having had enough, I stood and stomped over to the door only to find her missing from her desk. I pulled out my cell phone and typed her a text.

Thane: Where are you?

I heard the chime of a phone and found hers sitting atop her desk, the screen lit up.

Carthwright the Assholian: Where are you?

I blinked down at the screen before picking it up, but it faded away.

There was no way I read that right. No way she gave my contact that name.

Thane: Why did you leave your desk?

The phone buzzed in my hand and lit up again.

Carthwright the Assholian: Why did you leave your desk?

I blinked down at it. Was that really what she thought of me?

For some reason, that didn't sit right. It felt like a stone in my stomach.

I moved back into my office as I waited for her to return from wherever she'd run off to.

Yes, I was high-strung lately. Yes, I had taken my bad day out on her when she spilled coffee on me. But it was the clash of wills that had me playing with her. I enjoyed our back and forth, and as much as I knew she got annoyed, I didn't realize I was the only one having fun.

James was right—she wasn't a game. Verbal sparring was

one thing, but I didn't want her to think badly of me. Not when one of my goals was to have her.

Roe actually hating me was counterproductive. While I was certain the hate fuck would be spectacular, I craved more than that.

A few minutes later, she walked through my doorway with two bags in her hand.

"Where have you been?" I asked.

"I had to pick up your lunch," she replied, holding up a bag.

Well, that made fucking sense.

"Without your phone?"

I tossed it onto the table in the corner of my office where she set the bags, and she snatched it up.

"Were you looking through my phone?" she asked, an edge of accusation in her tone.

"Of course not. It's locked."

"And if it was unlocked?"

"I would never." Though I was tempted. "But I did see your screen when I texted you."

She froze.

"Is that really what you think of me?" I asked.

"If the shoe fits, buy it in every color," she said without missing a beat.

Another point for Roe.

I deserved the shot.

Still, it made my stomach twist. The woman had me falling all over myself, saying and doing things I would never do simply to get her attention, but now I was aware of how right James was.

What I thought of as exciting rubbed her wrong.

"Guess I'll have to work hard to change your mind."

"Do you really care what I think about you?"

"Yes," I answered honestly. "And more than just because we are working together."

She blinked at me and swallowed before turning her attention back to the bag in her hand.

"You know, I can get you this same salad for a fraction of the cost," she said, changing the topic.

"It's the best."

She rolled her eyes. "And you only do the best."

"Precisely. Did you get something for yourself?" I asked as I pulled two forks from a small liquor cabinet. I hated plastic utensils and kept a stash of stainless steel on hand.

"I can't afford that."

I lifted my head. "I told you earlier to pick something up."

"And I did at the deli I passed on the way there."

By the way she said it, I had a feeling she didn't go with the spirit of my offer—I wanted to buy her lunch.

A blaring alarm sound made me freeze. "Crap," she hissed as she set the container down on the table. After fumbling for her phone, she tapped the screen and blew out a breath.

"You didn't answer?" I asked, curiosity itching at me.

She shook her head. "Alarm."

"For what?"

She blinked at me, her cheeks pinking before she turned her attention back to the containers, pulling them from the bags.

"My pill," she said.

Pill? Why would she be embarrassed about—

Oh, fuck.

I clenched my fist and slammed my eyes closed. My dick was rock solid in seconds.

Birth control pill.

Bare.

I could fuck her bare and come inside her.

"You're killing me," I whispered as I tried to regain some semblance of professionalism before I bent her over the table and did just that.

Again and again and—

Fuck.

We'd already inadvertently had the "I'm clean, you're clean" conversation that first day, and now to find out she was on birth control?

I was screwed seven ways to Sunday.

"Your boyfriend likes that, I bet." The words were acid on my tongue, burning with each syllable. But I had to know, to be sure.

"No boyfriend."

"One-night stands?"

"None of those either."

"Hookups with exes?"

She straightened and huffed, glaring at me as she shoved a container at me.

"None of your business."

I grabbed her wrist when she moved to leave. "Why are you on it?"

"Fuck you." She twisted from my grip. "You don't get to know my reason, Carthwright, because it is mine."

"For an ex?" I pressed. I *needed* to know for some damn reason.

Her gaze narrowed on me. "Maybe in hopes that one day I'll find a guy worth fucking. Too bad it hasn't happened yet."

Lashed again.

I was sorely losing our game, but I began to wonder if that was a bad thing.

I stepped closer, looming over her. "Maybe you should come over and we can put that to the test."

"Hell and no," she hissed through clenched teeth.

I leaned down, my lips close to her ear. "Are you afraid to be alone with me?"

When I pulled back, that delicious pink was spread across her skin again. Her body was on my side—now to change her mind about me.

Eight

Roe

The adjustment to my temporary position wasn't nearly as difficult as it was to be close to him. That arrogant, cocky attitude rubbed me wrong, though I had to admit the attraction between us was strong. Our push and pull only made it more difficult.

I reluctantly had to exchange numbers with Carthwright, and I immediately labeled it as Carthwright the Assholian. Not that he saw at the time. All he paid attention to was making sure I added it to my contacts.

The name was fitting, I thought. However, he did seem upset when he saw it the other day.

The exchange was mostly for emergencies or call-offs, so I was quite surprised on Saturday when I was cutting up fruit for Kinsey's lunch when his nickname popped up on my screen.

Carthwright the Assholian: It has come to my attention that you don't particularly like me.

A harsh laugh left me, causing Kinsey to look at me oddly, which only made me laugh more. Her expressions were often comical, especially when she was surprised by something.

Not liking him was accurate. Sadly, that did little to deter the attraction that buzzed when he was within five feet. Or when his smug mouth opened and that deep, silky voice came out.

Roe: Been sending your spies around, have you? Besides, did you really think I did?

Was his message because of the contact name?

I set the fruit in front of Kinsey before popping a piece into my mouth.

Carthwright the Assholian: I'd like the opportunity to change your mind.

Yeah, right.

Roe: You forced me from a position I actually liked and a career accelerating project, demoting me to your errand girl, and after all that, you think the hatred coursing through me might subside with some conversation?

Carthwright the Assholian: One night. Dinner. Anywhere you want to go.

Dinner? He wanted to go on a date? No. Not just no, but hell, no.

For one thing, I knew it would end in sex because I wanted him, but there was also Kinsey to consider.

Roe: I mean this in the shittiest way…go fuck yourself.

A bold move, but was he serious? It wasn't happening.

Carthwright the Assholian: I'd rather discuss other alternatives.

That stopped me. It was almost as if I could hear him whispering the words into my ear, his breath blowing across my skin.

I crossed my legs, trying to ignore the feeling that was growing between my thighs.

How long had it been since I'd had other alternatives? There had also been enough instances to prove I was attracted to the man despite my words. The two of us alone, together, outside of the office only had one outcome—me ending up in his bed.

Why did I have to keep thinking about that? *Focus, Roe!*

Roe: Sexual harassment much? I'm not a notch kind of girl.

A ruse, because I refused to admit he piqued my interest past a romp between the sheets.

Or against the wall.

I wasn't picky so long as that mouth never left my skin.

What is wrong with me?

I shook my shoulders out and straightened up, clearing my mind and body of the constant dirty road they kept veering off into when it came to the man.

Because the sad fact was that my body very much wanted to play.

Carthwright the Assholian: You're so stubborn you won't even hear me out? Fine. I like a challenge.

Roe: Better get your boxing gloves on. I don't go down without a fight.

Carthwright the Assholian: Is that all you'll be wearing?

I meant everything I said, but I also loved screwing with him. There was something about the man that set my blood on fire, and not in a bad way.

I wasn't going to let him know that.

He was the epitome of the "I'm better than you" personality, from the set of his eyes as he looked at people, to the way he barked orders with neither a please or a thank you and the money he dropped left and right on things as simple as lunch.

The man did not need a fifty-dollar salad from Carmichael's. I could get him the same thing for ten at the deli a block away.

Still, our constant back and forth felt like more than just bickering. There was an underlying current that drew us closer and closer.

Kinsey let out a grunt of protest and I looked over to find the banana gone, the last piece smashed to a pulp in her tiny fist.

"More?" I asked. She kicked her legs and started babbling, smearing the banana bits across the tray.

All the scene did was remind me that it didn't matter how close we got, or if I did cave and have sex with him, he would run the second he laid eyes on her.

Nine

Thane

Every day at noon was torture. The musical reminder set my cock off at lightning speed, even with my mind engrossed in whatever task held my attention.

All thoughts were focused on what it would feel like slamming my hips against hers with no barrier, her tiny frame bouncing on my cock, squeezing around me. Imagining the high pitch of her moans, the heaviness of her eyelids as I made her come. The sweet milking of my cock until every drop of cum was inside her.

"If I cared about you, I might ask if you were okay."

I blinked and focused on the woman in front of me. When did she walk in, and how long had she been there?

"Why wouldn't I be?" I asked, noticing how low my voice was.

She shrugged. "Judging by your white knuckles, something is bothering you."

The something is the fucking hard dick that you cause every single day.

"Would it matter to you if something was?"

She quirked a brow. "If I cared, but like I said, I don't."

My chest clenched. I hated her detachment, especially when I was beginning to care about her for more than just a potential fuck. "Simply because I borrowed you?"

Was that why she was still angry?

"This isn't borrowing. This is punishment."

I thought by now she would have moved past all that.

"You did spill coffee all over me, and I'm not talking about the accidental initial splash." That shit burned, but thankfully nothing more than a reddening of my skin. She must have cooled it down with something.

"You were being an asshole. I'd had a really shitty day, and I'd had enough. Simple as that."

It occurred to me then that I had no idea what had gone on for her that day. No answer to the multiple stains on her white top. I only cared that they were there.

Thinking back, all I remembered was the agitation and anger that rolled inside me. Not at her, but at what had happened before I walked into that break room. To the phone call that caused me to slam the phone as hard as I could into the window. The glass was unbreakable, but I took some satisfaction from the destruction of the plastic on impact.

"I'm sorry I was an ass. It was a bad day for me too," I said and actually meant it.

The invisible wall that always surrounded her faded. Muscles that were usually coiled tight, ready to fight, relaxed.

Her jaw clenched, and she glanced around the room before sighing.

"I hate manipulators."

"It's not manipulation. It's truth. I really am sorry. I should have said something, alerted you. Instead, I took it out on you. All the stains on your shirt said that you were an easy target, and

I needed an outlet. I didn't know I was about to piss off a fire-cracker. You should come with a warning label."

Her lip twitched. "I'm quite friendly. It's not me—it's you."

I nodded. "It was." It really was. "And I don't want to be an asshole in your eyes any longer."

She shifted her weight from one foot to the other, her hands clasped in front of her. "What was it, then? The bad thing?" she asked, unable to squash her curiosity.

My chest clenched, and I had to look away for a moment. "My mother..."

I trailed off.

My mother was a subject that was rarely broached. Nobody in New York but my little brother new about that part of my past, and even then, Wyatt didn't know everything.

Most of the time when I talked about my mom, I was talking about my stepmother, Wyatt's mom. She raised me from the age of ten like her own, right before she had Wyatt, and at times I forgot she didn't give birth to me.

My biological mom, on the other hand, was a vile piece of human garbage that I refused to see. In fact, she hadn't contacted me in over a decade—and that had been a birthday card to celebrate my eighteenth birthday when it was in fact Christmas of my twentieth year. Wrong month and wrong year and I never figured out why, just lit the card on fire and watched it burn.

Imagine my shock when she hunted me down at the one time I didn't have someone around to screen my calls. How had she even found out I was in New York?

"What about her? Is she okay?" Roe asked, sounding genuinely concerned.

She chose drugs and affairs over her family. Over me. That was the gist of it. The short story.

"She's fine," I said simply, not wanting to get into my issues with my mother.

But Roe's expression said she wasn't buying it. She also wasn't digging deeper. Still, that furrow of her brow told me something that her words never would—she did care.

Despite all her bravado, Roe did have a soft spot for me.

She was just going to make me work damn hard for every inch.

But that was okay. I was up to the task. If I was being honest with myself, the motivation that I might get to call Roe mine? That was worth all the effort I could utilize in my arsenal. I'd always gotten what I wanted, and I wasn't afraid of hard work.

And I knew winning over my firecracker would be the prize of a lifetime.

Ten

Roe

I*, Roe Pierce, have a soft spot for Thane Carthwright.*

There. I said it. Admitted it.

Well, at least in my own mind.

He got me with his apology. Tugged me with talk of his mother because I could see the pain etched into his features, the distance and vulnerability in his beautiful blue eyes. He could fake a lot of things, but that raw emotion he didn't think was showing was on full display. Thane had a heart, but much like mine, he kept it guarded, hiding behind layers of arrogance.

Changing my attitude toward him took a few days, but it didn't change our jabs at each other, only my standoffish attitude. In truth, I knew I was being unfair. After the first few days he'd been mostly nice, except the few times I irritated him on purpose. And really, how else did I expect him to react when I was deliberately pushing his buttons?

That was when it really hit. I liked fighting with him. It was so stupid, but also freeing.

All day, every day, I was only ever given the opportunity to be one of two people—Roe the professional marketing associate, or Mama. I'd almost forgotten what being Roe the person felt like. Our fights were almost like a dance. It wasn't anger, but it wasn't entirely playful. What it was made me feel free, like I was waking up after a long slumber.

"Good morning," I said with a yawn as I set my bag down.

Thane was already at his desk, squinting at his monitor. I watched him, trying to hide my laughter as he cursed, pouted, then pulled a pair of glasses from his desk drawer.

I bit down on my bottom lip as I stared at him. Just when I thought he couldn't get better looking, he went and put on glasses. Seriously, he needed to just stop.

He glanced up and caught me. "They're for the blue light and the glare."

I shrugged. "No need to explain. I think you have a false impression that glasses make you look like something lesser. Let me just set you straight—they don't. You just look better, and that is so unfair to the rest of the world."

"How is it unfair?" he asked.

"Because nobody should look that damn good."

The insecurity melted away and he grinned at me. "You think I'm good looking?"

I rolled my eyes. "No. No, I don't."

"You just said I was."

I shook my head. "Maybe I did, but I refuse to feed your ego any more than that."

"Just admit it."

"I admit that you are full of yourself."

He groaned, and his head fell back. He whispered something, but it was hard for me to hear. I could have sworn it was something like "I want you to be full of me," but that didn't seem to make sense. At least that was what I told myself when my thighs clenched together at the thought.

Instead, I turned back to my computer and started in on the emails that had come in overnight and in the early hours of the morning.

In my regular position, it wasn't something that happened that much. Often, I took my laptop home to work, but I rarely sent out emails.

Working for Thane was different.

The late-night spinners, the different time zone letters, and the up-too-damn-early-in-the-morning writers were constant invaders of my email once I was gone for the day.

I'd cleaned up the work that had piled up since Crystal went on leave. It had taken just over a week, but I had everything running smoothly and efficiently. Which was good for my regular job.

It took a few minutes to go through the emails, then I jumped into the Worthington proposal.

After an hour of working and fielding a couple of calls, I let out a yawn. I could use another coffee.

"I want a coffee."

I jumped in my chair, my hand flying to my chest. "Crap, don't scare me like that!" Where did he come from? I turned my head two seconds ago and he was seated at his desk, and now he was suddenly hovering, entirely too close to me.

He just chuckled at my reaction. "I want a coffee."

"Okay..." It wasn't the usual way he ordered a drink, and the way he stood expectantly at my desk confused me.

"Are you coming with me?"

"Coming where?" I asked. He wasn't making much sense.

There was a flash of heat in his eyes that quickly faded. "To get coffee."

"You're going to get your own?" I narrowed my gaze at him. "What's your game?"

He smiled at me and held his hand out. "I need something

stronger, and by the three yawns you've let out since you arrived, so do you. And those are contagious, by the way, so you need to stop."

I stared at his hand and slipped mine in.

A shock ran up my arm the moment we connected, and I drew in a sharp breath. It wasn't a static discharge shock, but one that felt like a pulse of electricity beating between us.

I stood, my gaze catching Thane's. We were both frozen for a moment, my heart fluttering, beating double time. Neither one of us pulled away, his thumb brushing against my fingers and sending a cascade of electrified shivers through me. After a moment, he lifted my whole arm and pressed his lips to the top of my hand.

It felt like the floor shifted beneath my feet, and I reached out and grabbed his arm with my other hand.

"Ready?" he asked.

I blinked at him, my attention still focused on the tingling that radiated from his touch.

"What?"

"Coffee?"

"Right!" I said with a start, pulling my hand from his. I instantly missed the warm feeling, but I tried to shake off whatever had just happened.

"Purse, purse, where is my purse," I chanted. My brain was complete mush, and I was trying to hide how much I was affected by the man beside me.

"You don't need it. I'm buying."

I turned back to him. "Oh. Thank you."

He held out his arm, ushering me to walk ahead of him.

"What is your favorite coffee drink? Not what you drink, but your absolute favorite?" I asked, making sure to steer the conversation away from whatever had just happened.

"Hmm, probably a peppermint mocha."

"Really?"

He nodded, then patted his stomach. "But that's a lot of sugar. I'd have to spend an extra hour on the treadmill to work that off."

Internally I groaned, curious to see what he was hiding beneath his suit because I was pretty sure it was perfection. His suits were bespoke for sure and hugged his body perfectly. "Do you work out much?"

He nodded. "Six days a week. My building has a huge gym, which is very convenient."

"Must be nice."

"Do you work out?"

Did picking up a nineteen-pound eleven-month-old fifty times a day count? I'd definitely gotten stronger since she entered my life.

"I walk everywhere, so that's my exercise." There was truth to that, covering where my strength really came from. I easily walked two miles a day just going to and from work, then add in grocery runs and errands and just leaving the house in general.

"I drive."

I turned to him. "You *drive*? Here? In New York City? Manhattan?"

"Yes, I drive."

"Weirdo."

He chuckled and reached out to press the call button for the elevator when something on his wrist caught my eye.

"Is that a rooster on your cuff link?" I asked. Thane had a collection of cuff links, and I swore he wore a different pair every day.

His lips drew into a smirk. "It's a cock." He leaned down, his lips ghosting my ear. "Because I'm a cocky motherfucker."

A shudder rolled through me at how close he was. The spicy, woodsy cologne with a hint of citrus drew me closer. He smelled so good, and I wanted a taste. A little lick of his skin.

"Do you have a monthly budget for new links?" I asked, a little breathier than I meant, but I needed to stop the yearning circulating through my senses.

He quirked a brow. "Why do you ask?"

"Because I've seen half a dozen or more. One that looked like blue woven fabric, a fossilized shell, sleek black, polished turquoise, mother of pearl, and I swear one with black pavé diamonds."

He nodded, seemingly impressed. "You're perceptive, and yes, they were diamonds."

I shook my head. "You have a cuff link problem."

"If that's my issue, what's yours?"

"My what?"

He nudged my arm with his elbow. "Tit for tat. What is your spending vice?"

Once upon a time it was eating out and bracelets. I *loved* bracelets. The fact that I was only wearing three at that moment was only because too many was too casual for my business attire.

Since Kinsey, my splurging had become cute baby clothes. That wasn't something I could tell him, though.

I narrowed my eyes at him. "And why should I tell you?"

"Is it bad? Or naughty?" His eyes widened in excitement. "Do you have a collection of adult toys?"

I whipped my hand back, knocking him in the stomach. It did nothing to deter him, only made him laugh at my discomfort.

Over the past week or so, our spats had slowly morphed from anger and frustration to teasing and ribbing and more than a little flirting.

"I'll take that as a yes. Even if it's a no, that's all I'm going to believe," he said with a grin.

The elevator arrived and the doors slid open.

"Are your expensive cuff links trying to make up for some *shortcomings* in your life? Is that why you're such an ass? Because of your lack of endowment in other areas?" I asked as I stepped into the cab.

"Coming out swinging today, I see." He chuckled, a twinkle in his eye and a smirk on his lips.

"Tit for tat."

He leaned in and whispered, his breath against my neck sending shivers down my spine. He *really* needed to stop doing that.

"I'll show you mine if you show me yours."

Yes, things had definitely shifted between us.

I rolled my eyes at him and shook my head. "You know, you're not as slick as you think you are."

A groan left him. "Maybe, but I bet you're slick enough right now to take all of my *generous* endowment."

I leaned back to meet his eyes. "Keep dreaming that you're more than a Popsicle stick. The biggest assholes are always compensating for something."

"If I am, I guarantee it is not due to my size."

I bit down on my bottom lip as I felt the heat rising in my face.

We were on our way down to the lobby, having only passed a couple or so floors when the elevator jostled and shuddered to a stop. Looking up, I found we were stopped between the twelfth and fourteenth floors.

Fitting. We were in the void of level thirteen. Neither of us moved as we waited for it to pick back up and resume our descent.

A shiver rolled through me as I remembered a horror movie Pete made me watch where the elevator stuck in the same place, then shortly after plummeted to the bottom. It was déjà vu, and a loud screech of metal on metal from somewhere outside the cab did me in, igniting my fear. After a minute of nothing, the pressure that had settled in my chest blossomed, exploding into full-blown panic. I reached out and pressed the buttons, but nothing happened.

"Come on," I hissed under my breath as I took in shallow breaths, my jaw locked down as my heart hammered.

Oh, God, this thing needs to move!

My breath sped up and I closed my eyes for a moment as I leaned against the wall to steady myself.

Thane stepped forward and hit the *Door Open* button, and still nothing. He gripped the edge of the doors and pulled with all his strength, but they didn't budge.

"Fucking open!" he screamed before slamming his hand against them.

His jaw was tight, and he stepped back to stand next to me against the wall.

The heat of his body was comforting, and I inched closer until our arms touched.

"Are you okay?" he asked, his voice sounding strained.

I swallowed and shook my head. "I'm okay with elevators as long as they are moving, but we're not moving anymore."

My breath sped up even more, and I could feel the panic taking over.

Eleven

Thane

The air that seemed to crackle with sexual tension just mere minutes before was amping up into a Molotov cocktail of anxiety and panic.

My throat constricted and as hard as I attempted to settle myself, I was barely holding on. Weakness wasn't something I wanted to show anyone, but especially not Roe. Her fear was palpable and feeding my own, growing it at an exponential rate.

Flashes of lights, my mom passed out in the corner of a stalled elevator in a shady part of town, a needle in her arm.

Fuck.

I hated that memory and I was trying to tamp it down when I heard Roe whimper next to me.

"Hey, it's okay," I said as I stepped in front of her. I needed an anchor, and so did she.

The warmth of her body inches from mine was both calming and alarming at the same time. I cupped her face to get her to look at me, and her wide eyes met mine. She reached up and gripped my arms, momentarily distracting me with the fire that shot through me. It was gone as quickly as it had come, but the effects lingered.

It was enough to turn her attention to me, our eyes meeting before everything went dark.

"Shit!" I hissed, bracing for another wave of panic to pulse between us when the emergency lights flashed on.

Roe cried out. "Fucking horror movies!"

It was random, and almost made me laugh until I noticed she was drawing in quick, shallow breaths.

"Hey, hey. It's okay. I'm here," I soothed. "Open your eyes."

Our eyes met, and for a moment I forgot about my own tense muscles. My focus was solely on her and settling her down before she hyperventilated. The last thing we needed was two fucking passed-out adults when the elevator finally started moving again, because once she was gone, I wouldn't be able to calm myself.

The pucker of her lips and the crease that had settled between her brows drew my focus away from the phantom shift of the cab that wasn't really happening. I concentrated on the dusting of freckles across her cheeks and her nose. On the splashes of green and brown of her hazel eyes.

I reached up and smoothed the space between her brows with my thumb, but it didn't take the look away. Instead, her panic laced with confusion. I trailed my fingers down the side of her face, lightly cupping it as I dragged my thumb across her bottom lip.

Leaning down, I closed the inches that separated us and pressed my lips to hers. She gasped at the contact, her lips parting.

When the moment of shock subsided, I was graced with a moan that traveled from her mouth to mine. Her arms wrapped around my neck, pulling me even closer. Our battle of wills transferred from words to lips and tongues.

My whole body lit up as I pulled her tightly to me. We pulled apart for a breath, and a shiver ran through me at her heavy lids and clouded eyes. I was sure mine were the same, lust completely overtaking thought and driving my need for more.

I attacked her neck with my teeth, tongue, and lips, spurred on by her high-pitched moans of pleasure. The energy coursing through me needed an outlet, and I was desperate to pin her to the wall or the floor. Anywhere I could sink my hard cock between her thighs.

I roamed my hands around her body, taking in as much as I could, memorizing each sweet curve. Around her ass and up her sides, skimming her breasts.

My thumbs brushed across her nipples, hitting something hard as they moved. Again, two bumps, one on either side of her nipple. A groan left me, and my cock stiffened even more when I realized what it was—Roe had pierced nipples.

Digging deeper, pulling closer, I still couldn't get enough of her. Couldn't *feel* enough of her to satisfy the insatiable hunger that was driving me.

I'd craved women before, but never on the same level as I craved Roe. By her fervor, the way she clawed onto me, bit down on my neck, I knew it was the same for her.

We both needed a break in the tension that constantly swirled around us.

The elevator shook, and the power coming back to life was the reality check that had Roe pulling away. Her eyes were wide, lips swollen and pink, and her skin was flushed. The loose bun she always wore had strands flying everywhere.

She was absolutely stunning.

Before I could protest, she stepped back and out of my arms, resting against the opposite wall. We were both breathing hard, and it took everything in me to not close the distance between us and continue.

She looked away, her concentration on the screen over the door as she pulled her hair down, watching the numbers until the cab slowed before coming to a stop at the first floor.

As soon as the doors opened, she rushed out ahead of me.

Twelve

Roe

O*h my God, what did you just do?* I asked myself as I sped away from him. I was in the middle of the lobby before I even remembered why we were in the elevator in the first place, then continued my path across the marble floors to the coffee shop on the far side of the lobby.

I was trembling from the waning adrenaline and happy as hell to be out of that elevator, but that didn't change what happened inside that space.

My body was still heated—flaming hot—as we stood in line. The tingle of my lips reminded me that his had been pressed to mine, the lingering mint against my tongue, and the recurring whiff of his succulent spicy citrus scent that had rubbed off on me haunted me.

He had touched me, and now my skin crawled to have his touch again.

Desperate.

Wanting.

Needing.

We got our coffee in silence, but I didn't have the stomach for it anymore. What we'd done had my adrenaline pumping, and I was desiring something else entirely.

We kissed.

And I wanted it.

I wanted more.

We didn't just kiss—we made out like hormone-driven teenagers.

And it felt so unbelievably good.

It pulled me from my panic, brought me out of my fear, and filled me with a passion I'd never felt before.

The way back up was uneventful, but I noticed the tension in him.

Through my panic, I had seen my own emotions mirrored in his eyes. He was always so confident and put together, but now I was struck by the evidence of his vulnerability. If it wasn't for his rigid posture, part of me would have questioned if what happened wasn't just some elaborate act. Even the most cynical parts of my mind couldn't believe that.

He had needed an anchor as much as I did. It was a truth I could feel.

"About the elevator," he began the moment we were back in his office, the door behind us closing.

I shook my head and set my coffee down on his desk. "Please, don't mention it." Please, oh, please don't bring up that embarrassment.

Because I knew he wasn't talking about my anxiety. He was talking about the other thing. The thing that still crawled around my skin.

It was like I was another person, completely overtaken by the electricity that surged through me at his touch. The attraction I'd felt for him was pale to the way my nerves exploded under his hands.

"Don't mention how hard it made me, or how much I want you?" he asked.

I froze, lips parted, and I couldn't stop from looking to his waist, my eyes widening at the bulge down his right leg that strained against the fabric. Had he been in that state since then? Was I the only oblivious one?

"I… Wow." I bit down on my bottom lip as my thighs clenched. Heat pooled deep inside me and an ache began to spread.

"By your reaction, I know I'm not the only one."

"It is very much not a good idea. Remember how much I hate you?" Though it wasn't hate anymore. More likely that I hated what he did to me. I hated how much I wanted him.

Especially knowing we could never be more. I didn't want to just be his plaything.

His lips twitched. "You don't hate me. Besides, all of that was foreplay."

"Arguing is foreplay?"

"With you, it is."

"You do know you are technically my boss right now, and so that's just not a good idea," I argued, hoping it would make him back down. Him cooling off was the only thing that was going to stop us, because I'd already pulled away once and I didn't think I could do it a second time.

"Right now, or ever?"

"I really want to say ever, but I can't do it." He'd worn me down. After his lips had touched mine, I wanted nothing more than to be consumed by him.

"Let me take you to dinner tonight."

I shook my head. First off, did I even want to entertain the idea of going out with him? Yes, I did. Things had changed between us.

I even knew the answer to the follow up—I wanted to go out with him.

But then second, there was Kinsey. There was no way I'd be able to find a babysitter on such short notice.

"You can't just ask a woman to dinner the same night."

"Why not?"

"Preparation and stuff, and this high of making you wait. You are giving off this vibe like you want to pounce on me."

"Because I do."

I drew in a ragged breath. I couldn't remember a time I'd been so overtaken with the fantasy of what it would be like to have a man between my thighs. It'd been so long since I'd had sex, including a good amount of time before my ex-boyfriend and I split.

Suddenly, Thane rounded his desk and stalked toward me. I backed up, my eyes wide, but I didn't get far when his hands gripped my hips and spun me around, picking me up with ease. He took a few steps, not stopping until my back was pressed against the wall.

"Thane..."

"Tell me you don't want me."

"I..."

"Can't, can you?"

"We shouldn't." I was shaking, giving away what I tried to deny. Being surrounded by him crumbled what little resistance I had.

"Liar."

We were so close we were breathing each other in. The elevator had been a sort of foreplay, turning me on so that when his lips touched mine again, every cell in me exploded.

I gave in. To his touch, to the fire, and to him. I was going to take Lizzie's advice and fuck him. Maybe then the curiosity would die down and I could concentrate again on what mattered.

His mouth on mine was a euphoric relief that opened my body to him, desperate for more.

A whimper left me when he pulled back.

His dark eyes met mine as his hand moved up the outside of my thigh before shifting to the inside and under my skirt. I drew in a breath, lips parted when his fingers brushed my mound. My nails dug into my palms as he worked his way under the fabric of my thong, pushing it to the side to find the flesh beneath.

My head fell back when he slid between my pussy lips, running up and down my slit.

A groan left him. "So slick."

I wanted to protest, but I couldn't. He'd barely touched me, and it was better than I imagined.

"Tease," I hissed.

His lips twitched, and without warning two fingers slipped inside me. We both let out a groan before his lips found mine. Little bolts of electricity zinged across my chest, the residual heat pooling between my thighs.

My hips jutted forward, pushing his fingers deeper. Lips parted, I kept one hand pressed against the wall, while the other had a death grip on his sleeve as tiny moans slipped from me.

"Everything you dreamed of, baby?" he whispered.

I moved my gaze up until our eyes met. "Is that the best you can do?"

His lips pulled up into a devilish smirk. "I told you…" He pressed his palm against my clit and my back arched, pushing our chests together as I grabbed onto his arms for support. "I like a challenge."

My mind was relieved of all thought as my head fell back against the wall, every nerve focused on the pleasure. No man had ever touched me with such confidence and strength, and it made me melt into him. Each slide in, each strum against my clit with his thumb had me falling endlessly into a mindless state of pleasure.

Thane had an expert touch. He knew exactly where and how to drive me crazy.

My eyes flew open and my grip on his sleeves tightened when his other hand moved from my waist. Our gazes locked and I was enthralled by the dark, lust-filled heaviness of his eyes. The anticipation grew as his hand inched up, and when the tips of his fingers brushed against my nipple piercings, I heard a low groan.

The feeling was so intense that I struggled for breath. Only stunted little mewls escaped between my lips. He leaned down, his breath hot against my neck before he nipped at my skin.

"Soon I'll have my mouth on both of these," he said. He squeezed my breast and my pussy, then increased the pressure and speed of his fingers. "But first, I want to taste your cum on my fingers before I *fuck* you into the wall."

I couldn't stop my hips from rocking against him, chasing the orgasm that was building inside me. The tightness in my abdomen radiated out to all my muscles. A growl vibrated against my ear before he bit down on my neck as if he already knew my neck was my weak spot.

A wave of pleasure rocked my body and a strangled cry ripped from my chest.

"Fuck, that's it, baby. Come."

The most intense feeling ever whited my mind as I shook in his arms. I barely noticed as I came down that he'd grabbed hold of my thighs and lifted me against the wall. Still dazed from my orgasm, I didn't register the sounds of him freeing himself until I felt the hot head of his cock pressing against my sensitive clit.

"Oh, fuck," I whimpered, my legs flexing, pulling him closer until I felt the tip slip in, then his hips flexed, slamming himself all the way until his hips were firmly against me.

My vision became blurry, head back against the wall as a long, low keening left me.

"Fuck, yes. I've been dreaming about this for weeks," he groaned against my ear.

"What?" I asked, confused. I'd never felt so full.

"Being inside you."

When he slid out and then slammed back in, I suddenly felt on the edge of another orgasm. I didn't have time to think on it when he enacted on his promise of fucking me into the wall. Hard and fast, over and over, and I could do nothing but let out a litany of mewls.

"Fuck, fuck, fuck!" I whimpered as I held on for dear life. My lips parted and a silent scream caught in my throat as I clung to him, my body shaking.

An incomprehensible string of grunts and groans left him as his hips pinned me to the wall. They flexed, pushing me harder as I felt his cock twitch inside me.

He was coming. Oh, my God, he was coming. Filling me.

My head fell against his shoulder as strength abandoned me. A man making me come once was a miracle, but Thane proved just how much of a god he was by doing the impossible.

Now all I wanted to do was take a nap.

His breath was hot against my neck as he took in deep, labored breaths.

"Don't pull away," he whispered against my skin.

In my hazy state, I didn't understand the meaning of his words, but I would.

Thirteen

Thane

If I'd ever even questioned the attraction between me and Roe, that was completely blown out of the water when she came in my arms. Then when she came around me.

All night long, it was on replay.

And I had to be honest with myself—being with her was without a doubt the hottest sex of my life. It wasn't that we were in my office and anyone could hear or walk in, and it wasn't because we were mostly clothed. Weeks of pent-up sexual frustration had gotten an outlet, and I couldn't get enough of her. Every whimper, every touch made me want and need more, driving me to madness.

However, I did hate that she still ran out on me at four thirty. It was strange, but maybe she had a second job? Whatever it was, it was maddening.

After that, the woman consumed my every thought. My questions were piling up, even if I was no closer to getting answers.

I'd never wanted to take a woman out so badly before. To

date, and yes, to fuck, but definitely to get to know her outside of work. She had me completely captivated, and I had a need for all of her—a feeling I hadn't had in many years.

With the time she'd worked for me, it shouldn't have been a surprise to watch her make a mad dash to her desk nearly ten minutes late, looking flushed and gorgeous. Of course, the phone was already ringing. Her "Hello, Thane Carthwright's Office" rushed out after nearly six full rings.

I chuckled to myself, because obviously fucking the hottest woman I'd ever met against the wall of my office wasn't going to change the work environment we'd established.

I took the call, and once I was done, I forced my attention back to my email to keep from getting distracted by her. It was torture. Every movement she made, every sigh, had my skin crawling to be closer to her. Being near her was tormenting me. I just wanted to touch her again.

A few minutes later, movement caught my eye and I looked to the door. It was hard not to groan as I watched her hips pop with each step. She was wearing pants, and I desperately missed the view of her legs that her skirts provided.

"Your coffee," Roe said, setting the cup down next to me. There was no little snip or snide remark. Instead, a smile brightened her stunning features. A slight pink on her cheeks enticed me.

I smiled up at her as I picked up the cup. "Thank you."

She turned, a bounce in her step on the way back to her desk. I was so completely hypnotized that I was on my second sip before I spit the coffee back out into the cup. Bitter drain water was more the taste than coffee. I had no clue what the difference was between what Crystal got me and what Roe did, but I needed to text Crystal to find out.

The idea of a cappuccino from the lobby coffee shop crossed my mind. Maybe I could have her get me an espresso from there and avoid offending her. The last thing I wanted to do was upset her. That wouldn't help my mission to get inside her again—something I was desperate for.

Neither one of us made any sort of mention or allusion to what had happened, but each time our eyes connected, it simmered beneath the surface. She would turn me down again for a date without notice, but I'd discovered a loophole.

The next morning when she came in to drop off my coffee, I stopped her before she left.

"I need you to make a lunch reservation for two at noon."

"Two?" Her brow scrunched. I knew she was confused because the only meeting I had on my calendar was at three.

"If I can't take you to dinner, then I'm taking you to lunch."

She shook her head. "I can only take a half an hour."

Yes, that annoying secret to go with all the others.

"And maybe someday you'll tell me why, but that isn't a concern today. It's a work lunch with ulterior motives."

"Ulterior motives, huh? Does that mean I get to pick the restaurant?" she asked.

"When you agree to go to dinner with me, but lunch is mine."

A few hours later, I was holding the door open to The Capital Grille, one of my favorite places for a business lunch. And probably where I would have taken her to dinner if she'd agreed.

"I've never been here before," she whispered as we approached the hostess stand.

"You'll like it," I assured her.

"Are there fifty-dollar salads here?" she asked, her lips drawing up into a smirk.

"Probably."

Her eyes went wide and she slowly turned to look at me. "I ca—"

"I'm buying you lunch, so don't say another damn word about it. If you want the fifty-dollar salad, get it."

"Right this way," the hostess said.

I placed my hand on Roe's back as low as I could, keeping her close to me. It was a possessive move, but I wanted all the fucking eyes that were watching to know she was taken. Even if she hadn't agreed yet.

"I haven't been to a place like this in a long time," she admitted as she looked over the menu.

"Why not?"

She shrugged. "Time, mostly. No reason to go to such a nice place being another, but I also have a hard time spending so much on a meal."

"I don't."

She rolled her eyes. "I'm well aware of that. How much did today's cuff links cost you?"

I glanced down at the curved onyx and clenched my jaw. "No comment."

"Over a hundred?"

My lips thinned.

"Two hundred?"

Again, I remained silent.

"Five hundred?"

"They're my vice, okay?"

She smiled at me, her eyes skimming the menu again. "You said there was an ulterior motive. Are you going to tell me?"

I leaned back, having already decided on the filet mignon. "Where did you go to college?"

"NYU. You?"

"Same. Siblings?"

She paused. "Younger sister. You?"

"Much younger brother. Wyatt is almost eleven years younger than me. He's a senior at NYU right now."

"Following in his big brother's footsteps?"

I nodded. "Which is kind of strange, considering I moved out when he was seven."

"He must idolize you."

She hit the nail there. My little brother was a mini version of me. Definitely the Carthwright genes in play. "Where are you from?"

"I'm a New York girl. You?"

"North Carolina."

Her head tilted in surprise. "Really?"

"Yes. Why?"

She shrugged. "You seem to have the city life ingrained in you."

"After fourteen years, I would think so."

She shook her head. "Then again, you did say you drive everywhere."

The waitress came around for our orders, giving us a break.

"Twenty questions was the big motive driving you?" she asked when we were alone again. I nodded, engrossed in the smile that filled her face. "And here I was thinking by ulterior motive, you meant sex."

It wasn't meant to sound erotic, but somehow her offhand vocalization of such a small word had me shifting in my seat. Being close to her was an aphrodisiac in itself. The soft scent of roses and cherries tempted me, and it was taking a lot of self-restraint to keep from touching her. However, she was badly testing my weak hold.

"That is always on the table. Whenever, wherever. I wanted to get to know you, and you me. Maybe then you'll let me take you out on a real date instead of tricking you into lunch."

"I don't know. You have that 'I fuck a lot of women' vibe."

"It depends on what your definition of a lot is. Do I date? Occasionally. Does it last long? Not usually past a second date."

"And that makes me wonder. Is it you, or them? If you sleep with them, do they get off as well, or are you just another selfish prick?"

I smirked at her and leaned closer. "I'm pretty sure you already know the answer to that one."

Pink filled her cheeks, and I knew she was remembering all the ways I touched her. "True, I do have some experience with you in that area. But one time doesn't make a good case study."

She bit down on her bottom lip as she smiled, while I was struck stupid, my body rapidly rising to the challenge. That lip between her teeth was her biggest tell. I had a feeling she had no idea she did it every time the sexual tension rose between us, but I did.

I leaned closer, my voice low. "I'll drag you to the bathroom right now and give you another entry for your data collection."

"That's some big talk, but back to the subject at hand. What's wrong with you?"

I blinked at her, blindsided with the question. Weren't we just talking about my cock deep inside her in the bathroom? She had me completely unhinged. "Nothing is wrong with me."

"Then what is wrong with them?"

Oh, my exes. "It just didn't work out. Incompatible or schedules didn't mesh or no spark."

"Am I just a casual occasion?"

"There's only one way for us both to find out, but I'm fairly certain that the answer is no."

"Hmm, I think I liked you better when I hated you, before I knew you were good in bed. Though technically I haven't had you in bed, so I guess really you're good on the wall."

"I'd really like to add public bathroom to my list of places of accomplishment."

"What if I said no?" she asked.

Everything in me begged her to say yes, and the idea of no

hadn't entered my mind. "Then I would back off, but I really hope to have you screaming yes very soon."

"And then?"

"And then *maybe* you might say yes to an actual date." Getting through to her was like breaking into Fort Knox—impossible. Yes, I wanted to fuck her. Lots. Yes, I wanted to take her out.

What was so hard for her to accept?

"You keep harping on this actual date thing."

"Because there's something keeping you from saying yes, and that annoys me, so I'll continue asking until that word leaves your lips." Her secrets annoyed the fuck out of me because I wanted to know them. It drove me crazy.

"Why did you kiss me in the elevator?"

I froze, the playful energy leaving me, and I felt that tightness in my chest reemerge. "Because I wanted to."

"That's not what your reaction to my question says."

I nodded. The best thing for me to do was to tell the truth, but how much of that would satiate her curiosity? "I have the same issue as you. I don't do well in situations like that."

"Horror movies get you too?"

"Horror, yes. Movie, no," I admitted.

"You didn't seem like it was much of a problem for you." Her words said one thing, but her expression told me another. Perhaps I didn't do a good enough job stuffing down how affected I was.

"You don't remember me trying to tear the doors open? I was panicking as well, but you needed help. Touching you grounded me, and I had hoped it would do the same to you. Once I started, I didn't want to stop."

My eyes met hers, and I reached out for her hand. She drew in a sharp breath when we touched, and that wonderful vibration passed between us again. That was my cue, my proof that Roe was something special.

Fourteen

Roe

Lunch was filled with our regular banter with sprinkles of getting to know you and more than a few innuendos, the latter happening when I flattened my tongue against the dessert spoon, then flicked the tip.

At the time I laughed at the way his jaw dropped, but that laughter died down when his hand gripped my thigh and slipped under my skirt. I swallowed hard and he leaned closer to whisper in my ear, "Keep playing innocent and I'll have that tongue on my cock before we even make it back to the office."

My heart sped up and a whimper left me when the tips of his fingers lightly ran across my clit before disappearing. He paid, and we walked in tense silence, every nerve acutely aware of how close he was.

There was a burning ache between my legs that only pulsed stronger with each minute he was near.

I chuckled internally. It seemed my burning hatred had turned into a burning desire.

Could be worse.

The energy crackling between us was explosive, and if the elevator hadn't been full when we entered, it would have been a very different kind of ride. Instead, we stood in a corner and he worked his hand up the back of my skirt, right between my thighs, and slipped his fingers inside me. I was forced to turn into his shoulder in order not to embarrass myself with the moan that was sealed behind my lips.

When the elevator arrived at our floor, he motioned for me to walk in front of him before he moved to my other side and rested his hand on my lower back. We continued toward his office, but he made sure I didn't miss him sucking my juices from the tips of his fingers.

Heat flooded my cheeks, and as soon as we crossed the threshold of his office I grabbed at his waist, the hot head of his cock pressing against my palm. The sound of the door shutting and locking registered as I worked to get his belt unhooked. He tilted my head back, and a shock left me as his lips pressed against mine.

With his hands on my hips, he walked me backward while I continued with his belt. I had the loop out and the zipper down, my fingers popping the button, and I reached beneath the elastic waistband of his briefs. I grazed the hot, silky head, earning a hiss from him. His blue eyes were dark and the ache between my legs increased.

A moan left me as his large hands grabbed my thighs, lifting me over the edge of his desk.

"Your papers," I argued.

"Fuck them," he growled as he pushed my skirt up my thighs and over my hips. His fingers brushed against my clit, making me moan as he pushed my panties aside. "Fuck, you're so ready for me."

Before I could respond, I was silenced by his cock pressing all the way inside me. My jaw dropped and a guttural sound came from me at the sudden overwhelming pleasure that crashed down on me.

His thrusts were fast, hard, and I could feel the tightness in my abdomen growing. A shiver rolled through me as his hand snaked up my waist and across my breast to rest lightly at the base of my neck.

Just the closeness to my neck, the slight pressure pinning me down, sent a spike of heat blasting through me and I broke. I trembled beneath him as a strangled sob rocked me.

"Fuck," he hissed. His hard thrusts continued as my walls pulsed around him. With a few hard grunts and groans his hips stilled, and I felt each twitch as he came.

His hand slid from my collarbone to the desk beside my head, using that to prop himself up as his muscles loosened. We were both breathing hard, staring deep into each other's eyes.

Somehow, it didn't feel as if it was just some office romp to blow off steam. As his blue eyes bore into mine, it felt like something deep inside of me unlocked.

After a few moments, he stepped back and I felt a rush leave me, but he was quick to clean it up with some tissue. I sat up and worked on adjusting my clothes but stayed on the edge of his desk, not trusting my legs to hold me up.

"Are you available for dinner on Friday?" he asked as he pulled his pants back up.

My head snapped to him. "Are you asking me on a date?" I'd already turned him down once. Going on a date with him was everything I wanted.

And everything I feared.

"Yes… Is there a problem with that? I'm giving you multiple days of warning."

I brushed a lock of hair behind my ear. For weeks, we'd had banter and chemistry and a few explosive sessions of release I had desperately needed.

But that was all I could do, even if I wanted more.

"I don't think that's a good idea."

"Now why not?" he asked, clearly exasperated. "You're attracted to me. I'm attracted to you. I want to get to know you more. Is that so bad?"

I swallowed hard, and my chest tightened. As much as we'd connected, his words still haunted me. While he could accept me, experience had shown me there was no way he could accept Kinsey. Therefore, all we could have was what we had and nothing more.

"Look, this has been fun, but it's not going to work past that. We're not a good fit."

He stepped forward, forcing me to look up at him. "Oh, I think I just proved we are a *very* good fit."

"I can't. I just can't." *As much as I want to.*

"Why not?" he asked through clenched teeth.

"It just won't work." I hopped off the desk and pushed past him to make my way out. The knot in my stomach was tightening, and I had to get away.

"Roe..."

I didn't pause, just continued my way out of his office. "Goodnight, Mr. Carthwright. I'll see you tomorrow."

~

Walking out on Thane—*again*—was difficult. Shot down not once, but twice, and I couldn't seem to stop doing it. The fear that filled me took over and refused to even entertain the idea. My mind was beating out my body and my heart. I was trying to save myself by not getting close. If I didn't get close, he couldn't leave me.

As I rode the train, I blew out a breath as I pulled up my phone and typed out a message.

Roe: Are you ready for it? I did it. I fucked him. Twice. It was wonderful and glorious and hot and OMG I didn't know anything could feel THAT good. But then he asked me out to dinner. I turned him down because I know that as soon as he finds out about Kinsey, he's gone.

I hated the unease that filled me. Maybe I should have told him, but the longer I withheld, the longer I could keep hold of the lie to myself. If he didn't know… but what if he did? Part of me was curious, but the dark part of my heart already knew and silenced any hope that remained.

My phone buzzed right as the train stopped at the station.

Lizzie: YES! I'm so happy for you! Why are you hiding that beautiful baby from him? You're torn because you have feelings for him. Tell him, and then ask him if he's still interested. That's the only way you'll ever know. Now that your pussy is thoroughly used, stop being one and talk to him. Love you!

I loved Lizzie's exuberance, but I didn't like her pointing out that I had feelings for him.

Because I did, and it would hurt when he was no longer interested because of Kinsey.

The next morning, we had a meeting scheduled together with some of the Worthington executives. When I arrived, it was so silent I thought he wasn't in yet.

"Good morning," I said when I found him at his desk glued to his screen. There was no response so I stepped closer, thinking maybe he had earbuds in and couldn't hear me. "Good morning."

He picked something up from his desk and thrust it at me. "I need this sent to Shannon so he can get the contract going."

"Okay," I said as I took the folder from him. He still hadn't looked at me, and I didn't like the pit forming in my stomach. "Do you need some coffee?"

"I already have some," he replied, still not looking at me.

I didn't move, refusing to do so until he acknowledged me.

"Is there a reason you aren't getting that done?" he asked in a clipped tone.

"Is there a reason you won't look at me?"

His jaw flexed and he turned to me, a cool detachment in his gaze. "Now will you leave me alone?"

"That's something I've tried to do for weeks. Why so hostile now?"

"Because I was so stupid to think that maybe there was something between us, but my bad, I guess it isn't worth even trying," he spat.

It felt like he'd stabbed me in the chest, and I couldn't figure out why.

"I hate passive aggressive as much as I hate manipulation."

He abruptly stood, fire burning in his eyes. "You want to talk about manipulation? *You*. Because that is all you've done to me for weeks."

"I have not." *Have I?* It couldn't be.

"But you have. You may not have realized that was what you were doing, but you were. Twice I've had you in my arms, twice I've thought that finally you would tell me yes to fucking dinner! Only to be shot down as not fucking good enough." He sat back down and pulled his chair back into his desk. "So go file that and get out of my face, because I really don't want to see you right now."

I was in shock as I backed up and turned, holding the file close to my chest.

The pit in my stomach grew, and I stepped out of his office. Not good enough? Did he really think that? I was the one who wasn't good enough. Me.

I was the problem. He was… *perfect*.

There was a pang in my chest just thinking that I might have hurt him, that because I wasn't honest about my situation, I'd caused him pain. It was a feeling that deepened when I acknowledged that on some level, he cared about me. That was the only way he would be fazed. A hit to the ego wasn't enough for the backlash I was receiving.

It was a hard hit. One that I took personally. I'd hurt him, and he was lashing out at me.

Over the past few weeks I'd gotten to know him, know his true personality, and accept that I was judging him by our first interactions. By not being honest I had unintentionally played with his feelings, emotions I didn't even believe he had toward me.

After taking the file to Shannon, one of the in-house lawyers, I was welcoming officers of Worthington Exchange into the conference room. Once everyone was seated, Carthwright excused me from the meeting.

I retreated back to my desk, hating the unease I was feeling. But I just had to remind myself of one thing—it was better this way. If he hated me, then he couldn't leave me.

But in a way, he already had. I'd pushed him away as hard as I could, and I was paying the price for not taking his feelings seriously. The cold infiltrated everything, and I found myself desperately missing his touch.

For the rest of the day, every time Thane looked at me there was a cool detachment, a stark contrast to the day before. He didn't take my rejection well.

Neither did I.

~

All weekend long, that stone remained in my stomach.

We were halfway through Tuesday, or work-day three of the same attitude, when I realized I needed to inform him of my upcoming absence.

"Can I talk to you?" I asked as I stepped into his office.

He looked up and sat back in his chair. There was no expression on his face, his features blank. I wasn't used to the blanket indifference to me. The emotions that were normally so strong between us, simmering under the surface, were extinguished. I swallowed hard, my chest clenching, knowing I was the reason for that look. I missed the devilish smirk, the fire in his eyes, and the way we interacted.

I missed him.

"I'll be out on Friday," I said. It was a date I'd cleared with Matt long ago, but I realized Thane didn't know.

"I need you on Friday," he said, then turned his attention back to the work in front of him, effectively dismissing me with just five words.

"I won't be here," I stressed. A tightness began to wrap itself around my chest.

He pushed his keyboard back and stared at me. "Why not?"

My teeth mashed together. His attitude told me he was upset, but didn't he realize his behavior was hurting me? Maybe he wanted that, to punish me in another way for shutting him down.

All I wanted was to go back to how we were a week before, because every moment I was close to him had become torture.

"I'm taking a personal day, and that's all you need to know." I turned to walk away.

"Roe, wait."

I snapped back around. "You can't force me to tell you because I don't have to. I'll do what I can by the time I leave on Thursday, and then I'll see you on Monday."

He just stared at me and I turned to leave, settling back down in my chair.

A tear slipped down my cheek. Why did it hurt so much?

Fifteen

Thane

The last week and a half was complete shit. It started off fantastically between her thighs, and a minute later it fell apart.

I couldn't figure out why Roe was so adamant about Friday. She refused to tell me why, but when I looked at the calendar, the date hit me—September 11th.

I glanced at the door, to the profile of her face as she worked. Did she lose someone when the towers went down?

If she did, I would feel like a complete and total ass, earning the name in her phone.

I hated the feeling in my chest every time I even thought about her. The frustration and anger. I knew I just needed to try harder, but I also knew I couldn't *make* her go out with me, let alone like me.

Maybe her change in attitude had to do with Friday. Maybe I needed to get over thinking everything was about me—a hard thing to do when all my thoughts were on her. Remembering our lunch date and how well that went, how well we fit together.

Then the smack-down of cold, hard rejection that stung and resonated for days.

The first time she declined a date, her rationale was sound, though I knew there was something else. All the secrets that I wanted to know that hung around.

How was I supposed to make her mine if she kept slamming the proverbial door in my face? Shutting me down right after proving she wanted me was a hard blow.

Then again, I wasn't being very receptive. Processing these feelings that I'd never had before was proving more difficult than I believed.

For the next two days, I tried to tamp down the desire to get back to talking to her like I used to. To get back to the relationship we had been developing. My problem was that I'd never been in such a situation and I didn't know how to proceed. As much as I wanted to go after her relentlessly until she gave in, I had a feeling that would just push her further away.

"Where's Roe?" James asked from my doorway.

He'd barely stepped into my office when I laid into him. "Does she have a boyfriend?"

James froze at my sudden outburst, his brow furrowed. "I told you no."

"Then why doesn't she want to go out with me?"

His muscles relaxed, and he sat down in one of the chairs opposite my desk. "I can't tell you that."

"That's not an 'I don't know,' James."

He shrugged. "Roe has been through a lot lately, and that's all I can tell you."

"Why?"

"Because she trusts me, and if you want her to trust you,

you're going to have to wait until she's ready. If you keep harping on it, you'll just push her away."

I threw my hands up in frustration. "I already have! And now I don't know how to talk to her anymore. It's fucking frustrating as hell."

A small laugh left him as he watched me. "I'm having fun seeing you invested in a woman. In all the years I've known you, there has been interest but only enough for a night or two."

"You were the same, once upon a time." I ran my fingers through my hair. "She's under my skin."

"I'm very familiar with that feeling. The worst thing you can do for your case is to push her away. You want her to open up to you so you can be there for her."

Great—the one thing I'd done for the past week was push her away. I was completely fucked. Would she even trust me now? She probably thought I was only being nice to her so I could fuck her, and then I went back to being an asshole.

Shit. My goal was even further away now, and by my own damn doing. The woman had me a complete and utter mess.

"I fucking hate this secretive shit."

"Just remember it's not to torture you. Trust is hard earned, and you're going to need hers to get any further."

She didn't trust me? Or she didn't trust me with something specific?

"I need to prove myself," I said, finally understanding. Though that didn't make it any easier to take.

"Good luck."

"Thanks, man. Totally off the topic you came in for, I'm sure."

"Yes, but that doesn't change that you're my friend, Thane."

"She's your friend as well, which is weird, by the way."

He ignored me. "Roe is a much better match than your last real relationship. What was her name? Liz?"

"Liv."

"That's right."

He was completely right there. Liv was all about status and money, neither of which I had at the time only a year out of college. She was gorgeous and made great arm candy, but she was otherwise a boring, materialistic socialite—the complete opposite of Roe.

"How can one woman flip my life upside down so quickly?" I asked.

"That's what happens when you meet a good one. Now, sort yourself out. Get the girl. And tell me what you think about that email Worthington just sent."

My eyes widened and I turned my attention back to my computer, pulling up my email. I skimmed over the letter and cursed.

"We had this ironed out."

James sighed and ran his fingers through his hair. "They know how much we want the company," he grumbled.

We needed the company. They were a major lynchpin in the ten-year expansion plan we'd laid out.

"We are already the majority shareholder. This is asking for a hostile takeover." I ran my hand through my hair.

Fuck.

"Which it may become. I didn't want to do it that way."

I nodded. "I'll get on it, see what sense I can talk into them."

"I'll leave you to it. Give me a call if we need to press them harder."

"Will do."

After he walked out, I tilted my head, a loud crack emanating from my neck. It seemed there were two things I was going to be on the warpath for if the people involved didn't change their minds.

~

A few hours later, I was sitting at the bar with Jace wanting to bang my head on the counter until I bled. Worthington wasn't budging, and it would be a fight on Monday when their CEO was back in office. It seemed some of his senior management was trying to stage a coup, and I'd need his help getting everyone back on track.

That matter was on hold. However, the matter of the female variety had me at a standstill.

"How do you get a woman's trust?" I asked Jace as I stared at the bank of televisions in front of me.

A cold beer sat in my hand as I stared off. I needed help. Guidance. I didn't even know where to begin. I wasn't sure that Jace was the right person to be asking, either, but I was desperate for any insight.

"You're asking me?"

My lips formed a thin line. Yeah, Jace wasn't the best person, especially not after his last relationship, the one where he got caught fucking his girlfriend's best friend.

Ass.

I never understood how he, or how any man, could do that. If I was in a relationship, I would only sleep with my girl, fuck my girl, and not even consider another.

You're thinking about Roe.

A sigh left me. How could I want someone so much? Or was it just the memory of how good she felt around me driving me for more?

"I just… fuck, I don't even know what I need, but I need something."

"How about that blonde on your dick tonight?" he asked, nodding to the blonde at the end of the bar.

I gave him a side-eyed glance. "That's not going to help my issue." Bars weren't really my thing, but after a long week, I didn't really care where Jace wanted to go. I was just desperate for a drink. Or ten.

"Come on, man. The last year I've barely seen you show any interest in getting your dick wet."

"That's not my problem," I grumbled, trying not to remember the fucking perfection of Roe's body.

His eyes widened. "Oh, I see." He grinned and leaned in. "She hot?"

"Very." Natural beauty, curvy, petite body, and suckable pink lips.

"More than once?"

I groaned and let my head drop back before returning to look at him. "Yes, but now she's shut me out. She doesn't trust me, and I don't know how to fucking change that."

He shrugged. "Just play with her. Tell her whatever she wants to hear."

I narrowed my gaze on him. "When the fuck did you get so slimy?" Jace was never the devoted type, but I thought he had more integrity than that, and more respect for women.

"What? You're not looking for anything serious." His expression fell as he stared at me. "Holy shit, you are. This is the chick working for you, isn't it? The girl that hates you."

He was animated, excited, and it both amped me up to talk about her but also made me reserved. At least with Jace. The problem with talking to James was that he was also close to Roe.

"She has some secret, some hang-up. I know she's attracted to me."

"Yeah, otherwise why is she playing with your meat stick?"

I rolled my eyes. "My first impression isn't doing me any favors, and she seems stuck on that version of me."

"For starters, stop being this mopey ass with a chip on your shoulder. She turned you down? Hurt your little feelings? Be a fucking attack dog and keep going after her until she submits."

"While that is a graphic analogy I didn't really need, I understand its intent." I'd been called that before in business deals, which was why James entrusted me with his company's acquisitions, but I'd never applied that mentality to a woman. Never before had I wanted to, but Roe had me wanting so many things.

"And that is?"

"Don't give up, keep asking until she says yes."

He tilted his head from side to side as he thought over my interpretation. "Yeah, I suppose that works."

I quirked a brow at him. "What were you thinking?"

"Edge her until she says yes."

I rolled my eyes. "Dude, is pussy ever *not* on your mind?"

"Are you trying to tell me it's not on yours?"

I turned back to the screens. "Fair point. I'll try that way if the other doesn't work."

I really hoped the other way worked, because my appetite for her was more than just sexual.

Though the idea of edging her until she said yes did sound appealing.

Sixteen

Roe

The day was rough, as was every September 11th. Mom and I went to the memorial as we always did, but this time we had Kinsey in tow. After finding his name, I introduced him to her.

It was a bittersweet moment. It still floored me that something so devastating was now so long ago.

"What are you doing tonight?" I asked Mom as we walked back to the subway entrance together.

"I have a shift starting at midnight."

"So, nap?" I asked as I looked into the stroller. Kinsey was out like a light, fast asleep after a busy day.

She nodded, her arm threading with mine. "Any weekend plans?"

I shook my head. "The usual—laundry, groceries, and cleaning. Probably a walk in the park since the heat is supposed to break a little on Sunday. Kinsey loves the park."

"Any men in your life?"

I quirked my brow at her. "Really?" Inside I was really trying hard to not think about Thane today, and I was determined to keep it that way. After the pang subsided, I buried my feelings back down.

"What?"

I gestured to the stroller I was pushing and the infant inside. "I'm basically a single mother."

"I was a single mother and I dated."

"We weren't still in diapers." It took a few years before Mom had her first date. A firefighter she met in a nine-eleven support group.

She'd never had to go through the gamut of dating with a toddler. Hell, I couldn't even get a man interested enough to want to date.

Thane wants to date you, my brain reminded me. But he wouldn't once he found out.

We were almost to the subway entrance when I spotted a familiar profile standing against the railing. Her hair was bleached, the blonde long grown out, and looked like it hadn't been combed in weeks, and her clothes were riddled with rips and tears as well as some stains.

"Ryn."

She blinked at us and blew out a shaky breath. "Hi."

"You're late." I hated the tone in my voice, that edge of anger and rage that whipped across my words. Any other day, it would be cautious. The knot in my heart would loosen looking at her state, but not today.

It was with well-worn reason. Over the years I tried so hard to help her get clean, to help her have a life outside of drugs. I was the supportive older sister who did whatever I could to help. It failed every single time for one reason—she didn't want to get clean.

She traded sex for drugs and got pregnant with Kinsey, but never stopped.

While I hadn't given up on my sister, I had given up enabling her. Especially when one November morning I picked up a tiny bundle from Social Services.

"Ryn, baby…" Mom trailed off. The words had been said before. Over and over and over for nearly a decade, but they never penetrated. "How are you doing?"

Ryn chewed on her thumbnail, or rather what was left of it, and nodded. "I'm okay."

I ground my teeth. "You don't look okay."

She tried to smile, but she was fidgeting badly. "Well, you know, today." Her eyes flitted over the stroller, but she didn't even seem to register her child was in front of her.

"What are you on?" I asked.

"Roe!" Mom snapped.

"What?" I asked as I turned to her. "She's high as a kite, Mom."

I'd seen the different stages of high on her many times over the years. Whatever empathy I once had for my sister was nearly gone. It took a massive hit the day I took her abandoned daughter home. The same daughter she had yet to acknowledge.

"I just… you know… Daddy." Ryn blinked away a few tears.

It was like a stab to the heart. *Daddy*. Nearly two decades had passed, and I still missed him. My memories were limited, overwritten with time and age, but I still remembered his laugh and the smell of his aftershave.

We were all silent for a moment, but the more it stretched on, the more my anger grew.

I didn't want to hate my sister, but the drugs were making it nearly impossible to love her. It wasn't her, my baby sister, who grated on me. It was her high alter ego.

"You barely remember him. You're just using today as an excuse for why you're high when it doesn't matter anyway, because you're always high."

Ryn shook her head, tears filling her eyes. It was an act I'd seen many times.

"I've been clean for two weeks. I swear. I swear, Roe. I just… today. It's today for fuck's sake."

I closed my eyes and tried to push the memories from the day away. I'd gotten good over the years at putting that day in a box, separating it from the rest of my emotions. The pain, the fear, the unknown that filled me with terror as I watched the sky turn grey and block out the sun. The acrid smell that lasted for months.

He called. Told us he loved us. I begged him to come home. I was sorry. Just come home, then the line cut out and the screams echoed through the streets along with a roaring thunder.

I shook my head, a tear sliding down my cheek.

"This is no way to honor him," I said before turning and walking away.

"Roe!" she called out.

"It's been a rough day," Mom said in an attempt to soothe her.

"Love you, Mom," she said.

I turned back to see them hugging and waited for Mom. They separated, and Mom swiped a tear from Ryn's cheek. They talked for a moment, Mom probably asking if she'd eaten, then pulled money from her wallet.

I wanted to go and snatch it away because I caught the way Ryn brightened. The high was calling her.

"Why did you do that?" I asked when Mom caught back up to me.

Mom looked somewhat chastised. She was a nurse. She knew what drugs did to people.

We made our way down to the subway and onto the train that had just pulled in.

"You shouldn't say things like that to her," Mom said once we were seated on the train.

"Why not? Have I not done enough for her? Fights with my boyfriend because I spent our rent money getting her into rehab, her stealing my stuff, getting high in my apartment, and giving her more money than I can even count?"

"Don't give up on her."

"I'm not, Mom." I let out a sigh and looked down to the stroller and the chubby cheeks of the baby slumbering inside. "But I'm done coddling her. I don't have the energy for it. All of my love and empathy and caring transferred into her daughter."

Mom took my hand in hers and squeezed. "I know. I'm sorry. Seeing her like that, never knowing where she is or what she's doing. Every phone call I think will be the police to tell me she's dead."

It was a fear I had as well.

"We've tried, but she doesn't want to get better."

"I just don't understand why."

"Because then she'd have to become a functioning member of society with no means of escape. Ryn just wants to get high. That's all she's ever wanted." My chest clenched. All I wanted was for Ryn to get better, to come back to us, but I wasn't going to aid her habit any longer. Not until she came to me, sober, and asked for help. Just one fucking time to come to me when she wasn't high or itching to get high.

Just once.

"And Kinsey."

I ground my teeth together. "She never wanted Kinsey. She wanted to get high, and Kinsey was the outcome of that. She couldn't pay the hospital bill, and they knew she was pumped full of drugs so she ran out, leaving Kinsey there. I miss my little sister, but I don't miss the lying, stealing con-artist version."

She looked like she wanted to argue with me, but it was a conversation we'd had time and time again. As Ryn's mother, she wanted to defend her and keep working at it. She even tried to make me feel bad for cutting her off. All I had to do was point to Kinsey, and she stopped.

Days after my twenty-seventh birthday I had taken a tiny, underweight baby into my arms and made a solemn swear to protect her.

Even from her own mother.

No matter what.

Seventeen

Roe

Sunday was a complete and total waste. Kinsey spent most of the night screaming, and I spent the night bargaining with the banshee in my arms who likely didn't understand a word I said while trying to soothe her. Thankfully the old building had thick brick walls, but I knew her anguish leaked through the front door.

I just prayed it didn't disturb the neighbors too much.

We both spent the day napping on the couch, and when the evening rolled around, happy Kinsey was back.

"I'm so glad you're in such a good mood," I said as I looked down at her playing on the floor. "But can you sleep tonight so I'm not dead tomorrow when I see Thane?"

It wasn't until I said his name that I realized what I'd done. For so long, I'd simply called him Carthwright. It was formal, off-handed in a way, with no personal attachment.

But Thane… It was casual, friendly, and invited a different sense of propriety.

I liked him. A lot, to my surprise. And I'd upset him so much that I wasn't sure he could go back to the way it was.

Kinsey crawled over to me and pulled herself up, standing at the edge of the couch.

"Well look at you, nugget!" I smiled at the tiny tot before lifting her up. "I'm gonna have to baby proof more of this place, aren't I?"

"Mm-mama," she said.

A tear slipped from my eye and I pulled her against my chest. "Yes, beautiful girl, I'm Mama."

It wasn't the first time, because she always made that sound. I was only realizing that she said it while trying to get my attention.

I'd tried to keep a small amount of arm's length in my heart, not calling myself her mother, but the fact was clear—I was her mother. Maybe not genetically, but that didn't matter. I'd cared for her all but the first few weeks of her life, and I would care for her all the following days.

~

It was a new day, and a new attitude. Seeing Ryn reminded me why I said no to Thane, and I vowed to tell him this week. I just had to get back into his better graces.

For once, I actually arrived before him, and a few minutes before eight. Just as I set my bag down, I caught sight of him out of the corner of my eye.

He didn't glare at me when he saw me, but he didn't smile either. It was a neutral glance and that gave me hope that the week would be better than the one before.

"Good morning, Thane," I said as he passed me.

He stopped and turned toward me. "Roe?"

I tilted my head. "Hmm?"

"Say it again."

A smile broke out on my face. "Good morning, Thane."

He gave me a small, warm smile that was encouraging. "I like that. Keep it up."

I blew out a breath, happy that something so small could make him smile at me again. I still wasn't ready to tell him about Kinsey, but I also couldn't stand for the wall of last week to be between us any longer.

An hour later I tried to stifle a yawn, the back of my hand covering my mouth as I let out a high-pitched sound.

"Those are contagious," Thane said from behind me, his mouth opening wide, unable to stop a yawn from moving through him.

"Well, if you were at your desk where you're supposed to be, you wouldn't have even noticed."

"Maybe, but I came with a request."

"And that is?"

"I have a conference call in twenty minutes I need to get ready for, and I need something stronger than the piss water that comes from the break room. Can you please get me a cappuccino from downstairs?"

I stood and blinked at him. "Did you just say please?"

His brow furrowed. "I say it all the time."

I shook my head. "Not to me."

He pursed his lips. "Are you sure?"

"Oh, I'd know if that word ever came out of your mouth."

He stepped closer. "Forgive me for that."

I turned to him and drew in a shuddered breath. Spice, grapefruit, and musk invaded my senses whenever he was near, and it made me want to walk right into his arms. Every single day I was nearly taken out by his scent, even the week before when we barely interacted.

I was kidding myself. Every day I was nearly taken out by him. There was no one factor that beat out the others. No, he was the whole package.

"You're forgiven," I whispered.

He reached out, the back of his fingers brushing against my arm. Goose bumps rose on my skin, and a shiver rolled down my spine. The buzz of electricity that always hummed between us grew louder.

"Are you ever going to wear that blazer?" he asked, his deep voice almost a rumble in his chest.

"When you buy it."

"I'm still keeping score," he said as he stepped back, a twinkle in his eye.

"Score?"

He nodded. "You're winning, by the way. Handily. I just can't seem to keep up with your wit."

I stared at him, a bit confused. "I wasn't aware we were playing a game."

"The best never do. Cappuccino, one sugar. Get one for yourself. You look like you need it."

"Are you trying to say I don't look my normal spunky self?" I asked, realizing my mistaken word choice with the charge in the air between us.

"You know you can't say words like that to me. I'll spin it in a completely unprofessional way," he said with a wink before heading back into his office.

I rolled my eyes. "You avoided my question, perv."

He turned back around, a grin on his face. "You look beautiful, as always. You yawned before I came over, remember?"

Oh.

Right.

I bit down on my bottom lip and nodded. "Cappuccino, one sugar. Got it."

Our eyes locked for a moment, and I felt a calmness wash over me that I wasn't used to around him. With a tap of his hand on the door frame, he retreated back into his office and I headed off to the lobby coffee shop.

Things were already better and I wasn't quite sure why, but it seemed that somewhere between my time off and the weekend, the stick shoved up his butt had released. Which was good, because I wasn't sure how much more of that Thane I could take.

This Thane, though, I could definitely appreciate more of.

The week continued with our banter and flirtation back in place, but something still wasn't quite right. There was an invisible wall between us that fell from time to time, but never went away.

The weekend was hours away, and I was counting down the minutes. But before I could escape, he called out.

"Roe, can you come in here?"

I finished up my thought in an email to Donte, then stood and headed in.

"Hi." My smile dropped when I found Thane out of sorts and cursing under his breath. "Everything all right?"

He shook his head. "I need you to stay late tonight."

"I can't."

When his head snapped up, a deep scowl greeted me. Gone was the charming flirt, replaced by the assholian. What had him so worked up?

"You will," he growled through clenched teeth.

My spine straightened as I stared at him with wide eyes. Did he really want to have a day one fight with me?

Eighteen

Thane

Fuck. Fuck, fuck.

The stress had gotten to me and I was taking it out on her, which was *not* what I needed or wanted to be doing. And I knew my attitude would activate hers and it was going to be another battle.

"Or what? You read my contract."

"It also states that on occasion you can be requested to stay late." I *needed* her to stay late. Worthington was on the verge of *finally* going through, but I received a call stating that shareholder packets had to go out *today*.

No warning whatsoever.

"*With notice,*" she stressed.

"Here is your notice."

She wrapped her arms in front of her. "An hour before my end of day is not sufficient."

"These shareholder notifications have to go out by eight with the last courier and no later. I was just informed of this. I need you to stay."

She ground her teeth together, and while I loved our usual banter, that was not what was happening. Legitimate anger stewed beneath the surface.

"Fine, but if I do this, I'm taking a break now."

The muscles in my shoulders and back let go a small bit of their tension. "Don't worry, I'll get some dinner delivered."

She shook her head. "That's not what I'm saying. You want me to stay and help? Then you are going to give me time, an hour, and it's going to be paid."

I watched as she moved to her desk and pulled her purse from the bottom drawer.

"You never take breaks," I reminded her.

"I do today. Keep your panties on and wait."

I ground my teeth together as I watched her walk away. What the fuck was so damn important? It didn't make sense to me. We were losing valuable time that could push us to missing the deadline.

However, I would rather lose an hour of her help then only have an hour of it.

Every minute that passed, I stewed until I was focused on the task.

At an hour and sixteen minutes, Roe was speed walking to my office door. She tossed her purse onto my table and kicked off her shoes before pulling her hair up and twisting it into a bun. There was a slight sheen of sweat on her skin, a few lone beads gathering. Unable to look away, I was enthralled, watching a drop of sweat roll from her hairline, around her neck, then along the swell of her cleavage.

Fuck, I wanted to dive between her breasts and lick the droplet.

"Fucking heat wave," she said as she fanned her face. "It's mid-September."

"Did you have a good break?"

"I got done what I needed to, if that's what you're asking. And I'm ready to get this done now."

"Glad you're finally ready," I ground out, instantly regretting my tone.

"No."

"No?"

She folded her arms in front of her. "You can't give me shit, because I'm here, helping you, when I'm supposed to be somewhere else. Unlike you, work is not my life."

"With no boyfriend, I didn't think you had a life outside of work."

"It may not be much of one, but it's mine, and it includes obligations you can't even comprehend." There was conviction behind her words, as well as tears. She wiped them away with her palm, then cleared her throat. "Where were we?"

Her tears stripped me, tore at my chest. I'd done that, upset her, when I wasn't supposed to fucking be doing shit like that anymore.

"Roe… I'm sorry," I said, holding back the urge to touch her. "I've been an ass and taking my frustration out on you the last two weeks."

"I noticed."

"I'm trying to understand, to process it in a non-asshole way, but I don't get why you won't go out with me. Just once." It wasn't the time or place, but I needed some kind of answer.

Her brow scrunched. "You think I don't want that? Things aren't what they appear. You don't know what my life is like, and if you did, you'd run away. That's why. It's not that I don't want to, it's because you won't."

I froze, staring at her as my heart pounded. She did want me, but she assumed I wouldn't want her once her secret was revealed, whatever the fuck it was. "You don't know that."

"I do. You wouldn't be the first that couldn't handle it, and probably not the last, so… drop it."

I desperately wanted to know what secret she was keeping.

What it was that she was so convinced would make me bolt? All I wanted was a chance, but I would need to work harder for that.

By seven, we were almost done with the packets and sharing plates of sushi. Once the courier collected the envelopes, we cleaned up the trash and got ready to head out.

When they were gone and the tension of the day was over with, the bad vibes between us settled away. I glanced out the window and found the sky to be dark and the lights of the city glowing all around.

"It's late. Let me give you a ride home," I said as I watched her stuff her heels into her bag and slip on some flats she'd pulled out.

"It's okay. You don't have to."

"Yes, I do. Where do you live?"

"Lenox Hill. Upper East Side."

I froze as I stared at her. "How long have you lived there?"

"A while. Why?"

"I live in the Upper East Side." It was an upscale area of the city, and I had to imagine a one-bedroom apartment cost a small fortune and would be tiny. Probably the size of my first apartment when I moved to New York.

"Oh great, so you're telling me you invade my personal sanctuary outside of work hours?"

Her lip twitched up, and I finally believed she was no longer angry at me for making her stay late. Good. Of course, not being an ass probably helped my case, as well as airing out the tension.

As much as I loved to argue with her, I didn't like the stones that settled in my stomach when she was legitimately angry.

Living in the same neighborhood could definitely have some advantages. Maybe I could figure out why she was so set that we couldn't work, let alone go on a single fucking date that didn't involve me tricking her into lunch.

"Technically, you invaded my sanctuary. I've lived there for four years."

"Let me guess—one of the high rises?"

I grinned at her. "The twenty-ninth floor."

She nodded and stepped forward, our bodies inches apart as she looked up at me. My hands instinctively settled on her hips as I stared into her eyes. She didn't push them away, her palms resting against my chest.

The atmosphere around us shifted, and it took all my strength to resist kissing her.

"This is not me invading your space, by the way. I'm an LH girl for life."

Life? "What brought you to Lenox Hill?"

"My parents, when I was born."

"You grew up there?" I asked.

She nodded. "Seventieth and Second. Then after college I got a studio apartment with a loft up on Eighty-Third with my ex-boyfriend."

"Studio with a loft, that's not bad."

She shook her head. "By loft, I mean there was a space above the kitchen to throw a mattress into and literally crawl into bed. Then last year I moved down First Avenue."

"Why didn't you move someplace cheaper?" I asked. Granted, after I graduated, I stayed in Manhattan as well.

"Jersey or Brooklyn or Queens? I'm a Manhattan girl. Lenox Hill just has this down-to-earth feel. It surprises me you're not on the west end closer to Central Park. What brought you to my neighborhood?"

"I like the area."

"Me too."

"And I like it even more knowing you're there."

Her cheeks turned pink and she bit down on her lower lip before stepping out of my arms. "We should go," she said. I couldn't stop watching the harsh rise and fall of her chest.

Stepping forward, I cupped her face with one hand and

pulled at her waist with the other. She drew in a sharp breath right when my lips met hers.

There was no pushing away, no angry outburst, just a soft moan that moved from her to me. Pure, utter perfection. All I wanted to do was devour every inch of her. It took all my strength to pull away, but I managed.

"We should go," I said, mimicking her own words.

She nodded in agreement before walking back over to her bag and grabbing it and her phone. I put my hand on her lower back as we walked, desperate to feel her close.

Nineteen

Roe

The traffic had thinned out, shortening what I knew to be a longer drive and leaving me with less time with his spicy scent filling the small space of the car—the kind of scent that had me wanting to rub up against him. I was able to control myself when at the office, but being so close to him, staring at his hand resting on the gear shift, it was difficult to keep myself from climbing into his lap and pressing my lips to his. Or putting my hand on his crotch to tease him to hardness.

These were thoughts that were not supposed to be going through my mind, but I couldn't seem to stop.

"This is me," I said, pointing to a five-story brick building with a self-proclaimed best pizza pizzeria, a laundry, and a sushi place occupying the first floor. To their credit, the pizza was really good. Even better as leftovers after a night of drinking.

"Which one?" he asked as he swooped into a spot against the curb.

"I don't know if I should tell you. You might try to sneak over in the middle of the night and take advantage of me."

His tongue peeked out to wet his lips as they drew up into a grin. "I don't know where you got that idea, but it's a damn good one."

That small movement proved to be too much for me to handle.

I grabbed his neck and pulled his lips to mine. It was instinctual, and I could see the surprise in his eyes before they closed. A small moan left us both when our tongues met. When his hand slipped behind my back, I retreated. It was already escalating too much, and there was no way I could invite him up.

"If you're a good boy, maybe I'll tell you one day."

"Tease. You know I could just knock on every door until I find you." I believed that he would.

"Patience, Mr. Carthwright. Good things come to those who wait."

"If it gets your lips around my cock, I'll be the best boy in the office."

"Keep dreaming," I said with a wink before exiting the car. "Only boyfriends get those."

"It will happen. You will be mine."

My heart began to race at the determination in his words. "Goodnight, Thane."

He grinned at me. "See you later, beautiful."

My whole body felt charged, and I missed him the moment he sped away. A tingling lingered on my lips, and I couldn't keep the smile from my face as I entered my building. He was persistent, which I was enjoying, but my heart sank every time I remembered he'd run as fast as he could the moment he found out about Kinsey. After grabbing the mail, I ran up to the second floor and knocked on the door to apartment one.

A few moments later, the door creaked open and I was greeted by a sweet smile. "Roe. Good gracious, they worked you to the bone tonight."

"They did. Thank you so much for helping me today," I said as I stepped in, my gaze searching out my nugget.

"No problem, dear. She made my evening."

"Hey, chubby cheeks," I said with a smile. My heart settled when she crawled over to me, baby talking in high-pitched squeaks.

"Ma, ma, ma, ma," she babbled.

I scooped her up in my arms. "Were you a good girl for Mrs. Walsh?"

She kicked her feet in excitement.

"She was a doll, as always."

"Thank you so much for your help." I leaned over to pick up her diaper bag. "Say bye-bye," I said to Kinsey. She waved her open hand at her. "Thank you again."

"You're welcome, sweetie. See you later, Kinsey." Mrs. Walsh blew Kinsey a kiss and waved her arthritic hands.

I probably thanked her too many times, but she really saved me. It wasn't often I asked for her help, but the few times I had, she was always willing. We had a barter system going, and I knew a list of items she needed would show up under my door in a day or two. I didn't mind helping her at all and would have done it even without her help with Kinsey.

Kinsey waved back as we turned toward the staircase. "You ready for a bath?" I asked. I kissed her forehead, loving her giggle in response. "We'll get your little blue doggy. You'd like that, huh?"

We headed up the stairs, and I was hoping she would be out after her bath because I was dead tired and it was already past her bedtime.

"Roe," a familiar voice called out when I reached the landing.

In front of me stood Ryn, and my stomach dropped. *Why is she here?*

"I've had a really tough day. Can we not tonight?" I asked.

Her hands were shaking, and she couldn't stand still. The itch had her, and I really didn't want to let her in. I hated Kinsey seeing her like that, even if Kinsey had no clue who she was.

"You're high."

"Please, Roe. I just need a place to stay tonight. Please." A squeak drew her attention, and she finally looked down to the bundle in my arms. Her lips pulled up into a smile. "Hey, pumpkin." She leaned over and took Kinsey's hand. "How's my baby?"

"If you really cared, you'd be around more."

She looked back to me again. "Roe..."

I blew out a breath. "Are you hungry? There are some leftovers in the fridge."

"Thanks," she said, stepping back and allowing me to unlock the door.

We entered, and I threw my bags down on the coffee table and slipped my shoes off. There were some leftovers that might not be good anymore, so I pulled out my phone to order something for her. I was still full from sushi, but some junky and carb-filled appetizer to top it off wouldn't be bad. Just as I turned to ask what she wanted, Ryn opened the door and three men filed in.

My eyes widened as I tried to process what was going on. "Ryn?"

Ryn was looking at the ground not saying a word.

"Where's the shit, Ryn?" When she didn't answer, a man with greasy black hair yanked her hair back, making her scream out before he slapped her.

I watched as one of the men, who was as big as a linebacker, pushed Ryn to the ground.

"Bitch, where's the money?"

Ryn looked to me. "She knows where."

My eyes widened as the situation fully settled in. Movement caught the corner of my eye as the last man came through the threshold and headed straight for me. A heartbeat was all it took for instinct to take over and I turned around, rushing into the bathroom and slamming the door behind me. I pushed against the door to lock it and jumped after it clicked when someone slammed against the door.

"Open this door, bitch!"

Kinsey let out a cry, and I pulled her closer. I could hear Ryn screaming and some glass breaking, but whoever was on the other side continued to beat on the door.

With shaking fingers, I pulled up my contacts and hit the call button for the first person that came to mind.

"Couldn't last fifteen minutes without me, huh?" he answered.

"Thane," I said, my voice shaking. "I need help."

"Roe, what's wrong?"

The door shook with a slam, making me jump. A scream left me, and I pulled Kinsey tighter to me. "There are men in my apartment."

"Where are you?" he asked. What had been silence was suddenly filled with the sounds of the city in the background.

"The bathroom. Third floor, apartment four."

"Stay put. Find something to defend yourself just in case. I'll be right there."

"Please hurry," I whimpered as I watched the door shake.

My heart hammered in my chest as I grabbed the bottle of cleaner from the cabinet under the sink. It wasn't much, but it was something and the bleach would hopefully burn. The slams against the door grew harder and I climbed into the tub, sinking down, holding Kinsey close to my chest.

My eyes closed, pinching shut at another slam that shook the door. Kinsey let out a wail, tears sliding down her cheeks.

There were a few loud thumps, crashes, something breaking, and then I heard Thane yelling. My heart slammed in my chest. *What is he doing? He could get hurt!*

Another few heartbeats passed before it became silent, then footsteps became louder as they grew closer. A soft knock on the door made me freeze before the sound of Thane's voice filtered through.

"Roe? It's okay now. You can open the door."

With a shaking hand, I reached up and flipped the lock on the door, then turned the handle. I looked up as he passed through the doorway and stopped, his eyes wide.

At least Kinsey wasn't a secret anymore.

Twenty

Thane

A baby.

There was a baby in Roe's arms. She had the same hair color and same hazel eyes as Roe.

Roe was a mother.

I was struck stupid as I stared at them.

Everything suddenly made sense. The leaving early, late arrivals, refusal to stay late, rejecting my date invites, and even more so why she had disappeared that afternoon.

The child filled the stretching silence with a piercing scream. Roe pulled it tighter to her, bouncing slightly as she soothed. "Shh, it's okay. He's here to help us."

Tears slipped down Roe's cheeks, her bottom lip trembling.

I stepped forward and kneeled down beside the tub. The angle was awkward, but I was able to wrap my arms around them both and pull them close.

Roe shook as she let loose a sob. She reached up and gripped my neck, pulling me closer.

The child's cries subsided, a curious look on her face as she stared at her mother.

"The police will be here soon," I whispered.

"Thank you. Thank you so much."

"Mama," the baby cooed as she nuzzled into Roe's chest.

The police arrived a few minutes later and separated us as they took our statements. One of the intruders was still unconscious on the floor, and they cuffed him as they waited for an ambulance. He'd knocked his head pretty hard on the table when I punched him—hard—sending him to the ground.

Good.

He deserved more for the terror he put Roe through.

The others were unfortunately long gone. I'd seen two other men and a woman.

They didn't walk out with much, but what they did take was a hard hit to Roe. All that Roe could discern that they stole was her Blu-ray player, tablet, jewelry box, and her purse.

I'd stopped them before they got her TV, but it was broken in the process.

She had no prescription drugs, no video game console—though I did notice a few game boxes for a PS4 on a shelf. Her personal laptop had been on her bed when she got up that morning, the covers haphazardly thrown on top of it, putting it out of sight.

Her purse being gone was the worst, and she had to find the numbers to cancel her cards. Then came the realization of what was in the jewelry box. At first she brushed it off as costume jewelry, not worth anything really, just pieces she would miss. Then it hit her.

"My dad's watch." Her face crumpled and tears filled her eyes. By her reaction, it was the one thing that really mattered. Everything else could be replaced.

But I knew that couldn't.

"It's a Cartier Tank watch from the late nineties with gold trim and a leather band."

"Any distinguishing marks or engravings?" one officer asked.

She nodded. "On the back are the initials M.C.P."

After a few hours, the police left and I closed and locked the door after them. I'd tried to get Roe to come to my place or get a hotel, but she refused. The baby was fast asleep against Roe's chest as I sat down next to them on the couch.

I flexed my fingers, lifting the ice from my knuckles. They were a bit swollen and a few were split, but other than some pain, they were fine. All superficial.

Roe smiled, and I could tell it was a struggle. She looked down at the baby in her arms and brushed a few stray locks from the tiny girl's face.

"Thane, meet Kinsey."

I stared at her in stunned silence. Putting a name to her baby made her all the more real and made me question many things, the most prominent being why she never told me about her.

"Where is her father?" I asked. A burning curiosity filled me.

Roe shrugged. "Who knows?"

"You're not still with him?"

She blinked at me, then looked around like she suddenly remembered something. "My work laptop."

I pointed to the floor a few feet from the door. "I managed to pry it from one of the guys as he ran out. I'm sorry I couldn't stop them from taking more."

She shook her head. "It's fine. As long as we're okay. That's my work laptop and has so much sensitive information on it."

"And it would still be fine if they'd taken it. Better it than you."

She settled back down, her hand absently stroking Kinsey's back.

"How old is she?"

"Eleven months."

"Roe, the door wasn't broken in, so how did they get in?"

"Ryn. They were with Ryn." Her voice was distant, her eyes too. It made my chest clench, seeing her beaten down emotionally.

"Who is Ryn?"

She pointed to a framed photo sitting below her now smashed television. I walked over and picked it up before returning to her side. In the wooden frame was a woman who was maybe in her forties with a teenage girl on either side. One was obviously Roe, and the other had to be Ryn. They had similar facial features as well as hair and eye color, making it obvious they were related.

She must have been the woman I saw.

"Your sister?" I asked. She nodded. There was a time for tiptoeing and letting her push me aside, but no more. "I know it's been a hard night, so I can't tell if it's due to that or if you have a hard time opening up, or just opening up to me."

Abruptly, she stood. "I'm going to go put her in bed. There is a bottle of tequila in that cabinet and some limes in the basket on the table. Hopefully you know how to make a margarita."

I watched her walk down the hall, hating that she had to hold Kinsey protectively to her out of fear from what happened. I stepped over to the large wooden cabinet she pointed to. The tequila was close to empty, but I located a smaller bottle in the back of the cabinet.

I knew vaguely how to make a margarita, but still engaged in the power of the internet for help.

The shards that fell from her television were scattered across the tabletop. It took a moment to locate a trashcan to sweep them into, and then I found a broom and swept the floor around the table.

Once the debris was cleaned, I started in on her drink.

When she stepped out of the bedroom, her work clothes

were gone and replaced by an oversized T-shirt and shorts that I could barely see.

I held out a glass to her, and she took a few long gulps. "Thank you."

"You called me."

She nodded. "I'm sorry."

I locked my eyes with hers. "Don't be."

She looked down at the tabletop, her fingers swirling along a grove in the wood. "I didn't know who else to call."

"You don't have any friends?"

She shrugged. "I lost a lot after Kinsey. I have Lizzie and James, but they are in Midtown. I knew you weren't far."

"I'm glad you could count on me." I needed to assure her that she was right to call me. It would kill me to find out what happened on Monday knowing I was so close and she didn't call. I didn't even want to think about what would have happened if I'd been a few minutes later. The bathroom door was solid wood, but they'd managed to crack it. Much more, and then what? I shuddered to think, and the anger rose in me.

She set her hand on mine and squeezed. "Me too."

That calmed me and brought me back to what was important. "You have a beautiful daughter. She looks just like you."

She made an odd chuff that reminded me of the tigers at the zoo, but the sound was more of a bad emotion than the good emotion my memory evoked.

"You're a good mom."

She reached up and swiped a tear from her cheek.

"Hey, none of that," I said as I took her hand in mine and tipped her head up so that she'd look at me. "You did good today. They're gone, and you're both safe."

"It was a situation that I shouldn't have even been in!" She pulled back, and I watched the anger move through her. She stood and began pacing, which, given the size of the room, meant she walked about two steps before she turned around. "For fuck's sake, she can't stay clean for a day, and I'm done! Just fucking done! She brought that into my home, to where her fucking daughter sleeps, to fucking rob me! After all I've fucking done for her!"

I narrowed my gaze at her as I tried to unscramble what she was saying, not knowing what fueled her sudden burst of anger. "Your sister?"

"Yes." She was shaking her head back and forth. "I'm done with her. I can't do it anymore and after tonight, she's never getting Kinsey. Ever. I'll make sure of it."

Once again, everything clicked. Kinsey wasn't her daughter. Kinsey was her niece. That was why she'd never mentioned a child. That was why the baby resembled her.

"Your sister is a drug addict, and you're raising her baby."

That realization hit me hard. My own mother had abandoned me for drugs, and the beautiful woman before me was doing everything to shield Kinsey from the same experience.

"Not many people at the office know that I'm her guardian."

"How long have you had her?"

"She wasn't very old when I took her, a couple of weeks. With no father, a crackhead mother, and a traveling nurse grandmother, I was the best candidate. There was no way in hell I was going to let her fall into the system. She didn't deserve that just because her mother is a piece of shit." She tipped back her glass, polishing off the liquid before slamming the glass down in front of me. "Barkeep, another."

"As you wish," I said as I moved back over to the tiny kitchen that ran along one wall. There was "open concept," and then there was her apartment. The kitchen, dining room, and living room were all scrunched into a room that was maybe twelve feet by fifteen feet, which was smaller than my bedroom.

"It didn't take much for the court to grant me guardianship, especially with all that Social Services had on the situation." She went silent, her gaze far off before she drew in a stunted breath. "I defended Ryn for so long. Helped her get into rehab clinics, gave her a place to stay. Food, money—whatever to help her. Put strain on my life and my relationships. Now I see that she doesn't want it. She'd rather put her family—her own *daughter*—in jeopardy for a hit. She probably would have sold Kinsey for a couple bags of heroin by now. She couldn't even quit while she was pregnant, so Kinsey had neonatal abstinence syndrome and had to be in the hospital those first few weeks."

My chest constricted. The baby had done nothing and was born into immeasurable pain because of her mother's vices. I poured the remainder of the mixture I'd created into her glass, though it didn't even fill it halfway, then handed it over.

"She couldn't even give her a damn name."

Seriously? "Who named her?"

"I did," she said with a sad sigh. "She was born on our dad's birthday. His name was Mac, short for Malcolm, so I named her Mackinsey. Somewhere along the line, it just got shortened to Kinsey."

"That's a sweet tribute."

She gave me a sad smile and swiped another tear away, confirming my suspicion that her father was dead. "Mom thought so, too." She took a deep breath. "I hoped Ryn would get clean one day and could really be a mother to Kinsey, but I've lost hope of that ever happening."

"Why don't many know about her?" I asked. It was that omission I'd felt when we talked, the reluctance to open up.

"Because I lost people I trusted, people I loved, when I took in Kinsey. Good riddance, but it's caused me some unintentional issues."

"Boyfriend?" I knew she didn't have one, but I wondered if she lost one.

She opened her hand and made the explosion sound. "Four years down the drain. When I told him I was taking her in, he was out. No discussion, just gone."

"That had to be hard."

She stared down at her glass. "At one time, I thought we would get married someday, but at the first challenge to the norm, he was gone. He gave me an ultimatum, but I didn't budge." She polished off her glass and pushed it toward me. "Barkeep, my glass is empty."

"I'll make another if it will keep you talking."

"Dam is open now."

"He wasn't the one, you know."

She raised a brow at me. "The one? A little romantic sounding for you."

"You think I don't know what romance is?"

"No, not really."

Ouch. Have I really given her that bad of an impression of me? No wonder she didn't want to go out with me.

"I may have never been in a long-term relationship like yours, but that doesn't mean I don't want it."

"You don't like kids, so I figured you weren't a love kind of guy," she said with a shrug.

I froze. "When did I say I don't like kids?" And how in the hell did she get that idea?

"You were bitching about Crystal being gone so long so she could take care of her baby. You were pissed she chose the baby over work."

Fuck. Once again, my own issues were messing things up. That wasn't it at all.

"Is that why you wouldn't go out with me? Because of Kinsey?"

She nodded. "I'm surprised you're still here."

My heart sank. She had no faith that I would be able to handle her having a baby.

We'd gotten closer, learned more about each other, but she didn't know my past, just my assholish behavior in the beginning, which drew a very unlikeable portrait of me. One, it seemed, I was never able to fully erase in her mind.

"You're not the only one who's had to deal with a drug-addict relative," I admitted, hoping that opening up to her might help her see me as someone other than the man she'd known those first few days.

The bristles from her emotional explosion settled and softened. "You, too?"

I nodded. "But I'm not you in this situation. I'm Kinsey." Her eyes widened as she stared at me. "I'm going to ask you a question, but it's a little different than before—will you and Kinsey go out with me tomorrow?"

She blinked at me, her brow furrowed. It had been a long, hard night and I knew her emotions were everywhere, but I needed her to know that having a baby didn't scare me away.

"I… Why?" she asked.

"Why what?"

"Why would you want that?"

"I thought that was obvious—because I want you."

She blinked at me. "But I have a baby."

Had she not been listening to me? Or had it just not sunk in? "And?"

"And…" she trailed off, her arguments losing the ground that held them up.

I took her hands in mine. "If you haven't figured it out yet, I'm kind of enamored with you. I'm sorry for the way I've acted. Honestly, I was just so happy to have a sparring partner that I kept egging you on to keep it up."

"You like fighting with me?"

I nodded and smiled. "You have a wicked wit, and I'm always on the edge of my seat for your reactions."

"It has been fun," she admitted with a smile. "And sexy."

"So hot," I agreed. "You are also dense sometimes, you know."

"What?"

"I can't tell you how many times I've tried to buy you lunch and you haven't gotten the hint."

She shrugged. "I didn't want to have to owe you anything."

A groan left me. "I wasn't doing it so that you'd owe me. I was doing it so that you'd see that I liked you."

"And after all this, you still like me?" she asked, and I could hear the waver of uncertainty in her voice.

I moved closer to her and cupped her face. "Even more now."

Leaning down, I pressed my lips to hers. At first, she didn't respond, but her arms quickly wrapped around my waist, pulling me closer and spreading warmth through me. Her lips parted, and my tongue lapped against hers.

My grip around her waist was loose. The last thing I wanted to do was take advantage of her, despite how much I wanted her.

"I should get to bed."

I nodded. "I'll sleep on the couch."

"Really?"

"You already said no to my place or a hotel before the police left. I'm not leaving you here alone." She was insane if she thought I was leaving.

She disappeared and returned with a pillow, sheet, and blanket.

"Goodnight, Thane," she whispered as she stood on the tips of her toes, her neck straining to reach my lips. Soft and sensual and completely too short. "Thank you again."

"Always."

She headed to the bedroom and turned to look at me before she closed the door. I blew out a breath and stripped out of my clothes, then set up my makeshift bed for the night before turning off the light and crawling in.

I stared up at the ceiling, lost in thought. The infatuation I held had morphed in one evening to complete and total desire for her. It scared me that she had a child, but not in the way one would think. It scared me because I could see how much she loved Kinsey, and losing her due to one of her parents taking custody would devastate Roe.

I didn't want to see her heart break like that. Her smile was too beautiful.

I'd been so frustrated with her earlier in the day because I couldn't understand her logic, but now I knew. All I'd ever seen was the surface. That was all she ever showed, and I never dug deeper.

So much rested on her shoulders. Responsibility she wasn't anticipating that she took in stride. She found a way to become the mother Kinsey deserved.

At some time in the night, I was startled awake by the blanket moving. Roe crawled under, her legs twining with mine as she laid her head on my chest. I was confused, but when she let out a sigh and relaxed against me, I understood. There wasn't a lot of extra room, so I wrapped my arms around her and held her close.

The normally feisty and strong woman had let her guard down and shown me a fragility she kept hidden.

Hours later, Roe stretched against me, rousing me. She hadn't even opened her eyes, just snuggled into my chest. The last year couldn't have been easy on her, and I was curious if she was desperate for comfort or if she genuinely wanted comfort from me.

I'd given her little reason to trust me, and I could tell it I would have a hard road ahead of me.

"Good morning," I whispered, kissing the top of her head. It was a mistake and she froze, her body no longer pliant against mine.

"I'm sorry," she said as she pushed against my chest to sit up.

"Don't be." I pulled her back down to me despite her reluctance and wrapped my arms around her. "I'm here for whatever you need."

We lay there for a few minutes until a cry and "Mamamamama" came from the bedroom.

"Be right back," she said as she left my arms.

I couldn't help but smile at her disheveled appearance. Her hair was everywhere and the neck of her T-shirt was stretched, revealing her collarbone and the top of her shoulder.

So cute and sexy, but what drove me wild was realizing the small shorts she had worn the night before were gone, leaving me a perfect view of her thong-clad ass when she bent over to pick the blanket up.

"You're killing me, Roe," I groaned as I palmed my hard cock—the hard cock I'd been trying to ignore since I woke up.

She turned, finally noticing I was only in my underwear—a pair of low-cut trunks and a white undershirt—and I watched pink spread across her cheeks. She bit down on her bottom lip, her eyes locked on mine as she pulled up the front of her T-shirt, exposing her thong and sensuous hips.

A groan left me, and the wicked woman simply smiled before letting out a giggle and walking away.

Twenty-One

Roe

Leaving the warmth of Thane's arms was difficult, especially seeing him nearly naked on my couch. I couldn't help but tease before another cry from Kinsey made my chest clench and I quickly headed to her.

All night I kept wondering what would have happened if he hadn't been so close. The police couldn't have gotten here as fast as he did.

"Good morning, sunshine," I said as I stepped into the walk-in closet that held her crib. The bedroom wasn't large enough—none of the rooms were—but there was an oddly large walk-in closet with a window that faced the street.

Once Pete had moved out, there was room, and it was the perfect spot.

Kinsey smiled at me and lifted her arms, babbling.

"You hungry?"

Fingers whapped against my chin and lips as legs kicked.

"Let's get you changed first, stinky girl."

I moved back into the bedroom and the makeshift changing table that was simply the top of my dresser.

My mind took over as I went on auto pilot.

From the time I left Thane to the time I crawled into bed with him, all I could think about were the what-ifs. That was the anxiety that had me seeking out comfort in the first person in so long who didn't let me down.

The way Ryn was pushed to the ground and the strength they used to try and bust into the bathroom made me fear greatly for my life and for Kinsey's. What did they want with us? What were they going to do to me? To Kinsey? What did they do to Ryn?

What if Thane hadn't been so close?

He hadn't run away yet, which surprised me, but I was guarded for when he did. It would happen, just like it had happened before.

Getting even more attached to him than I already was would only end in heartbreak.

Thane didn't deny that he didn't like kids, and it didn't matter how much he liked me; I was a package deal. Kinsey was mine, and she wasn't going anywhere.

"You want to go see Thane?" I asked her. The thought that he might have already skipped out crossed my mind, but the front door was heavy and I didn't hear it shut.

His head snapped to me when I walked in with Kinsey on my hip. I was struck by how good looking he was with bed head. His dark locks were longer on top, and they had curled and kinked in the night, sticking up and out everywhere. His blue eyes almost glowed from the light pouring in through the windows.

I hadn't even looked at my own appearance, but I knew I had to be a mess.

"Cappuccino?" I asked as I set Kinsey down in her high chair.

"Sure," he said as he stood, pulling his pants up as he did.

I nabbed a stray ponytail holder and threw my hair up in a quick messy bun.

After sprinkling some O's onto her tray, I turned to my cappuccino machine. Thankfully the assholes didn't take that along with my purse.

We were halfway done drinking our coffee when he locked eyes with me.

"I don't feel right leaving you yet."

I quirked a brow at him. Honestly, I was confused he'd stayed so long, especially after finding out about Kinsey.

"I'm surprised you stayed."

"Why?"

"It's not that I keep her a secret, but my situation isn't what I led on."

"Actually, I think it's spot on. All your little idiosyncrasies and OCD about leaving on time, not staying after. Your tardiness and sometimes rumpled demeanor make complete sense. Before, I wondered if you partied too hard at night."

A strangled laugh erupted from me. "Major party person right here."

"If this is an attempt to forget what I said last night and throw your walls back up, I'm going to have to stop you."

"What you said?"

"I know you didn't get black-out drunk on those two margaritas last night. You were barely tipsy when you went to bed."

"It was just lip service," I said, turning my attention back to the cup in my hand.

"No, it wasn't. I'm taking you two out today. I already got us tickets."

My head snapped up. "You what?"

"You heard me. I bought us tickets to the zoo. And little miss gets in for free because she's under two."

My chest clenched and I swallowed hard. "You want to go on a date with me and bring Kinsey?"

"Is that not all right?"

I stepped forward and wrapped my arms around his waist. "It's perfect."

He leaned down and placed a kiss to the top of my head.

"She's going to be so excited," I said as I pulled back. "She loves when I put Animal Planet or Discovery Channel on. She's enamored with the animals."

"How long does it take you to get ready?"

I pursed my lips and looked at the chubby-cheeked baby stuffing another O in her mouth. I needed a shower, and there was a whole day's worth of stuff I'd need for her diaper bag.

"Two hours?" I said, though it was more of a question. An hour was definitely too short.

He nodded. "I'll go take a shower and change and come back."

He wrapped his arms around me, and I relaxed into the warmth. A whimper left me when he stepped away.

"I'll be back soon." He picked up his dress shirt and jacket, then slipped his shoes on. "Lock the door after me."

I did as he requested, not that I wouldn't after what happened. It still felt like a dream, but the evidence of my nightmare was everywhere—including my lack of a purse.

Shit.

What was in it? I didn't keep a lot in it because Kinsey's baby bag and my laptop bag held a lot of the unnecessary extras.

After a quick shower, I put Kinsey on the bed while I dug through the closet for clothes for both of us. Then, I pulled an older small leather bag from my closet and grabbed my bedside lip balm, tossing it in.

We moved back out to the main area, where I dug through my kitchen cabinet until I found the small cosmetic bag tucked in the back. After years of Ryn stealing from me, I'd gotten better at hiding valuables.

Inside was my other credit card, my passport, and a stack of cash. I tossed some of the cash into my purse, with the ID and card. At least I had some identification.

Shit.

I was going to spend half the week trying to get replacements for everything, and some things were going to require taking personal time.

It was the first time that day I'd thought about the previous night. Despite everything that happened, my chest clenched, hoping she was okay. The men she was with weren't the type to care about her life at all. She was gone before the police arrived, but I had no problem implicating her in what happened. I only hoped they found her before those men took their anger out on her.

I busied myself with gathering up diapers, bottles, formula, O's, a change of clothes, and every little thing we might need. Luckily, it was pretty close to what I packed up every day for her when I took her to daycare.

Thane arrived soon after, his eyes wide as he stared down at the stroller. "That is elaborate."

"This is the arsenal you need for a day out with a baby," I explained.

When he said he bought zoo tickets, I'd assumed the Central Park Zoo since it was just a few blocks away. But no, Thane went all out and got tickets to the Bronx Zoo. At least a decade had passed since I'd visited and I was more excited than Kinsey, if Kinsey understood what was going on.

"Tell me again why we didn't just drive?" Thane asked when we got off the train and continued walking.

"Because I don't have a car seat."

He shook his head. "That just sounds weird."

"Why? I don't have a car, so why would I need one?"

"Just in case."

"And where would I store it? The stroller takes up enough room as it is."

He nodded. "Fair point."

The sun was high in the sky when we made it through the entrance, and we'd only walked a few steps before I veered us off to the right.

"Everything okay?" he asked.

"I almost forgot the sunscreen," I said, stopping the stroller before digging into one of the bags I had with me.

Once I had the bottle, I crouched in front of Kinsey, whose eyes were wide as she looked around. Her brow scrunched and she grunted in annoyance when I applied the sunscreen to her face.

When she was covered, I squeezed more into my palm and spread it on my arms and face.

I glanced to Thane, who'd been watching me the whole time, and stepped to him. His eyes widened as I began to smooth the sunscreen around his face. I'd barely covered his forehead and cheeks when he yanked me to him and pressed his lips to mine.

A squeak left me, allowing him to slip his tongue against mine. With hands still covered in lotion and getting caught up in his touch, I cupped his neck and wiped the remaining on the back of his neck.

He pulled back, a brow raised as he looked down at me. "Did you just lotion up my neck?"

I gave him a small smile and nodded. "Yes."

"Oh, wow."

"What?"

"I didn't realize I was such a terrible kisser. I mean, I thought I was pretty good, but that... I couldn't distract you."

"Was that your goal?"

"No. I simply wanted to kiss you because you are amazing."

"It was a good kiss." I stood up on my toes, and he leaned down to meet me. When I cupped his neck, it wasn't to wipe my hands. It was to pull him closer.

When we parted, we were both breathing hard and the space between my thighs tingled. "Very good."

He dipped his face into the crook of my neck, his strong arms wrapping around me and holding me tight to him. A shudder rolled through me, and I drew in a sharp breath at the feel of his tongue lapping at my skin. Little nips from his teeth had my thighs clenching.

His breath was hot against my ear, a low moan rumbling in his chest as he placed open-mouthed kisses on my neck. "I could just eat you up."

My heart hammered in my chest, and I had to force myself to pull away. "Okay, big bad wolf, settle down. There are children around."

He chuckled and pulled back before we merged in with the people entering.

Walking around with Thane drew more attention than I ever would have expected. More than once I heard someone say what a cute family we were. I knew Thane heard it as well, because he wrapped his arm around my waist and smirked down at me.

Kinsey practically bounced in her seat, squealing at all the animals and reaching out for them. She would look to me and it was a readable expression of, "See it, Mama?"

"That's a big giraffe, isn't it?"

After walking around for an hour or two, we decided to get some lunch. Thane grabbed our trays while I parked us at a table.

Kinsey fussed, not liking that we had stopped. It was close to nap time and tired baby was taking over, but there was just so much stimuli.

Before I could reach down and pick her up, Thane was unbuckling the seatbelt and pulling her up into his arms. I was stunned, unable to speak as he smiled at her, tucking her against him.

"Is this better?" he asked her with a smile.

She stared up at him with wide eyes for a moment, trying to figure out just who he was. The expression was adorable, and I couldn't help pulling out my phone and snapping a quick picture.

Kinsey started kicking her legs like she wanted to bounce, and Thane picked up on that. He placed her on his thighs and I watched as he held her steady, helping to propel her. A sweet giggle left her.

I couldn't tear my eyes away from the sight in front of me. My chest clenched and so did my thighs. The man was delicious looking on most days, but with a baby in his arms?

I was ready to jump him right then.

Just as I was about to say something Thane cursed, his eyes widened as big as saucers. He pulled Kinsey back to him and closed his eyes as his hand moved to his crotch.

Did she…

I brought my fingers up to hide my amusement. I knew exactly what had just happened because it happened to me a lot, but little feet slipping off my leg between my thighs didn't affect me much. However, a man was a different story.

"Did she just kick you in a sensitive area?"

He blew out a breath. "I think you have a soccer player on your hands."

I tried to feel bad, but I couldn't stop my shoulders from shaking.

"Not funny." His gaze narrowed on me.

"I'll make them feel better later. Give them a nice massage."

"They would appreciate that. Maybe a kiss or two."

"I think I told you last night."

He snatched a fry from the tray. "I know what you told me last night, but I'm hoping you'll finally say yes to me, and not when I have you pinned to a wall."

"You want to date me that badly? To become my boyfriend? For a blow job?"

He shook his head. "Not for a blow job. I'm playing for something much more valuable than that."

"What would that be?" I asked

"You. All of you."

I blinked at him, unsure of how to respond.

"What about her?"

His brow scrunched. "She's part of you, isn't she? So that includes her."

I swallowed hard, my chest clenching as I watched him make silly faces at her. Maybe I was wrong about him after all.

After lunch we walked around again, and after about an hour Kinsey gave up the fight and fell asleep.

Thane chuckled as he looked at her passed out. "She's adorable."

"Wish I could say I had something to do with it."

"She's happy because of you. Anyone can see that."

"You're being awfully nice, and I'm having a hard time processing it."

Another chuckle. "I am a nice guy once you get to know me, when I'm not being a total prick."

"And I'm a nice girl as long as you're not a prick."

He grinned at me before leaning down and pressing his lips to mine.

"Roe?" a familiar voice called out.

I stopped dead in my tracks. Brown eyes that I'd once stared at lovingly at met mine. Eyes that had been filled with anger when he left me. "Pete."

Twenty-Two

Roe

"Hey." Pete glanced down to the stroller. "You kept it."

It. We never talked again after he walked out that day. Well, nothing past a few "is this yours or mine" conversations when he cleared out the following week. Every time he spoke about Kinsey he always called her "it," and I wanted to punch that sneer right off his face.

The eyes of the girl beside him widened. "You got a kid?"

He shook his head. "Nah, that's something she was stupid enough to get stuck with."

His comment burned and ignited something inside me. Once upon a time, I'd thought we'd spend our lives together, but as I looked at him I couldn't remember why I ever wanted that.

He was self-absorbed and never really cared about what I wanted. What I wanted that day was the baby in my arms, no matter the cost.

"I chose her. I wasn't stuck with her. I chose her, dipshit," I spat back.

"Once a sucker, always a sucker." Pete glanced to Thane, who was glaring at him. He looked Thane down, then up, his lips curling. "And you suckered some dope."

Thane stepped forward, towering over Pete much like he did me. The move was so sexy, that little bit of intimidation, that heat rushed through me and it wasn't weather related.

"Only half right on that word, but she didn't need to suck me for me to be a man. Only a boy would run away from a baby."

I took a little too much joy in watching Pete give a hard swallow. "Whatever, man."

I shook my head. "How did I stay with someone like you for so long?"

"Because I'm a beast in bed," he replied with a smirk. So full of himself, so sure that he was "*the man*." An attitude he never showed before. My guess was that it was for the clueless girl on his arm and to get back some of the ground he'd lost with Thane's overpowering presence.

A bark of a laugh escaped me. He was nothing compared to Thane. Thane was caring and kind and strong and sensual and so sexy that I was having a hard time not jumping him right then.

A really hard time because the protective aura he was emitting was working me up. Wow.

"Keep dreaming," I said with a roll of my eyes.

Thane made a sound and narrowed his gaze on Pete. It was as if he was sizing him up and found him to be a weak opponent. The kill shot was easy. Pete had left himself open for it.

Thane set his hand on the small of my back, his fingers dipping into my back pocket before squeezing my ass. "From what I've gathered in the last few minutes, you are a selfish lover who has probably never gotten a woman off. You're a pussy of a boy who can't step out of your own self-centeredness to help anyone. And she probably stayed with you so long out of habit and pity."

Pete's anger and ego stepped up but Thane was a shark,

and sharks could smell blood in the water. It was what kept Pete from opening his mouth and cutting Thane off.

"Bingo," I confirmed. It wasn't entirely true. I'd deluded myself into thinking Pete was the one, settling on him.

Thane looked at me. "How many times did I make you come last night?" he asked.

"Hmm, five? Or was it six?" I shook my head. "Honestly after two in five minutes, my brain was mush. I mean, you weren't even inside me until the last two." I let out a moan, my lip quirking up into a smirk as I glanced at the wide-eyed look of the woman with Pete.

Our little fake conversation was turning me on even more. I really needed to cool down.

"It was seven by my count, though you were almost passed out by the last one. I had to hold all of your weight up against the glass. Probably gave someone a show."

I bit down on my lip, pulling him closer. He leaned down and pulled my bottom lip free with his teeth before pressing his lips to mine.

The fire that burned between us flamed high, and we pulled each other closer. I couldn't stop the moans and was consumed by Thane. His display, his arrogance and strength set me off and I wanted the lie we told them. Desperately. When we separated, we were both breathing hard and I didn't want to let go.

"Oh, sorry, I forgot you were there," I said to Pete.

I had. Thane had the ability to wipe my mind of all thoughts.

Pete's girl stared at us. Her cheeks were pink, lips parted.

"Come on, Amy."

"See you, Pete," Thane said with a wave, then winked. "Bye, Amy."

I smacked him on the stomach, making him laugh. "What was that for?"

He grinned down at me. "Just to get her more pissed off at him."

"That was an elaborate description you gave them," I said, feeling my face flame, and I looked back to them.

"Did you see the look on her face?" he asked with a chuckle.

"I saw the glare she gave him. Now you have quite a reputation to uphold." I pulled him close again, the heat between us almost intoxicating. "Are you up to the task?"

He held me tightly to him, and I was lost in his gaze. "With you? No problem. Give me a day and I'll triple it."

"You're just digging yourself a deeper hole," I said a little breathier than intended.

He leaned down, his lips ghosting mine. "I like a challenge."

A moan left me, and I arched into him when our lips met again. There was a high-pitched whistle followed by "Get a room" being shouted that pulled us from our lust-filled bubble.

I felt my face flame as many sets of eyes looked our way. Reluctantly I stepped out of his arms and grabbed hold of the stroller, checking on Kinsey before walking again.

"Was that really why you stayed with him?" Thane asked after a minute.

I shrugged. "First love, so it held that romanticized idea that we'd be together forever. Then we graduated college and started working. I was angry and sad when he left, especially because I think he was sleeping with someone else, but once he was gone, after those initial painful emotions settled, I realized how much better I felt without him around. It's not that he was some bad guy, or that we fought a lot, but we had become more like roommates. It took me a while to admit there hadn't been love there in a while."

Every time I said the word "love" while looking at Thane my heart jumped, as if it was pumping that emotion back to life. As if *he* was bringing it back to life.

"Sounds like you were comfortable."

I nodded in agreement. "Since then, my situation has led to an inability to date, because most guys run when they find out you have a baby."

Thane took my hand and pulled me to him. "Fuck them all, because they have no idea what they're missing."

I rolled my eyes, which earned me a swat to the butt. "They're missing two a.m. scream fests, milk throw up, and poop. *Lots* of poop."

"And the beauty that is seeing the way you look at her. The way she reaches out for you, her cute little giggles when you do something silly. They're missing your feistiness and fierce loyalty. Your beauty and your cock-teasing body."

I could feel my eyes filling with tears. "You really need to stop."

"Why?" His brow scrunched.

"Because I'm really starting to like you when you do that."

A chuckle left him. "And that's a bad thing?"

"Maybe." I stared at his chest, afraid of what would happen if I looked directly at him.

"Kiss me again and I'll make you change your tune."

All I needed was that edge of arrogance in his tone to pull me from whatever schoolgirl crush embarrassment had taken hold.

My lip twitched up as I looked up at him from under my lashes. "I think you'll have to make that night we talked about real if you think you want to change my tune."

His pupils dilated and his hold tightened on me. I could *feel* how much he wanted me pressed against my stomach. "All you have to do is name a time and a place."

"Slow your roll, Casanova."

"Oh, you want it slow?" He leaned in closer, his lips against my ear sending a shiver down my spine. "I can do slow, baby. Long, slow fucking all night long."

I swatted his chest and he backed up, chuckling at me.

"You, Mr. Carthwright, are a bad boy."

He threw his head back in laughter. "I can be a good boy, just let me prove it."

"Uh-huh, right. Come on," I said, pushing the stroller and continuing our walk around the zoo. He sidled up close to me and slipped his hand back into my back pocket.

"And here I thought fighting with you was fun and arousing. Teasing you is even better, plus I get the added bonus of turning you on."

"Who said I was turned on?" I asked, trying not to give away how right he was.

"You want me, just stop pretending you don't."

"Wanting you has never been a problem."

He grinned down at me and pulled me in closer, his lips pressing against the top of my head. "Ditto."

Four hours later we were exiting the subway station.

"Let me walk you home," Thane said.

"Really? It's only a few blocks." Though I didn't want him to go. I wasn't ready for him to leave.

"And more time I get to spend with you."

"You've spent a lot of time with me the last few days."

"That's what happens when you're infatuated with someone—you want to spend all your time with them."

He'd already won me over, and I felt the same. "Infatuated, huh?"

"Is it so bad that I don't want to leave you?"

"You don't?"

He shook his head. "Yeah, I kinda like you, and my bigger-than-a-Popsicle-stick friend really likes you."

I rolled my eyes at him. "Well, I'm beat, so if he's expecting any loving, you can just go on home."

He reached up and slipped a loose lock of hair behind my ear. The action had me looking up at him, and I drew in a sharp breath at the beautiful smile that held none of the sexual banter of the day.

"Where should we order dinner from?" he asked.

I could only blink up at him, completely taken aback by the soft sincerity of his expression. He agreed without saying the words, knowing nothing sexual would be happening.

We decided on some Greek, and when I put Kinsey to bed, we snuggled on the couch together, watching a movie on my laptop since the TV was busted. It was simple but intimate, curled up against him.

Besides a few soft kisses, he kept the evening tame, and around midnight he headed toward the door.

"Can I see you tomorrow?" he asked, turning back to me. "I really don't like leaving you alone."

I swallowed. It scared me, being alone after the other night, but I couldn't ask more from him. "It has to happen at some point."

He cupped my cheek and leaned down, his lips softly pressing against mine and then moving up to my forehead. "Call me if you need anything. And I do mean *anything*. If you're scared or just want someone to talk to or someone to sing you to sleep."

"Can you even carry a tune?"

"Surprisingly well."

I rested my hand on his chest. "Thank you. For everything. Today was wonderful. Best day ever."

A huge smile broke out on his face. "Good. I'm glad. Goodnight, beautiful. I'll see you tomorrow for brunch."

"Brunch? I never agreed to that. I don't know. Kinsey..."

"I'll bring the food. We can picnic on the floor."

I nodded. "Okay." I smiled at him and pulled my bottom lip between my teeth. "Goodnight."

When the door closed behind Thane, I let out a groan. I was so screwed. Completely and totally off my rocker.

Thane was nothing like I expected and yet everything I never knew I wanted. I didn't know things could be so amazing physically between two people.

While my experience was limited, I knew Thane was the kind of man who was the boyfriend every woman wanted—whether they knew it or not.

Owning up to my mistakes, my initial assessment of him was completely off base. Thane wasn't afraid of commitment, and Kinsey didn't scare him away. He was amazing with her and without a doubt, I was terrified that I was going to fall for him.

I was definitely screwed because I realized I was too late—I was already falling for him. He was acquiring my heart a little more each day.

At noon, Thane arrived with his arms full of bags of the most delicious-smelling food. It was the standard brunch fare, but after a long day the day before, it was nice to just relax at home.

Three hours later, someone knocked and I opened the door to find three delivery men with their arms full. They immediately went to work taking my broken TV down from the wall.

"What is going on?" I asked as I looked to Thane.

He just smiled and shrugged. "New TV."

I blinked at him, understanding clicking. "You bought me a new TV? Thane… Why?"

He stepped closer and wrapped his arms around me. "I couldn't let you be without."

"I have renter's insurance to cover it."

"Yes, but that could take weeks. Besides, it was my fault the television was broken."

"And not stolen," I said as I glared at him. "None of it was your fault."

"Maybe not, but I do have a sense of responsibility since I don't know if your policy would replace that."

One man handed me a bag and a box containing a Playstation4, which I had no clue how he knew I'd once had since Pete took it when he left. I looked inside the bag to find a new ten-inch tablet and case.

My eyes were wide as I looked at him and shook my head. "This is too much."

"It's not. I just won't get new cuff links this week," he said with a wink.

"Let me at least give you some money to cover the expense." Tears welled in my eyes and I tried to pull them back, but then it all hit me. I'd never had a man do things for me like Thane had. He accepted Kinsey without pause and thought about ways he could see me without having to exclude her—something that would have put more stress on me. "You suck," I cried as the tears streamed down my face and I hiccupped a sob.

He pulled me into his arms. "If this is the reaction I get from me sucking, I'll do it again and again. Now, did I earn that dinner date?"

I nodded against his chest. "Yes."

A few hours later, he reluctantly headed home, and I had to admit that I was reluctant about it as well.

After giving Kinsey a bath and putting her to bed, I cozied into the couch and started playing with my new TV.

I was thankful for the TV, but the rest was unnecessary. We could have done without the tablet for a while, and definitely without the PS4. Though, it would be nice to watch one of my movies, and I couldn't do that without some sort of Blu-ray player.

My mouth dropped open when I realized it was a smart TV and immediately entered my Wi-Fi password. I was logging into my Netflix account when my phone buzzed beside me.

Carthwright the Assholian: Goodnight beautiful.

I smiled at the message, my heart swelling with so many emotions. However, regret did catch me at the name. I quickly clicked on his name and erased all the letters, typing in five new ones.

Roe: Goodnight. I'm half tempted to call you my savior, but I don't want it to give you a big head so instead I'll send you this.

I attached a screen shot of our conversation with one glaring change.

Thane: That name change looks good on me. You look good on me too.

Thane: Great, now I'm thinking about you on me. And me on you. Me all over you in more ways than one.

Thane: I just wanted to say goodnight and now you have me contemplating sending you a dick pic because you made me so hard.

A giggle left me, and my heart soared.

Roe: I'm not entirely sure I'd be against that. Just imagine me playing with all those imaginary toys you think I have.

Thane: Fuck.

Thane: Fuck. Fuck…did you really have to tease me like that?

Roe: Yes.

Thane: So, how about that date?

Roe: I'm turning my phone off now.

I ran to my room with a wicked idea. Grabbing the one and only toy I actually had, I set the dildo between my breasts and squeezed them together before snapping a photo and sending it off.

Roe: And about that date—yes.

Twenty-Three

Thane

All I'd been able to think about in the week since Roe finally said yes to our date was that fucking photo. Every time I grabbed her at the office, she slapped my hands away and told me to wait until the weekend.

It was fucking torture. She was torturing me and getting off on it. I could tell by that sexy little smirk she'd give me as I sulked away. Though one time I refused to let her get away with teasing me as I pressed her against the glass window in my office. One hand under her shirt grabbing her breast and pulling at her piercing while two fingers slipped in and out of her incredibly wet pussy.

I loved hearing her sighs of ecstasy and her cries when she spasmed in my arms as her orgasm rocked through her.

I tried to be a good boy, but I could only take so much.

Finally, the weekend arrived and I was ecstatic that we could have a proper first date. Nothing against all the other times we'd spent together, but I wanted to do things right because I wanted her to trust me. The haphazard way we came together just wasn't good enough.

Thankfully Roe's mom was able to watch Kinsey on Saturday for the entire night, allowing us to go out to dinner without her having to worry about getting back by a certain time.

"Where are we going?" I asked. We were walking down First Avenue, my car still parked at my building.

Like I'd promised weeks ago, Roe chose where we were going to dinner. What I didn't count on was her refusing to tell me where we were going or what kind of food it was. She simply said to lose the suit jacket.

It was hard to keep my eyes on the sidewalk in front of me. I'd expected her to open the door in some sleek dress that hugged her skin. Something similar to her work attire, and probably black.

Then again, if I really thought about it, many of her blouses had a ruffled edge. The peasant top she wore to the zoo should have also clued me in to her casual wardrobe. It gave me insight into Roe outside of work and pre-Mom.

She surprised me when she walked out in a flowy floral peach dress with ruffles and a high waist. There were tiny strings that made up the shoulder straps that were tied in bows at the top, and I could imagine one small tug and the dress would fall to the ground.

More than just a vision, it was a plan. I was going to see that dress slip from her shoulders, exposing every succulent inch of the skin she was taunting me with.

It was already bad enough that I could see down the top and tell she wasn't wearing a strapless bra. Which was where my inability to focus on the sidewalk came in—I was unable to tear my eyes away from her breasts. With each step in her wedge heels they gave a jiggle, and it made me wonder if her nipples were hard from the friction of the fabric.

"Not far."

I cleared my throat in an effort to focus on our surroundings. "Considering we are walking, I figured as much."

"Trust me, you're going to want to work up an appetite." I grinned down at her, and she rolled her eyes. "For the food."

"And for later activities."

She rolled her eyes. "So sure of yourself."

I was damn sure. In fact, I was pretty certain I wasn't going to make it through dinner without slipping my hand up her dress to find out if she was devoid of all undergarments.

"How do you know I've never been where we're going?"

"Have you ever been to Le Relais de l'Entrecôte?"

My brain scrambled, trying to figure out what she said. Languages were not my strong suit, but I was pretty sure it was French.

"Bless you?" I said to cover my inadequacy. Her giggle told me I was spot on.

"It's French," she confirmed. She reached up to brush a lock of hair behind her ear. Half a dozen bangle bracelets slid down her arm, then back to her wrist when she lowered her arm. There must have been more than were in her jewelry box.

I wasn't used to seeing her with her hair down and styled, and I was completely blown away. Long brunette waves cascaded halfway down her back and perfectly framed her face.

All I could think about was running my hands through it, twisting it, grabbing it.

It'd been weeks since we'd had sex on my desk, and she had me completely wrapped around her finger. I'd practically begged her to go out with me, but I was struck with my desire to stay in with her.

One I had to push down. I was not going to mess this up.

After a few blocks we arrived at a red awning and Roe pulled at my hand, unfortunately separating us as we moved through the spinning door.

It was quite a tight establishment with not a lot of room between tables, but that didn't seem to bother anyone. Luckily, we were able to get the end of a long booth-like bench so there was only the table next to us, which was empty.

The hostess set a menu down and when I picked it up, my brow scrunched. Listed on one side was only one item, then on the other were desserts. The wine menu was ten times the size.

"Wait, so there's only one thing on the menu?"

"Uh-huh."

It wasn't the type of steakhouse I was used to. There was no picking of a cut of beef, elaborate sides, or alterations.

Salad. Steak. Fries. Sauce.

That was it.

Roe reached out and took my hand in hers. "Trust me."

"I do, but this is weird."

"I've been getting your lunch for a month."

"And?"

"You're going to love this."

It seemed the only thing I was able to pick was the wine, and decided to just go with the flow, allowing the waitress to pick her favorite.

"If I haven't said it yet, you look beautiful. I like this look on you."

"You did say 'Wow' when I opened the door, and your eyes nearly fell out of your head. And good, because regular Roe has a lot of things like this in her wardrobe."

That didn't surprise me. While it wasn't a normal look that would have attracted me, I loved it on her. She had a hippie, free vibe to her.

"Does she? I can't wait to see more."

"Me too."

"You don't know what's in your closet?"

She let out a cute little giggle. "I meant on *you*. The zoo trip was the only time I've ever seen you in anything that wasn't a suit. Though, even in jeans and a T-shirt, you looked like you just walked out of a boardroom. You scream money and power with just a glance."

"Is that a bad thing?"

She shrugged. "No, but I'm not sure you noticed that even when you're casual, you are commanding."

"Was that why your ex seemed intimidated?"

"That, and you really are too sexy for your own good."

I grinned at her and brought her hand to my lips. "I'm not sure I've ever heard that before."

She leaned back. "Uh-oh, I just blew your ego up. Your head might not make it through the door."

I nipped at her knuckle. "I like hearing that you find me irresistible."

She shook her head and pursed her lips. "I didn't say that."

"You did." I leaned in. "I'm pretty sure I can get you wet with just a look."

She blinked at me, pink spreading across her cheeks.

"You get me hard with just a look. I find you more irresistible than you find me, I guarantee it."

"Guarantee, huh?"

"And I plan to show you how much more all night long."

She swallowed hard, the pink in her cheeks deepening. "All night? I don't know if you've got the stamina to keep up."

Even being playful, she kept it up with the hits. I think the score was Roe—25 to Thane—6.

And I planned to prove to her all night long just how wrong she was, and to make true the lie we told her ex.

"After tonight, you're going to wish you said yes to me a month ago."

"There's that ego again."

When Roe said I would love the food, I was dubious. The

place wasn't posh or modern, and the menu was the most limited I'd seen. However, it seemed very popular as people flowed in constantly. Our food took hardly any time to arrive, and one bite in I almost proposed.

There was this weird green sauce that the sirloin was sitting in and at first I didn't know what to think about it, but then I couldn't stop eating it or dipping the perfectly crisp fries in it.

"How did you get to become the President of Acquisitions?" she asked when I was about halfway through stuffing my face.

"James."

She rolled her eyes. "Well, yes, I gathered that much."

A chuckle left me. "I worked with him in a different role, but then he needed a person who could handle the acquisitions because it was taking too much of his time. He wanted to focus on other aspects of the business, so I was named President and I have been growing the company ever since."

"Is that when you bought your condo?" she asked.

"I'd been renting in the East Village and when I got the promotion, my lease was also ending and it was the perfect time to buy myself a place."

"How long did you live there?"

"About six years. So it was a stretch when I first started working, but wasn't by the time I left."

We polished off a second bottle of wine, and I finished a second plate of steak and fries before paying the check. I patted my stomach as we headed back toward home.

Time to eat my dessert.

Twenty-Four

Thane

I had never taken a woman back to my place. Not since the days of my ex-girlfriend, Liv. Knowing that it would never be more than a night or two, I didn't see the point. They would never be part of my life.

Roe was different. I wanted her to be part of my life.

"Fuck, I am full."

"So, I did good?" she asked.

I stopped and turned to her, pulling her arm up until I could place a light kiss against the inside of her wrist.

"You did unbelievably good, baby."

"Baby, huh?"

I nodded. "Work for you?"

She stepped away, pulling me with her. "Baby could work."

"Still playing hard to get?"

She turned back and shot me that sexy minx smile that drove me crazy. "Maybe."

"Now I need to go work off all this food. I wonder how I can do that?" I grinned down at her.

"I might know of something."

The walk from the restaurant to my place only took a few minutes, and we passed her apartment on the way. She tried to play that she was going in, but I kept a firm grip on her as I continued on.

"Nope, I've been to your place. Now you're going to see mine."

When we arrived at my building, her eyes widened. "Very posh."

"You're the first woman I've brought here," I said as I held the door open.

"In the last month?"

"Ever."

She blinked up at me. "Ever?"

I nodded. "Though technically, there has been one woman, but she's my mom so she doesn't count."

"Making a girl feel special over here."

"I'm trying."

"Evening, Mr. Carthwright," Adriane, the concierge, said as we headed toward the elevators.

I gave her a wave before stepping onto one of the waiting elevators.

"What floor again?"

I moved my wallet in front of the sensor and hit the button. "Twenty-ninth."

"Wow."

My stomach clenched and my heart was beating faster than normal. Why was I nervous?

When we entered, she took a second to slip off her shoes, but once she was passed the entryway her eyes popped wide. "Holy shit." She stepped forward, passing the library that was empty of any objects, then the kitchen, and then living room and dining room.

Her lips were parted as she turned back to me. "Half this space is the size of my entire apartment. How big is this place?"

"Too big," I admitted. With the money came the need to have actual space in New York City, which was expensive. Instead of the two bedroom that was about fourteen hundred square feet, I doubled down for twice the size. It left me with lots of *empty* space.

I was lost in thought when the click of a door caught my attention, and I watched the skirt of Roe's dress fly up from the breeze as she stepped out onto the terrace.

"Holy shit," I heard her whisper again as I stepped out behind her. "Even your terrace is bigger than my apartment!"

I looked around as I thought about it. "Damn, I think you're right." She stood at the edge looking out at the twinkling lights that blanketed the skyline. I stepped up behind her and placed my hands next to hers, caging her against the railing. "What do you think?"

She turned in my arms. "Is this the show condo?"

"What?"

"It's just kind of... cold. Don't get me wrong, it's nice if you like modern."

My lip twitched. "Don't pull any punches."

"No warmth. Zero. Zilch."

I grabbed hold of her hips and tugged her against me. "You want warmth? I'll fucking show you warmth."

"Promises, promises," she said with a grin before twisting out of my grip and continuing her perusal. She stopped at the door before going back in and stared out. "This view is worth every penny."

I swallowed hard as I stared at her. Four years, and only Jace and James and my family had seen my home. I'd never noticed the cold she spoke of until the space was filled with her light and warmth.

"The most beautiful view ever," I said as I stared at her.

Her gaze met mine. "You aren't even looking."

"I'm looking at what matters." I stepped forward and pushed her through the door before pulling her close and getting lost in her beautiful eyes. Leaning down, I pressed my lips to hers.

All night I'd held off on doing that because I knew once we kissed, I would need my lips on every inch of her. It was soft, sensual, and unlike our previous encounters. I couldn't stop the moan from leaving me or my arms from pulling her closer. Her lips parted, and I caressed her tongue with my own.

She shook in my arms, and I pulled back. "What's wrong?"

"Nothing. I'm just overwhelmed."

I stroked down her neck and across her collarbone. "What overwhelms you?" We'd already had sex, so I didn't believe that was the issue.

"The anticipation," she said, her gaze trained on my chest. "This terrifies me because I've never felt this depth of intimacy with anyone before. Never."

A low chuckle left me, and I brushed her hair behind her shoulder. "It's the same for me. I've never felt this way before, and I'm afraid of fucking something up because you aren't some casual fuck or a conquest."

"What am I?"

I was locked with her beautiful hazel eyes, my thumb brushing against her jaw. "You're everything I've been waiting for."

That seemed to be the correct answer, and she threw her arms around my shoulders and pulled my lips to hers.

The hunger coming off her was intoxicating, and I found myself drowning in her. I held her close, one hand on her ass, the other near her shoulder, keeping our bodies completely connected.

"You are so unbelievably beautiful."

"You're just saying that to get in my panties."

"Doesn't make it any less true." I leaned back and admired the way her dress accentuated her chest and the fact that she wasn't wearing a bra. "Are you even wearing panties?"

She smiled and bit down on her lower lip. "Only one way to find out."

I tugged at the string, releasing the tie that held the strap together. The fabric fell, revealing one perfect, pert breast. My mouth watered as a groan left me, finally viewing the piercing I'd felt over and over through her clothes.

"Oops." I cupped her breast, my thumb brushing over her nipple and the balls of her piercing. She drew in a sharp breath, her body bowing into mine.

"Wow," she said with an uneven breath.

"Wow, what?"

She shook her head. "It's just that nobody has played with them since I got them."

"Nobody? Not even your ex?"

She shook her head. "They were healing, and then he just liked to look."

I bent down and took her nipple between my lips, my tongue lapping at the hardening flesh. A high-pitched moan hit my ears, and her grip on my arm tightened.

"Nobody's ever done that?"

"N-no."

"Good." There was a lot of things I planned to do to her that nobody had done before, and making her come as many times as possible was number one on my list.

A groan left me at the feel of her small hand cupping my hard cock. "What do you have there, little girl?"

She moved her hand slowly up to my belt and used both hands to unfasten it. "I'm bringing your friend to the party."

"Oh, he's been here since you opened your door."

"But you kept him locked away," she said. A groan left me at the feel of her fingers on my cock as she pulled me free.

When she began to lean over, I stopped her. "What happened to no blow jobs?"

She squeezed down on me, making me hiss.

"Is my mouth on your cock?" she asked. The way she accentuated the word cock had my grip on her waist tightening.

"No." I'd fucking know if it was.

"What part of my body is on your cock?" She did it again, and I leaned in and pressed my teeth into her shoulder.

"It's a fucking hand job, and you're a fucking tease." I was going out of my mind with want. She was driving me mad with each slow tug on my cock.

She took her bottom lip between her teeth again and smiled up at me. "Good things come—"

"If you fucking finish that with 'to those who wait,' I'm going to throw you onto that couch and pound you into the cushions." My cock was so hard I could barely hold myself back any longer.

Without warning, I slid my hand between her thighs, making her cry out as I slipped a finger under the edge of her thong and inside her wet warmth. Part of me was sad she wasn't bare under her dress, but part of me was happy because I didn't want even the slightest possibility of some fucker accidentally viewing what was mine.

"So you better stop because I have a promise to keep."

"What promise is that?"

"That I'll have your tit and your pussy in my mouth, and I won't fucking stop until your thighs are so tight they try to pry my head off."

"That sounds like a challenge," she whispered against my lips.

A growl left me and I grabbed her hand, taking it from my cock as I pulled her down the hallway to the bedroom.

"Then I'm going to fucking make it a challenge."

The moment we entered the bedroom I began stripping, giving my cock a tug when I noticed her staring at it with parted lips and pink cheeks. Her breast was still out in the open and when I stepped forward, I reached out and tugged the string on her other shoulder. Once the knot released, the fabric slid from her body, pooling around her feet.

We stood in front of each other, naked except for the thong still covering her. She was breathtaking. My heart sped up and my cock hardened even more.

Setting my hands on her hips, I hooked my thumbs under the waistband and tugged the last scrap of clothing down her legs. She lifted one leg to get free and I took the opportunity to hook my arm under her leg and lift it, causing her to grab hold of me to keep from falling.

She started to say something, but I cut her off as my hands took firm hold of her waist and drew her closer until my mouth covered her pussy.

"Fuck," she cried out, her body curling in.

There was no pause. I dove right in ready to drink from the source what I'd only had teasing licks of. I groaned against her, my tongue lapping against her slit, then sucking at her clit. That move had her nearly ripping my hair out and almost toppled us to the ground.

I pulled back, my dark eyes on hers as I licked my lips. "I couldn't help myself," I said with a smirk as I stood. Her lips were parted, and her eyes seemed a bit unfocused.

"Do it again."

I leaned down and pressed my lips to hers, drawing her tightly into my arms. I loved the way she gripped onto me and I straightened, lifting her from the floor. She giggled against my lips and drew her legs up to wrap around my hips. A groan left me at the feel of her hot pussy against my shaft.

It was so intense I nearly dropped her on my cock right then.

I climbed onto the bed and caged her beneath me, and her hips rocked against me.

"Baby, you need to stop or you're going to be stuffed with my cock in one thrust of my hips."

"Yes," she hissed, her tongue swiping against her lips.

She was a goddess of lust beneath me. A growl left me and I buried my face into her neck, drawing in her delicious scent of roses and cherries. I ran my hands up her sides until I was cupping both of her breasts. A whimper left her, and she moved against me again. Gripping her piercings, I pulled, loving the way she pulled in a sharp breath before melting beneath me, her body giving a jerk.

"These are so fucking enticing," I said as I lowered my head, sucking one of her hard nipples into my mouth. The softness of her breast in contrast with the hardness of the balls had me licking, biting, and sucking, pulling at the piercing with my teeth. I switched to the other, earning another cascade of whimpers.

I trailed my mouth down her body, licking and sucking before shifting until I was staring at her pretty pink pussy. A groan left me and I flattened my tongue against her slit, dipping into her opening before reaching her swollen clit and flicking it with my tongue. She cried out and I retreated, turning my head to bite down on the soft skin of her inner thigh.

My cock ached, desperate to be buried inside her. I covered her mound with my mouth, again flicking my tongue against her clit, encircling in as I took in her hitched breath and passionate cries. I kicked up the pace, alternating with sucking as I reached up and tugged at her piercings.

A keening moan left her as she fisted my hair, shoving me harder against her mound as her hips rocked. It only spurred me on, making me more aggressive as I pushed her closer to coming.

I felt her legs begin to shake as her muscles tightened and suddenly, just as I wanted, her thighs clamped down on either side of my head as her back arched. Then I heard the glorious sound of her screaming as she came.

I didn't stop, instead I groaned against her as I lapped up my dessert. Her muscles relaxed and her body jerked with aftershocks, but I kept up even as she tried to push me away.

"Wait," she whimpered.

But I was done waiting. I released my mouth from her, and in one fluid motion settled my hips between her thighs and sank into her in one hard thrust.

Her eyes widened before rolling back as she shook.

"You're so delicious, baby," I whispered against her ear as I soaked up the feeling of her tight warmth surrounding me.

"Thane," she whispered. It was almost a desperate sound, and it moved through me with the force of a sledgehammer.

I flexed my hips. "Yeah, baby?"

Each slam in elicited another cry and she turned her head, her tongue peeking out to swipe against the inside of my wrist. It was such a little thing, but that tiny lick had me dropping down and linking my fingers with hers as our lips met.

Soon the only thing I registered was the pleasure piercing through me with each thrust of my hips, causing my balls to tighten and the thick, heavy slaps of my cock pounding her wet pussy.

My muscles coiled, and a low groan left me.

"So good, baby," she whispered as she attempted to raise her hips in time with my thrusts.

Calling me that did something to me, setting off an ache in my chest. My thrusts sped up, and I buried my head into the crook of her neck.

"Roe… Coming," I cried out with a roar. My hips slammed against her as I exploded, sending thick ropes of cum deep inside her.

I nearly blacked out from the pleasure, never having come so hard in my life. Feeling the strength fading, I rolled us so that she was on top of me before every muscle went lax.

"I think I got the star treatment tonight," she whispered as she placed a kiss to my chest.

"No, that was just the warm-up. I plan to make you come and come often, or you'll think I'm all ego."

She giggled against my chest, and I finally had enough strength return to wrap my arms around her and hold her close.

"You are a bit full of yourself."

"And what are you filled with?" I asked with a sly grin, flexing my cock that was still at half-mast and still inside her along with my cum.

Her already pink cheeks darkened, and she bit down on her lower lip. "You."

"That's right, baby," I said as my lips captured hers.

It was the best night of my life, and it was only beginning.

~

When was the last time I had lain contentedly after sex? Had I ever? No feelings before compared to having her naked body wrapped with mine, the peace that filled me having her so close to me.

Roe Pierce had officially blown my mind.

In the last few hours, I'd managed to make her come four times—twice in the span of five minutes. We both needed a small break, though I planned to coax more from her before we both collapsed for the night.

After a little while, I got up to go to the bathroom and when I returned, Roe was lying almost completely on her stomach, giving me an unobstructed view of her back and the black lines etched into her skin. I climbed onto the bed and stared down. On her back was the most intricate and delicate tattoo I'd ever seen. Starting at the base of her neck, a jewel shape started a line down her spine before exploding into a phoenix between her shoulder blades. The line continued with more shapes and jewels.

I traced it with my fingers. "Beautiful."

"It's not done."

"No?"

She shook her head. "It still needs some color, but the last session I had was around the time Kinsey was born. When everything went down, I didn't have the time or money to get it finished."

I'd seen the one inside her wrist—Never Forget—and with the view of another of her tattoos, my mind began to piece things together, confirming what I'd already gathered.

"You lost someone on September eleventh."

She froze momentarily before nodding. The phoenix, the words, and her insistence to have that date off—it was the only answer.

Her mom was still alive, so that left…

"Your father?" That was why the watch was so important to her.

She nodded. "I was seven. Ryn was five. He worked for an investment banking company on the eighty-ninth floor of the south tower. Normally he was gone by eight, but he'd been up late working, so he slept in. He was going to head to the office for a meeting at ten, but I accidentally spilled my orange juice on his papers. When the plane hit, he was supposed to have been getting ready to go, but he'd had to go in early to reprint what I destroyed."

"Shit," I hissed. I couldn't even imagine the devastation that faced a seven-year-old watching that unfold, not knowing if her daddy was coming home. "It wasn't your fault, you know."

"If I just hadn't bumped the juice glass."

"Or if it had been a normal day. It was an act of terror," I said as I pressed my lips against her shoulder. "Guilt has no place in you for what happened."

"I know, and that took me a while to understand. As a child, though, it wasn't the same."

My experience was different. I saw the smoke and ash from the distance of a TV screen. Even when I moved to New York for school, it didn't hit me.

"Tell me something good," she whispered.

"Something good?"

She nodded. "I don't want to talk about then."

"Well, I met a woman," I began, my fingers trailing lightly up and down her back. "Complete and total pain in my ass. She fights me at every turn."

"That doesn't sound good."

"Hmm, maybe not to some, but I love it. Fighting with her is like an aphrodisiac. I've gotten to know another side of her recently, the side she hides, and I'm in awe of her. I've never met anyone like her before, and I can't stop thinking about her."

"She sounds like a catch," she teased.

I nodded against her shoulder. "She is. Best of all, she puts up with me."

"She comes with baggage."

"Who doesn't?"

"You, apparently."

"I have my fair share," I whispered.

"Do I get to know?"

I pressed my lips against her skin, breathing her in. Compared to many, my life had been a breeze. Well, my life after age five. We had so much to learn about each other, and I realized she'd gotten the short end of the knowledge stick.

"I told you about my mom, and I'll tell you more later. After my parents got divorced and my dad got full custody, we moved to an upper-middle-class suburban area. He got remarried, they had a kid, and we were a happy little family. In college, I was in a fraternity, and I landed a good job once I was out. I met a girl at a coffee shop soon after, and we hit it off. She was an Upper East Side socialite from a wealthy family. We'd only been dating a few months when a broken condom changed our lives."

I could tell by her rigid posture she was holding herself back from asking questions. Liv was the last woman I'd had any type of relationship with, and what I'd felt for her couldn't hold a candle to my feelings for Roe.

"She moved in, and we prepared to be a family. We found out it was a boy and started prepping the second bedroom for his arrival. Around the twenty-fifth week, he stopped moving."

Roe turned around, brow knitted and lips parted as she adjusted her position and straddled my thighs. I met her eyes as I told her about the most painful loss of my life.

"He was gone."

"Oh, Thane." She threw her arms around my shoulders and pulled me to her. I gladly nestled my head into her neck. A tear fell from my eye, landing on her skin. Her warm hands cupped my face, bringing my gaze back to hers. The warm swipe of her thumb across my cheek had me leaning into her touch.

"When did you break up?"

"A few weeks later. It took that long to realize that the baby was the only thing that held us together. It didn't help that I didn't make enough money at the time for her standards."

I'd dated many women in the last seven years, but I'd never told a single one. None of them were worthy of knowing me to that level. Roe was different.

For years I was solid in the belief that I didn't want a relationship, that I didn't need love. With each encounter, she was changing me. When we were apart, I wanted to be with her.

The way my chest burned, I understood the need for her—I loved her. It didn't matter that it was new. My feelings went well beyond like and beyond anything I'd ever felt before.

I was in love with Roe.

Twenty-Five

Roe

Thane made a mean omelet filled with gooey cheese, spinach, and tomatoes. He could also cook bacon to that perfectly crispy, melt-in-your-mouth stage.

Maybe I'll keep him. He can cook.

"What time do we have to pick Kinsey up?" he asked between bites.

I was surprised by his question. "We?"

"Is that not okay?"

I blinked at him. "I just… I thought you'd want your Sunday to relax."

"I can't do that with you two?"

Yes, he could. "Noon. We're meeting her for lunch."

He glanced at the clock, and it was almost nine. We'd slept until seven thirty—the latest I'd slept in ages.

"Good."

"Good?"

He nodded and grinned at me. "That means we have time for another round."

I returned his smile, my heart full and happy for the first time in years, if ever.

"If I remember correctly, the number is seven. I only counted five last night."

His eyes darkened and his tongue slipped out to wet his lips. "Seems I need to do better."

I could barely walk because of the mind-blowing orgasms he'd given me, and I honestly wasn't sure if I could take the challenge I'd just issued.

He wiped his mouth before taking a sip of orange juice. Without warning he ducked under the table. He gripped my knees and parted my thighs. I drew in a sharp breath, my eyes wide as I looked down at him.

Without a word he popped the buttons of the dress shirt I was wearing—his shirt. His fingers caressed my nipple, giving my piercing a light tug. A soft mewl left me, one that turned into a high-pitched cry. In an instant, my legs were on his shoulders while his mouth was attached to my pussy.

"Fuck," I hissed. Unrelenting and unmovable, my mind went white with pleasure.

One of his hands squeezed my breast as he moaned against my mound. He ate me like a starving man and in no time, I was gripping his hair, pushing him harder against me as my muscles shuddered in release.

I was a mess of jelly muscles as I slid down to lay on the banquette bench. He chuckled against my skin, giving me one last long lick before placing a kiss on my inner thigh. He gave a little tap to my clit, making me jump.

"Six now. I'll get number seven in the shower."

"You... you..."

"Are great? Fantastic? The best lover you've ever had or could ever dream of having?"

I waved my hand in the air. "Yeah, whatever. All of that."

Once we finished breakfast, I took my cup of coffee and walked around the living room, getting a better feel for it in the morning light. It was bright for sure.

"Is this you?" I asked as I picked up a framed photo from the bookshelf. There were a man and a woman standing on either side of a much younger, preppy-looking Thane. "Are you wearing chinos?" The collar of his polo was popped and he had a smug look on his face.

"Yes, that's me, and probably on the chinos. That's my dad, and that is my mom," he said as he pointed to the couple on either side of him.

"That's your mom?" I asked.

"Why do you say it like that?"

I turned to him. "Because I was under the impression she wasn't in your life."

He shook his head. "Sorry, no, that's my stepmother. My dad married Sandy when I was ten. She always treated me like her own, never like I was a burden. Even when she gave birth to my brother, Wyatt, she never treated me any differently. She's my mom in all the ways that count."

I remembered him mentioning his younger brother weeks ago when we had lunch. "So they're still married?"

A smile lit up his face. "Still madly in love. Now, you've seen mine, so show me yours."

"I think you saw mine last night. Intimately."

He chuckled at that. "What were you like in high school?"

"Oh." I felt the heat rise in my cheeks. "Well, I can tell you we were in different crowds and probably wouldn't have been friends."

"Why do you say that?"

"I was an emo girl."

His head tilted to the side as he stared at me, then straightened. "I don't believe it. Proof is needed to believe this whopper."

I picked my phone up from the counter and pulled up

Facebook. After flipping through my photographs, I found the one I was looking for.

Black hair with pink highlights, lip ring, heavy black eyeliner, and black clothes.

"No way. That's not you," he said.

"It very much is an embarrassing part of my past." I pulled the phone away.

After that Thane pulled me into the shower and made good on his number seven promise, and when I could barely stand after, he picked me up and pinned me to the shower wall. He used his cock to pull number eight out of me.

"You win."

He chuckled against my throat. "I didn't realize there was something to win."

"You proved your manliness."

Once we were dried off, I slipped my dress on but I couldn't find my thong. My legs shook as I searched the floor.

"Have you seen—"

"You're not getting it back," Thane interrupted.

I quirked a brow at him. "A trophy?"

He shook his head. "A token. A reminder of the best night of my life."

"Best night?"

His eyes were wide as he nodded adamantly. "And I can see each day we are together getting better and better."

"Sounds like you want to see me again."

He chuckled and pulled his bottom lip between his teeth as he yanked me against his chest. "Oh, I want there to be no doubt that this was just the beginning. I want to call you mine." He leaned down and pressed his lips against my neck, working his way up until he was ghosting my lips. "So there is no misunderstanding, I'm going to pretend we are in high school—Roe Pierce, will you be my girlfriend?"

"Since you asked so nicely, I suppose so."

My heart was beating double time and I was shocked at how easy it felt, how right, to agree. Still, inside the insecurity rumbled, and while I attempted to push it down, I also waited for the other shoe to drop. I wanted to bask in the warmth that filled me when we were together. That safety I'd only ever felt in his arms.

We walked down to my apartment where I changed into some black leggings, a flowing, long-sleeved dusty rose top, and some black booties before throwing my hair up into a ponytail. A quick swipe of some mascara and I topped the look off with an eclectic mix of the few bangle bracelets I had left.

I really wanted to go shopping for replacements.

"How do I look?" I asked, holding my arms out. It was definitely a casual look, and I knew he wasn't used to seeing me with little to no makeup.

A grin broke out on his face, and he pulled me into his chest. "With every look I decide you can't get more beautiful, and then you top it."

I rolled my eyes. "This is barely caring casual."

"And I love it." He leaned down and pressed his lips to mine.

The heat made me bow into him. Whenever he did that, I lost all thought.

"Ready?" he asked.

I blinked at him. "Huh?"

"Kinsey?"

I straightened and pulled away from him. "Yes! Now stop being so distracting."

"Me? Distracting?"

I turned away from him and grabbed my purse. "Yes. With your hypnotizing eyes, your smell-so-good, too-gorgeous-for-your-own-good, sexy-as-fuck self."

He leaned down and whispered against my ear, "The feeling is mutual, you know. You've been distracting me for over a month."

I reached back, cupping his neck and holding him close, reveling in his presence and drowning in the warm emotions he filled me with.

Twenty-Six

Thane

When we arrived to lunch, an older version of Roe with brown eyes stood from a table. Her eyes were wide as she stared up at me, then back to her daughter.

"Mom, this is Thane. Thane, my mom."

"Pleased to meet you," I said, holding out my hand.

She swallowed, seemingly at a loss for words. "Please, call me Linda."

Kinsey cooed from her stroller, and I leaned over to pick her up. When I straightened, Roe and her mom were whispering to each other, but I couldn't make out their words due to the noise in the restaurant.

Whatever they said must not have been bad as Linda's cheeks pinked when she looked back to me holding Kinsey.

Lunch was pleasant, with Linda sharing embarrassing moments of her eldest daughter, including the time she got caught trying to sneak out to see a boy when she was fifteen. She apparently yelled at her mom about having no idea what it was like to be in love.

Roe simply covered her face and shook her head while saying, "I was a teenager!"

Afterwards, we returned to Roe's apartment and put Kinsey down for her afternoon nap. It was then that I got to see where Kinsey slept.

Roe's apartment was small, her bedroom tight, and when I entered, there was no crib. I watched her walk through another doorway and followed, surprised to find a decent-sized walk-in closet. At the end, under a window, sat a white crib. The walls around were filled with Roe's stuff, and I looked back into the bedroom to find she was using her dresser as a changing table. One drawer was partially open, and inside there were lots of tiny clothes.

It was tight, but she managed to make it work. But what happened when Kinsey got older?

A vision of one of my spare bedrooms flashed into my mind, but I pushed it back. We were way too early for that idea. *Right?*

Once she was down, Roe closed the door to the bedroom most of the way, and we moved out into the main room.

"What now?" she asked.

I took her into my arms and grinned down at her. "I can think of a few things."

She rolled her eyes and stepped away, flinging herself onto the chaise end of her couch. She tugged at her shoes and tossed them onto the floor, then patted the space next to her.

"Talk? Movie? Game? Which reminds me—why did you get me a PS4?"

I sat down next to her, then pointed to the built-in hutch. "You have a couple of games."

She nodded. "Good eye. Those are my games. The PlayStation was Pete's."

"It plays Blu-rays as well, so it seemed perfect. How long did he live here with you?" I asked. The curiosity had been burning ever since we bumped into him. Knowing Roe the way I did, I was a bit surprised to see who she dated before me. Maybe they were different when they met. After all, I was certain Roe had changed since she took in Kinsey, just as I knew I changed when I found out I was going to be a father—a loss that still hurt seven years later.

"We moved in last July, and the first week of November I brought Kinsey home, so not quite four months." She pursed her lips. "I should have clued in during that time."

"Clued into what?"

"We never had sex here. If he wasn't getting it with me..."

"He was getting it somewhere." A fucking cheater. "Wait, so this place isn't christened?"

Her hand flew back into my stomach. "Four times in less than twenty-four hours and eight orgasms—you have to give me a small break. I'm not used to it."

All of her weight had been in my arms, but I managed to squeeze two more out of her in the shower, topping the promised seven.

I slipped my fingers between hers and loved the sigh she let out as she leaned to rest her head against my arm.

"All the time you need." I turned and pressed my lips to the top of her head. "I like your mom."

"You definitely impressed her."

"Good."

"Can I ask you something about your mom?"

I stiffened but was determined not to close that part of my life off to her. It was a step in gaining her trust and if I wanted to be with her, she would know one day.

I nodded and swallowed hard. "Okay."

"When you were upset that day with the coffee because your mom called, what happened?"

I squeezed her hand and lifted my leg onto the chaise, getting full contact with hers. The comfort was a must with the subject, and a momentary distraction when I noticed how much further my leg went past the end of her toes.

"That was my birth mom. She's contacted me half a dozen times over the years."

"Birth mom?"

I'd told Roe I was once in a situation like Kinsey, but she didn't know the details of how or why. "My father had full custody since I was little."

"How long had it been since you'd heard from her?"

"Eleven years this time."

She ran her hand up and down my arm. "No wonder you were upset. That's a long time."

"She never told me why, but I also didn't really give her the chance before I hung up."

"When did she leave?"

"When I was five. Dad kicked her out after..." I closed my eyes to push back the image that was trying to surface.

Roe ran her fingers through my hair, and a groan left me as I leaned into her touch.

"After what?" she asked.

"She started out with opioids after a car accident on her way home from work when I was two. It quickly progressed, and she was always running after that high. I don't have many memories of her, but the few I do have aren't good. My dad has filled me in a lot."

"What made him kick her out?"

I blew out a breath. The subject was difficult. I was so young, but that day scared me in ways I couldn't voice.

"Do you remember after the elevator and how I said I don't do well in ones that aren't moving, just like you?" I asked.

She nodded. "You said it was horror, but not a movie."

I adjusted my position and took hold of her other hand so I was holding both. "She chased that high all the way to a broken-down high-rise in a shady part of town. After she got what she needed, we got back into the elevator. It had barely moved when she was shooting up. Then the elevator violently rocked and came to an abrupt stop."

I could still feel the shake, being thrown against the wall of the cab. The emptiness and the fear were overpowering.

"The light flickered and I was so scared, trapped in that small space. I was just a little boy needing his mother, and no matter how much I screamed and cried, it couldn't pull the needle from her vein or the glassy look out of her eyes. Eventually my cries alerted someone, and the police were called."

Roe lunged at me, swinging her leg across mine and straddling my hips. Her arms wrapped tightly around me, holding me close.

"Thane. Oh, my God, Thane."

I held her with all my strength, using her to ground me, to remind me that while there were people like my mother in the world, there were also angels like Roe.

And that was what I saw when I looked at her. What would have happened to Kinsey if Roe hadn't been so selfless and hadn't taken her in? What would have happened if Kinsey's mom ever had custody of her? Would she end up in situations like the ones that haunted my dreams, or something worse?

I lost track of time, but eventually the emotions subsided and I pulled back.

"Enough on me. Tell me more about Ryn."

She ground her teeth together. "I feel for your dad. To love someone and watch them totally change, completely succumb to the high, hurting friends and family for their next fix. Trying to help them, spending so much time and energy only to have them leave rehab within days and sending your money down the drain. Waiting for that call from the police, whether it be jail or the morgue."

The heaviness in her voice must have been made of stones that had piled high over years. I ran my hand up and down her back, soothing her as she did for me.

"Ryn got with the wrong crowd in high school. But her issues started before that. We knew a lot of kids who lost parents, but with Ryn, it was like she thought she was the only one. That only *her* father died that day. She barely remembered him, but still, she used him dying as an excuse for everything, and people let her get away with it."

"You don't like manipulators," I said, remembering what she'd once told me.

She shook her head. "Ryn was a master manipulator even as a child. But like with your dad, a child was in danger and I had to cut her off. She's only seen Kinsey a few times, and once she didn't even notice she was in front of her. For Kinsey's well-being, I can't even with Ryn anymore."

I nodded. We hadn't talked much about that night, but despite her anger, I could tell Roe still cared about her sister. "It's completely understandable. And I don't want her anywhere near you. What she did was unforgivable."

Roe nodded against my neck. "I just hope wherever she is, she's okay and that she stays there."

The air was heavy and thick, but also filled with comfort and peace. Neither of us moved. We simply held each other. After a while, a sigh left her.

She pulled back, and our eyes met. "Do you want to stay for dinner?"

It was the middle of the afternoon, but I knew my answer. "I'd stay forever if you'd let me."

She shook her head and rolled her eyes. "I've officially been your girlfriend for eight hours."

"Has it been long enough to move on to the next step?"

"Unless that step is a blow job, the answer is no."

"Well, in that case…" I grinned at her, then leaned forward to capture her lips with mine. "I'll wait until I've proven my boyfriend status, but that doesn't mean later I'm not going to try and get between these thighs."

"Technically, you are between them."

"Don't say that."

"Why not?"

I bit down on her bottom lip and pulled. "Because I have no problem ripping them open and sinking you down on my dick."

She popped up from my lap and was across the room, leaving me with my arms out reaching for her.

"You're not ruining my favorite leggings. So…" She stepped over to the built-in hutch. "Game or Netflix?"

Twenty-Seven

Thane

"This is still weird," Roe said as she slipped into the passenger's seat. It wasn't the first time I'd picked her up at the daycare she took Kinsey to every morning.

I pulled away from the curb and into traffic before slipping my hand in hers. "It's been three days now. Why is it weird?"

On Monday she'd been late again, and that was when the idea hit me. I knew the daycare was close, so why not just pick her up?

I pulled her hand to my lips and kissed it. "I like driving with you to work."

"I do too. It's just that this is New York City. You take public transportation. That's just how it works. You don't *drive* to work." She shook her head. It wasn't the first time she brought up my driving, but I didn't think it was as strange as she did. To me it was odd to *not* drive, but it was the opposite for her, having grown up in a city with such a huge transportation infrastructure.

"Well, I do."

"You do realize that just highlights how much of an outsider you are, right?"

I shrugged. "I rode the trains for years. I don't need the experience or whatever you're thinking I might be missing."

"It's not that. It's just—" She waved her hand in front of her to the stopped traffic. "How can you stand the stop and start?"

"The train does the same."

"I suppose, but the only thing I have to pay attention to is which stop is mine."

A thought occurred to me. Having lived in Manhattan her entire life, had she ever left the city? Not only that, did she even know how to drive?

"Have you ever driven a car?"

She shook her head. "Never been a need."

"Have you ever left the city?"

"I've been to Italy once, and I went on a Caribbean cruise a few years back. Then there was the time we went to a family reunion in Iowa, but Mom drove."

I almost wanted to say she'd led a sheltered life, but New York was the original concrete jungle.

"When we go to North Carolina, I'll teach you to drive. You never know when you'll need it."

"We're going to North Carolina?" she asked.

"I hope someday. Maybe next summer, we can spend a week at the lake house. There is a sandy shore that I bet Kinsey would love to play at," I said, smiling as I envision us making sand castles. She seemed stunned. "What is it?"

"I just… I guess I hadn't thought that far into our future."

"Would you not want to go?"

She shook her head. "No, no, that's not it." She reached over and placed her hand on mine. "I would love to go, and you're right. Kinsey would love it too."

I was happy she agreed, and suddenly my mind was awash

with all the things we could do. I couldn't wait for my family to meet her.

Twenty minutes later, we pulled into the parking garage and headed to the elevator.

"What can I cook my girls for dinner tonight?" I asked as we walked.

"Well, that's not something I'm used to hearing."

I shrugged. "My dad worked a lot and before my mom came into our lives, I kind of had to fend for myself. Luckily, the neighbor that watched me a lot taught me. She always told me that there wasn't much a woman found sexier than a man who could cook."

Roe leaned in and whispered so that none of the bystanders would hear her while we waited for an elevator. "She was right. And you really don't need to get any sexier. I promise you've reached sexy enough. In fact, you blew right past it."

A chuckle left me. "Am I too sexy for my shirt?"

That earned me a laugh, and she leaned against me. There was another guy watching us, or rather, staring at Roe. I wrapped my arm around her waist and held her close to ward him off.

When the hell did I become the jealous type? Probably from the moment her hazel eyes met mine.

"We should get some coffee on our way up," I said in an effort to avoid the bitter brown water from the break room.

"We'll be late."

I grinned down at her. "I don't think your boss will mind."

"Abusing your status again, I see," a familiar voice said from behind us.

I turned and shrugged at him. "Morning, James."

He smiled as he looked at us, noting my arm around Roe's waist. "Two months ago, I would have never imagined you two would get together."

"Because I'm an arrogant ass and she's the queen of wit smacking me down at every turn?"

He chuckled. "Pretty much."

The elevator arrived, and at least twelve people loaded in. I pulled Roe close to me as we crammed in.

When we arrived on the lobby floor and squeezed out, James waved at us. "See you at ten."

I looked down at Roe as we moved to the line for the coffee shop. "Do I have a meeting with James at ten?"

She shrugged. "Do I look like your assistant?"

My lips formed a thin line. "There is a likeness, but you are much prettier than Crystal."

"Bias. She's married and I'm your girlfriend, so you have to say that."

Pride filled me when "I'm your girlfriend" flowed from her easily as she spoke.

For over a week, I spent all of my free time with Roe. I was happy, ecstatic. But every night I went home to my cold condo, missing the warmth of her tiny apartment. After some time alone, I couldn't help texting her or calling her.

Our working relationship was running smoother than ever, but the banter wasn't completely gone. Now it was laced with innuendos of what we would do to each other that night.

I hated at the end of the day when Roe left without me. I often had to stay late, sometimes only half an hour, but other times it was a few hours. I was trying to keep down the longer nights because I wanted to spend my evenings with Roe. Have dinner together.

We'd fallen right into a routine of sorts, and I was fairly certain it had to do with our proximity. Being two blocks away, there weren't really any barriers to spending even an hour together.

"Are you sure you want to come over every night?" she asked with a scowl as she answered the door.

I froze mid-step, and my stomach clenched. Was I overdoing it? I'd admitted to myself earlier in the week that I was acting like a lovesick puppy, but I didn't give a fuck because I'd never felt this way before. "Do you not want me to come over so much?"

She rolled her eyes before grabbing my hand and pulling me in for a kiss. "It's not that. I just thought you'd want some you time."

I wrapped my arms around her and held her tight to my chest. "I'd much rather have us time."

"You're going to get sick of me."

I'd sensed for a while, especially after our run-in with Pete, that Roe's trust issues were deeply ingrained. Only time would earn her trust, and I'd have to show her that I wanted her.

A grunt followed by "Mamama" drew our attention to the toddler crawling toward us. Seemed she wanted to be part of the action. I scooped her up and held her high in the air, a drooly smile filling her face.

"Better put her down before that drool ends up in your mouth," Roe said with a laugh as she looked up.

"You wouldn't do that to me, would you, Kins?" I asked, and she answered with a long thread of drool slipping from her chubby cheeks. I quickly righted her, the line becoming a wet spot on her clothes. "Or you would."

I breathed in a strong garlic smell and looked to the kitchen wall.

"See, I mentioned pasta yesterday and what is Mommy making? Spaghetti." I growled the last word while playing that I was eating her belly. A peal of laughter left her, and she patted her hands against my face.

When I looked back to Roe, I was stunned by the soft,

sweet smile on her face. It was completely unguarded and took my breath away.

The sudden need to know what caused such an expression took over so that I could get her to replicate it.

"What is it?" I asked.

"I like this."

"Me too, but you have this sweet smile that is in contradiction to the woman I know."

She threw her hand into my stomach. It was a common move I'd come to expect when I said something I knew would embarrass her.

"You were saying?"

"I like this."

"And what is this?"

She stepped up and wrapped her arms around my waist. "I like that I can be a balance of myself with you. Old Roe and Mommy Roe. It feels good."

"I like it too. Seeing you free, unafraid to show your devotion to Kinsey, because if you didn't get it already, I'm not going anywhere. Kinda stuck with me."

"Like a bad tattoo. No regerts."

I tilted my head back in laughter. It was the quintessential reminder to check the spelling before it was forever etched into your skin—misspelling no regrets to read no regerts. "Did you just say I was a bad tattoo?"

"I may have likened you to one."

"So sassy. I feel like tonight I really am going to have to show you who's boss in this relationship."

She poked Kinsey in the belly, tickling her. "Kinsey will, right when you're mid-stoke. She'll let you know who the boss is. She has impeccable timing."

"Challenge accepted."

After eating, we put Kinsey down for the night. She'd

become more accustomed to my presence, making bedtime a little easier each night.

"How does your guardianship work?" I asked as we cuddled on the couch together.

"It's called Kinship Care. Kind of like fostering. I was awarded guardianship by a judge, but after what happened, I've decided I'm going to petition for adoption. I'll lose some of the financial aid I receive and her Medicaid, but I don't think Ryn is ever going to get clean and if she does, who knows how old Kinsey will be. I couldn't bear raising her until she's ten or twelve and then handing her over to someone who is essentially a stranger."

I looked down at her, stunned. The court wouldn't do that, would they? "Could that happen?"

She shrugged. "It's possible. But there are a lot of what-ifs and possibilities I don't even want to think about. I want to adopt her. I want to be her mom always."

"I'll help you in any way I can."

She tilted her head back to look up at me. "Why?"

"Because *you* are her mother. Your love and devotion... growing up, I wished I had a quarter of the love from my mother that you give Kinsey."

She stretched up and pressed her lips to mine. A moan left me when she straddled my hips and deepened the kiss.

From the moment her lips touched mine, the passion we shared exploded.

It was no longer gentle, but frenzied movements that had us peeling off clothing. I barely had my pants to my thighs when she straddled me again and sank down on my cock.

"Fuck," I hissed. My eyes rolled back at the feel of flesh on flesh for the first time all week, thanks to her period.

Her hips rolled, and I groaned out. I pulled her to me, smashing her breast right into my mouth. She drew in a sharp breath, her arms wrapping around my shoulders and into my hair. With each flex of my hips up, a stunted cry fell from her lips as she tried not to wake the baby.

We moved as one, tightly wrapped up in each other as she rode me. I tugged on her piercing, groaning as she squeezed around me. I wanted her to come, but the slow, sensual pace with no barrier had my cum threatening to burst out before she got there.

Reaching between us, I ran my hand down and strummed my fingers against her clit. The roll of her hips increased, and she bit down on her bottom lip as our eyes locked. Her pussy tightened, and I needed her to come before I lost it.

"Come on, baby. Come around my cock. Show me how good I make you feel."

Her forehead fell against mine, a sign she was close. I took control, gripping her hips and changing the angle so that I could thrust up faster, drilling her. She slid down and hid her face in my neck to muffle her cries. A growl left me as I pushed and pulled her along my length in time with my thrusts at a maddening speed.

When her teeth sank into my neck, I lost all control. She was shaking in my arms as she came, and I pushed into her as deep as I could as wave after wave of cum exploded.

As we came down, I relaxed back into the cushion. She was boneless on me, and I stroked her back.

"I won the challenge," I said as I turned to kiss her cheek. A small giggle left her, but a moment later, my exhausted girlfriend was asleep with my dick still buried inside her.

I hoped I was proving to her that her insecurities about me were unfounded, because now that I had her, I wasn't going to let her go.

Twenty-Eight

Roe

I loved spending time with Thane at home, but I also found I loved spending time with him at the office. All the tension aside, I found we worked quite well together. Two weeks of relative ease had passed, making the first few weeks seem like a bad dream.

"I have your coffee, Mr. Carthwright."

A groan left him and he licked his lips, his hand reaching out to squeeze my ass.

"You really need to not do that."

"Do what?" I asked.

"Cut the innocent act. You know you're a tease."

I leaned down and pressed my lips to his, then again. The phone rang and he pulled away, but I grabbed onto his tie and pulled him back.

"Roe," he chuckled against my lips.

I stood and picked up the receiver. "Thane Carthwright's office, how may I help you?"

It was one of the Worthington people, and I handed the phone over before walking out of the office.

I couldn't keep the smile from my face. I was so happy. Happier than I'd even been before. I'd never been more thrilled to be proven wrong, because every day with him was better than the one before.

After looking over Thane's schedule and his assistant's email, I found the rare time where I could work on my real work.

Donte had been doing a fantastic job on his own, but I hated that I wasn't there to help as much as I should have been. He'd come over a few times and we hashed some things out, but it wasn't the same.

The idea did come to me to talk to Thane about releasing me back to Marketing, but every time I thought about bringing it up, I couldn't get the words out. As much as I missed my work, I couldn't bring myself to leave him before Crystal returned.

The past few weeks had been unbelievable. It was incredibly difficult not to fall for him. Smart, charismatic, kind, sweet, protective, sexy, and he could cook—the complete package.

When we ate lunch together, another common occurrence, I was always stunned that the man I once thought of as an asshole was all mine.

"What should we do for dinner tonight?" he asked as he forked a piece of chicken from my container.

"Hey!" I cried in protest.

He just gave me a cheeky smile and licked his lips.

It was Friday, a normal day normal couples would go and spend the evening out. We'd only had one of those, and it was weeks ago.

"I'm sorry."

His brow scrunched, confused since he was the one who'd stolen from my plate. "For what?"

"That we can't go out more just the two of us."

He placed his hand on mine and rubbed his thumb across my fingers. "While I would like that, just being with you is all I need."

"But Kinsey—"

He cut me off. "Is adorable and—"

"And always with me," I finished for him.

He scrunched his brow and leaned back. "Why are you trying to fight me on this?"

I picked at the edge of my napkin, unable to meet his gaze. "Because dating me isn't normal."

"Who defines normal? So we spend more nights in than out—who cares?" He cupped my face and leaned in closer. "As long as I'm with you. Kinsey is just a bonus."

"Don't you want to go out on a date?" I asked. Old insecurities were rearing their ugly heads and I began to doubt.

"Of course I do. You've just seemed reluctant and I didn't want to push it. My goal is to make your life better, not give you more stress."

It seemed like a legitimate argument, but still that doubt nagged at me. "Getting a babysitter is hard, and my mom's schedule is all over the place."

"You know we don't need all that, right? We can take her with us."

"A toddler at a restaurant?"

He shrugged. "Why not?"

"The screaming. The crying. They tend to do what they want at whatever volume they want."

He nodded. "True, but why should that stop us? Why should a baby stop us from doing anything we want?"

It was instinct. One moment I was in my chair and the next I was in his lap, my lips smashed against his.

A groan left him and his arms wrapped around me. "Keep throwing yourself at me like that, and you're going to be the lunch I'm eating off this table."

"Then what will I eat?" I asked innocently.

His eyes widened and he swallowed hard. "Fuck, Roe, don't tease me like that."

I let my hand trail down between us and cupped his cock, which was hardening in my hand. In all the weeks we'd been together, I still hadn't given him a blow job and his reaction was tempting me to do it right now.

I removed my hand and sighed. "I'm sorry. You have a meeting in fifteen minutes and I'm getting you all worked up."

"Put your lips around me for the first time and I guarantee it'll be five minutes max."

"Only five minutes?"

"After weeks of anticipation, hell, yes."

"Challenge accepted," I said as I pulled his belt through the loops. With each movement his breath sped up, lips parted. When I slid down to my knees and pulled him free, he began cursing up a storm.

He watched in rapt attention as my lips wrapped around the head. A deep groan left him when I took more of him in my mouth.

"Fuck, that's a beautiful sight," he said as he stared down at me.

I took more of him in, opening my throat to get as much as I could before pulling back. I bobbed up and down, moaning at all the grunts and groans leaving him. When his hips started pulsing up into my mouth, I knew he was close.

I pulled back and swirled my tongue around the tip, earning a few pleas before I took all of him in my mouth again. He grabbed hold of my head and held me in place as he cried out. I felt each twitch as he came.

Five minutes? I had him coming down my throat in less than four.

He stared down at me in awe, trying to regain his breath. "That was un-fucking-believable."

I licked the tip, giving it one last kiss before tucking it back into his pants.

"You earned it."

"How do I earn another? Because you just blew my mind."

I pushed against his thighs as I stood. "Come on, we need to finish and get to the meeting," I said. As I sat, I tried to ignore the dampness of my panties and instead focused on finishing my lunch.

After we cleaned up and popped a couple of mints, we gathered up our laptops and headed down the hall. We had barely made it out of his office on our way to the conference room when someone I didn't recognize stopped us mid-step with a snide comment. "It's frowned upon to be dating a subordinate."

Thane stopped and turned back to him. "Good thing I'm not her boss."

"She's working for you," he sneered.

I'd never seen him before, and I wondered what department he was from. By the way Thane interacted with him, I had a feeling they knew each other. From Thane's attitude, I also had a feeling he wasn't a fan of the man.

"Temporarily. When Crystal gets back, Roe will be back in Marketing where she belongs."

"Why not send her back now and use the temp agency like you're supposed to?"

Thane stepped forward, his glare making the man slink back. "Do I answer to you?"

"N-no."

"That's right."

"But Mr. Donovan—"

"Is well aware of the situation. Obviously, he has no issue."

We continued on and just to make certain everyone knew, Thane wrapped his arm around me and pulled me tightly into his side.

"You know what's hot?" I asked him as we walked.

"Besides you?"

I gave his ass a pinch. "Pretending that it's forbidden."

His steps faltered, and I knew his mind was swirling. "Fucking in secluded areas, trying not to get caught?" His voice was tight and low, causing a spike of heat to rush through me.

"I knew you'd like that," I said with a giggle.

"You're going to kill me, woman."

"Woman? What happened to baby?"

He smirked down at me. "Baby entices. Woman fucking wrecks my whole day."

I pretended to ponder his statement, but the reality was that I loved both. *His*. I just loved that I was his and that he was mine.

Twenty-Nine

Thane

Over the weekend I stayed at Roe's for the first time. It was possibly the best night sleep I'd had in years. There was something so cozy about her bedroom mixed with having her in my arms.

Being with Roe was… hard to describe. In her arms, there was peace but also an edge of protection and love that I didn't even know I craved. She was quickly becoming my everything, which was why when I woke in my own bed on Monday morning, a single text caused my anxiety to spike and race through me.

Roe: I can't work today.

Immediately, I pressed call. "Is everything all right?" I asked as soon as she picked up.

She made a murmuring sound. "I don't feel good."

"What's wrong?"

Another inarticulate sound. "Sinuses and headache."

That didn't sound good. "Okay. Take some medicine and crawl back into bed. I'll call you later to check on you, and then be by after work."

"'Kay."

Unease and random worry invaded me constantly throughout the day, but especially after I hadn't received a response to my texts in three hours. The entire day I felt off. Not having Roe nearby was a strange, empty feeling that I didn't care for. By hour five with no response and Roe not picking up my calls, I left before three. My schedule was clear, and I took advantage of it.

When I arrived at Roe's, she answered the door more unkempt than I'd ever seen her. Her hair was a tangled rat's nest around her head, eyes barely open, nose red, and she looked like she could hardly hold herself up.

"What are you doing here?" she asked, her sinuses sounding completely stuffed.

"I came to take care of you."

She blinked at me. "What time is it?"

"Just after four," I said as I stepped in, making sure to lock the door behind me.

She blinked slowly, not really looking at anything. "I need to go get Kinsey."

Kinsey wasn't there? "How in the hell did you get her to daycare this morning?"

She shook her head. "I wasn't so bad then. I came back and laid down, and when I woke up it was like someone ran me over."

"You're not going anywhere right now."

She shook her head. "I have to pick her up by five thirty."

"Call them and tell them I'm coming to get her."

Her brow scrunched. "You?"

"Yes." I directed her to the couch and sat her down. "I'll go pick her up and bring her back here while you rest."

"But..." she trailed off, her sick brain unable to fire off on all its usual cylinders.

"Just do it."

I went into the bedroom and located her phone. After handing it to her, I went back into the bedroom and pulled mine out to call her mom. I'd only been sick twice in the last eight years, so I had no clue what Roe might need.

She answered on the second ring, an unsure edge to her voice. "Hello?"

"Hey, Linda, it's Thane," I said.

"Thane, hi," she said, relieved, and then her tone turned grave. "Is everything okay?"

"Pretty much. Your daughter is a disaster right now, and I wanted to see what you thought was best for her." I described Roe's symptoms, and Linda rattled off a list of items that were thankfully in Roe's medicine cabinet.

"Have her take all of those at the doses listed. I think I should be able to get Kinsey in time."

"Don't worry, I'm going."

"You are?" she asked in surprise.

"Yeah, she was calling them while I called you. I just hope they understood."

"Thank you," Linda said.

"For what?"

"You care about them a lot, don't you?"

Warmth filled my chest. "More than you know."

"I'll call later to check in, then. Thanks for calling me. Sometimes Roe is just too independent for her own good."

She was spot on there. Roe had trouble asking for help, even from me. Trying to anticipate her needs was difficult. I would not fail her now.

After helping Roe with the meds, I grabbed her keys and gave her a kiss, then headed out to pick up Kinsey.

Thankfully, even in Roe's sickness she had called the daycare, but when I arrived they were wary. Roe sent them a photo, but the real proof came when Kinsey's face lit up and she crawled to me when I walked through the door. That solidified it for them, and I loaded her into the stroller and headed back to Roe's.

Stairs. How the fuck did my tiny girlfriend manage to lug the stroller with a twenty-pound baby inside up two flights of stairs? Not only just for her building, but she constantly did it for the subway as well.

Kinsey was half asleep when I pulled her from the stroller and to my chest. I quietly stepped over to the bedroom door, hoping all the ruckus hadn't woken Roe up. Thankfully I heard little snores, confirming she was out.

We moved back into the main room, and I kicked off my shoes and lost my dress shirt, which was difficult with Kinsey in my arms. While I'd spent a lot of time with them, I still wasn't confident of her schedule, but I knew Roe liked to keep to it.

Kinsey nuzzled into my chest, and it felt like I'd been hit by lightning. It was an intense shock to my heart that I could hardly contain. An intense paternal love for her tugged at me. That little movement that said she trusted me, was comfortable with me.

It gave me a sense of completeness I didn't know I was lacking. I sat on the couch and pulled her close, pressing my lips to the top of her head.

"I'll make you a deal, okay?" I whispered. "You help me get your mama to fall in love with me, and I'll be the best dada ever."

Kinsey had reawakened a part of my heart I'd locked away. I'd been excited to be a father, to welcome my son into the world, and when he was gone, I shut that part of my heart down.

I was head over heels for Roe, and I wanted to be with her always. And like her mother, I'd fallen for the beautiful creature in my arms. Roe and Kinsey were a package deal. One that I'd gladly accept—after all, I wanted to be Kinsey's daddy.

Thirty

Roe

I wasn't sure how long I was asleep but when I woke up, I heard a baby giggling. Immediately I sat up as confusion washed over me.

Kinsey. Did I pick her up?

There was music coming from the other room, and I climbed out of bed. As soon as I opened the door, the sight had my chest clenching and my ovaries exploding.

Thane stood in the middle of the room with Kinsey in his arms. They were dancing to the music, and she was giggling at him like mad.

A few steps in, I leaned against the wall to watch them.

It wasn't until they spun around that either one of them noticed me. Kinsey let out a squeal while Thane shot me a megawatt smile.

"Look who's up, Kinsey," he said to her.

"Mama." Grabby little hands reached out for me. I stepped closer, but when I did, she just grabbed my hair and pulled me closer to them, making me chuckle.

"You look like you're having a good time," I said.

"The meds worked, huh?"

I nodded. They had helped greatly. The symptoms were only tamped down, but that alone was huge. I wondered how he knew. "I'm a little confused on what's going on, though."

He laughed and told me about a conversation that I could only kind of vaguely remember, and also about the conversation with my mom.

I still had a sinus migraine, but the pain in my face was less and I could breathe, and that was a huge improvement.

"Thank you," I said as I slipped my hand in his. "It means so much to me."

"Me as well."

"How so?"

He looked to Kinsey, then back to me. "You trusted me with your daughter. You trusted me to take care of you."

"Well, you're kind of a great guy."

"I'd like to think after today, I earned a better title than a great guy."

"Is that why you did it? Brownie points?" I asked, my hackles coming out.

He shook his head. "Calm down, Mama bear. I did it because, well." He heaved a sigh and stroked my thumb with his. A hard swallow made his Adam's apple bob. "I've got it bad for you. For both of you. I'd do anything you need, because I care so much about you."

"Oh," I said, suddenly feeling like shit. Then what he said hit. The butterflies in my stomach kicked back into action, and I took my bottom lip between my teeth. "Well, you're not so bad yourself."

"Not so bad? I think that's a backslide from a great guy."

"Keep talking, and I'll demote you to lackey." I stepped forward and leaned in to press my lips against his chest, right over his heart. "I'm falling for you, too."

He pulled me close and let out a sigh, his body relaxing into mine. "About time."

~

The next morning I once again woke to giggling in the other room, and I bolted up when I saw the time—it was almost noon.

Thane was on the floor with Kinsey, playing with her, and she was giggling away.

"You're missing work?" I asked as I pulled my robe on.

"It can wait. You needed me."

Warmth spread through my chest. I'd never had a boyfriend take such care of me. "Why didn't you wake me?" I asked.

"You're sick, baby. You needed rest."

My brow furrowed as I looked over to the couch. He'd spent the night, slept on the couch. Did Kinsey wake up in the night? "I probably got you sick."

"I can take your cooties."

"Oh, yeah?" I asked as I curled up on the couch.

He nodded. "Iron immune system. I haven't been sick since 2015."

"There's a toddler in the house; just you wait. She's going to bring home all sorts of wonderful things." I smiled as I said it, then my expression dropped when I realized what I implied. "I mean—"

"Stop," he cut in, his eyes narrowed on me. "Don't you dare take those beautiful words back, or I'll kidnap you both and make them a full-time reality."

The butterflies in my stomach really liked that idea, but I tried to brush it off and stood back up.

"I should probably get her diaper changed before there's poo all over the place. Right, baby boo?"

"Already done," Thane said.

I turned to him with wide eyes. "You changed her diaper?"

He nodded. "It was a stinky one, wasn't it?" he said to Kinsey, who was chomping on one of her blocks. "And then we had breakfast."

"You fed her, too?"

He nodded. "It's not hard to figure out when it's something you want to do."

My heart felt like it was going to burst.

"Don't forget, I was almost eleven when Wyatt was born. I've changed a good number of shitty diapers," he said with a chuckle.

He was making it almost impossible not to fall for him. He was amazing and perfect.

"Are you hungry?" he asked before getting up and filling a glass of water.

I looked up at him as he handed it to me. "Thank you, and I could eat."

"What are you feeling? There isn't a lot in the fridge or freezer. I think I saw some toaster pastries, or there is toast. Maybe pasta? Or we can order in?"

I shrugged. When was the last time I ate anything? I couldn't remember. "Is there any chicken-flavored rice in the cabinet?"

He turned and opened the one cabinet that I used as a pantry. It wasn't very big, so I didn't keep much extra stuff in it.

"Hmm, doesn't look like there's anything but some white rice." He turned to me. "I can go get some, or we can order some. There's fried rice, Mexican rice..."

The last one hit me, and my stomach grumbled thinking about a cheesy enchilada. "Let's order."

An hour later I was popping the last of my enchilada meal into my mouth. It was amazing how much better I felt with some food in me. I still didn't feel the greatest, but I felt like I could hold myself up again.

Later that afternoon, there was a knock on the door. Thane

went to answer it while I stayed snuggled on the couch. The officers that had come weeks before stepped in.

They had information. While one of the men had been arrested, my sister was being detained while they figured out her involvement, and they were searching for the other two. I didn't know what there was to figure out, since she let them in, but maybe they thought she was coerced. Either way, they never should have been *here*. That was definitely Ryn's idea.

It did settle a deep emotion in me to find out she was okay, though I really hoped she'd be given jail time. That was the only thing I could think of that would get her off the drugs.

"We were able to get this back," one of them said as he held out a familiar gold and leather watch.

I took hold of it, tears brimming in my eyes as I flipped it around—M.C.P.

Malcolm Christopher Pierce.

"They tried to pawn it. Owner spotted it for what it was and called us."

A sob left me, and I looked up at them with tears streaming down my face and a smile on my lips. "Thank you so much."

"You're welcome, ma'am."

With that, they left. Thane sat down next to me and held me in his arms as I cried, happy to have my precious reminder of my father returned.

Thirty-one

Thane

Fall was definitely upon us, but while the air held a crisp edge to it, the sun kept us warm. Roe was better, and we spent all the following week trying to make up for taking time off. It was totally worth it to be able to help her, to show her I was there for her. To see the distrust fade in her eyes as something entirely new took up residence. She said she was falling for me… and I couldn't wait until I could claim her forever. To earn that privilege was worth the time it took to prove myself.

And I would prove myself.

We could finally relax and decided to take a stroll around the park. It was something I didn't do that often, and considering how close we were, it surprised me. Then again, until Roe, I was all work.

Roe definitely was a walker. The nine blocks just to the entrance was more than I usually walked, but to her that was life. You wanted to go somewhere, you walked or took public transportation.

While it was a great advantage to city life, I preferred to drive most places.

"It's just easier sometimes. Ride a bus for a mile with ten stops in between, or walk?" she said as we walked. "Every time I visit Lizzie and James, I walk. It's not that far."

By car I knew it took a while, but walking? Maybe it was just the city traffic that made it feel like a long time. "What do you do when it rains or there is snow?"

"That's what rain boots and snow boots and umbrellas are for. Plus, a long puffer coat for the winter. They aren't the most stylish, but I don't care because it keeps me nice and toasty. And I've got a rain cover and a cozy cover for the stroller."

It was a beautiful day, and there were a lot of people out enjoying the crisp weather.

"The leaves are starting to change. We should come back in about a week when they pop."

"You seem to be the park expert, so lead the way."

"There are so many places to see. I think we need to take it slow, but we can start with one of the most iconic places—the Mall. We're really close."

"I didn't know there was a mall in the park."

"Not that kind of mall. You'll recognize it when we get there. I think it's in every New York-centered movie."

She was right that it wasn't far and when we got there, I did instantly know it: the extra-wide, straight path with a canopy of green leaves that were turning yellow. Benches lined the pathway, and I wanted to kick myself for not seeing it sooner.

I'd visited the park many times over the years, but it seemed I'd missed many parts of it. When we reached the end of the mall, I took her hand in mine and lifted it to my lips. Her fingers were cold, and I rubbed them between my hands to warm them up.

It was possibly the first time I hated the stroller because I was unable to hold her hand while we walked.

"The Loeb Boathouse has an express cafe we can get lunch

at. They've got good sandwiches," she said after my stomach rumbled.

I laughed and nodded. "After you."

The lake was filled with people in boats, and I couldn't help but think maybe when Kinsey was older we could do that.

We enjoyed a nice lunch while discussing where to go next, and Kinsey enjoyed munching on the fry she stole from Roe. Obviously she was not content with her cheese stick and berries, and wanted to experience what we were eating.

When we stood to leave, my feet let out a twinge of pain. I should have worn better shoes.

"You're going to wear me out before we get home."

She giggled. "Oh, come on, you're just soft."

"Maybe right now, but give me a minute and I'll be hard as a rock if you want."

She rolled her eyes, and I smiled down at her.

We were just on our way when I heard my name. Turning toward the sound, I was struck by a familiar blonde walking toward me.

"Thane!" Liv cried out before she swung her arms around my shoulders.

I was taken aback. The shock of seeing her for the first time in years. Since...

She pulled me close, and I placed my hands on her hips before pushing her back.

"Liv, how are you?" I asked in surprise.

"Better now that I've seen you, stranger. How long has it been?"

"Years."

"Too long, if I do say so. You're looking dashing. What have you been up to these days?"

"I'm the President of Acquisitions at Donovan Trading and Investment."

Her lips drew up into a huge smile. "Really? Well, my, my, you have certainly gotten better with age."

My lips formed a thin line. The last thing I wanted was her trying to get her gold-digging claws into me. I wasn't good enough for her then, and she wasn't good enough for me now. By the fake nails, overly done makeup and hair, and what I knew to be expensive tastes, she hadn't changed any.

What did I see in her in the first place?

"Do you need something?" Liv said. My brow furrowed when I realized she was talking to Roe.

Roe's gaze narrowed, and I realized my mistake too late. I'd taken too long to introduce her. I wrapped my arm around her waist and pulled her close before placing a kiss to the top of her head.

"Liv, this is my girlfriend, Roe."

Liv's eyes widened. "Girlfriend? *Really?*"

I noticed the way Roe's hand tightened on the stroller handle. Liv was proving to be just as vapid as I remembered.

I gave Liv a huge smile, so proud to call Roe mine. "Yes."

"Is the baby yours, too?" she asked, glancing down at Kinsey.

"No, she's Roe's." The words didn't feel right at all, like acid on my tongue, but they were already out.

"Oh," Liv said, her lips pulling up into a devilish grin. "Thank God."

My grip on Roe tightened. "Yes, thank God for sending her my way."

She gave Roe another condescending lift of her eyebrow, then focused back on me.

"Is your number still the same?"

"Yes," I reluctantly confirmed.

Her face lit up. "Good! I'll give you a call."

I hope not.

As I watched her walk away, I imagined how my life would

be different if she hadn't lost the baby. Hopefully I would have given up trying to be noble, unable to take her uppity personality, and broken it off.

I'd probably spend the weekends with my son. I smiled at that, wondering how he would take to Kinsey. Roe would have opened up to me sooner instead of being afraid I'd bail at the first showing of Kinsey.

I was lost in thought when a precursor to a tear-filled explosion caught my attention, and I moved around to the front of the stroller.

"What's wrong, sweetheart? Diaper?" I asked. Glancing up to Roe, it felt like a knife hit my chest. Her eyes seemed unfocused and lost, sad almost.

Did I fuck up? Cleary the atmosphere had shifted, and I couldn't help but worry.

Thirty-Two

Roe

I knew he didn't mean it the way it came out, but it was still a slap in the face. While not wrong, he'd also spent so much time trying to convince me that we meant more than his flippant response.

"No, she's Roe's."

Again, not wrong, but I hated the sour taste it left in my mouth. It was a bitter reminder that no matter what, that would always be the answer.

Still, I couldn't get mad. I knew it was irrational, though I, for some reason, felt angry inside. Kinsey was mine, but she also wasn't. So me saying, "No, she's my sister Ryn's," wasn't exactly something I would say, but it was something I had said many times before, in the beginning.

I hated the way it made me look at him differently, when it shouldn't. Maybe it was her. *Liv*. She was that perfect, rich Manhattan socialite, a good complement to Thane. The perfect arm candy for an executive of his standing.

Why couldn't he just claim us as his? What stopped him?

Then she was gone, and Thane stood there, appearing lost in thought.

"You okay?" I managed to ask, curiosity winning out.

He nodded and gave a wistful sigh. "I was just thinking about how things could have been."

It felt like his words were a knife, spearing my chest and twisting in my heart. How things could have been with *her*. Not having to degrade himself with someone with a lower social standing.

Was I just a placeholder, like with Pete? Someone to play house with until he found the right one?

She had his number. She was going to call him. He wished things hadn't ended.

I didn't mean enough to him.

"Everything all right?"

I smiled at him, but it was a forced smile. "Yep."

Inside, my heart was breaking. While I tried not to get too hopeful, too attached, it was obvious I had. I always knew I couldn't rank high in Thane's social or financial hierarchy. I made decent money, but nowhere near the level of his salary. Add in that he was a sexy single man, and me being a single mom, we didn't mix.

My feelings went far deeper than I imagined. No, that wasn't right. They were deeper than I had acknowledged to myself. I'd long surpassed falling, and was unequivocally in love with him.

Yet, I couldn't help but question everything—our relationship especially—now that I'd met Liv. *She's the one he should be with.* They were a perfect match. The only baggage she came with was a trauma they shared.

My heart was heavy, and I needed space. My chest felt tight and breathing was hard. I needed to take a moment to myself, and with that I said to Thane, "I need to run back to my place real quick."

Thane's surprise was apparent. We were cutting the day short. "Did you forget something?"

"I'm just not feeling very well."

"What's wrong?" he asked, coming to stand in front of me. He looked me over, but it was too close, too much.

I stepped back to give myself the illusion of space. "I have a headache." The most cliché excuse ever.

We walked together out of the park in silence. I closed myself off, a wall of tension rising between us.

"See you soon," I said, trying to give him a reassuring smile, but I knew I was failing.

He pulled me close, holding me tightly in his arms. "Why don't I take care of Kinsey while you rest?"

I tried to force a smile. "It's okay, it's her nap time, so we'll both sleep."

"Then how about I come over in a few hours with dinner?"

I could almost feel the desperation in his tone. "That sounds good."

With a last kiss to my lips, then to my forehead, he reluctantly stepped away.

A dark pit formed in my stomach as I watched him leave. Thane seemed so affected by her. And that thought terrified me. I needed a chance to rebuild my walls.

He was just biding his time until he got back together with her. It was like what Pete said—I just wasn't worth it.

After I locked the door, I lay down on my bed with Kinsey, hoping she'd fall asleep faster beside me.

Meeting Liv, Thane's ex who had once carried his child, had drained me. Thick, toxic thoughts had poured into my mind and heart, and I was struggling to rise above them. To believe in the feelings I knew we shared.

But it was easier to believe the bad over the good.

The week passed in a blur, and then Kinsey was officially one year old.

The party was planned and her presents were wrapped. It wasn't going to be much, because honestly, it was true that I had lost a lot of people when I took Kinsey in. Longtime friends stopped calling when I was no longer able to go out. People who I thought had my back had disappeared when I was no longer convenient.

It always made me wonder what Pete told them, if he had badmouthed me, or if it really was just all because I had a baby.

Kinsey's birthday wouldn't have much fanfare to it, and even though she wasn't going to remember it, I was determined to make it a special day.

Mom was coming over, as was Thane, and we were all going to the Central Park Zoo. Mom was making her a cake, and I couldn't wait to watch her eat it.

Her baby bestie, Oliver, was also coming with Lizzie and James, along with their older daughter, Bailey.

By nine thirty we were almost ready to go.

"It's a very special day today," I said to Kinsey as she looked up at me from the floor, a bottle in one hand and a block in the other. There was formula soaking into her onesie, and I was happy I hadn't put her birthday dress on. "You're a mess, nugget."

There was a knock on the door, and I gave Kinsey a surprised look. "Who is it? Grandma or Thane?"

Thane had slept over, but he'd run back to his place for a shower and change. My heart was still heavy about him, and while we'd returned to some semblance of normal, I knew he could feel the shift. Was that why he slept with a near death grip on me?

She kicked her feet excitedly and looked to the door. I smiled at her as I pulled the door open, but my good mood was instantly squashed.

Her hair was almost brushed, but I could tell she was coming down from a high.

"Hi, Roe," Ryn said.

"Ryn." My jaw locked down as I glared at my sister. "What are you doing here?"

"Um, well, it's her birthday, right?" Ryn said, but it sounded like she wasn't quite sure. "My baby's."

"What if it is?"

"Can I... can I please just tell her happy birthday? Please, Roe, she's *my* baby."

Hearing her say it was like nails on a chalkboard. Yes, Ryn carried her for nine months, but I was Kinsey's mother.

"Five minutes," I said, knowing I shouldn't. The last time she showed up, it was a disaster. "That's it."

"Thank yo—"

"And you're going to tell me how you're not in jail right now."

She nodded and stepped forward. With reluctance, I stepped back. Everything was screaming in me that it was a bad idea, but then the part of me that cared about my sister reminded me that it was her daughter's first birthday.

"Hi, baby," she said as she sat on the floor in front of Kinsey. Did she even know what her daughter's name was?

I rolled my eyes as I sat next to her.

Kinsey's attention was on the toy in her hand, but she looked up at Ryn, giving a high-pitched screech.

"A year ago today it was just you and me, little one."

"Kinsey," I said through clenched teeth.

"What?" she asked.

"Her name."

"Oh," she said as she looked down at Kinsey. "I was going to name her Emma."

"Well, then you shouldn't have abandoned her. Now tell me why you're not in jail."

She swallowed hard. "I took a plea deal. Community service and parole to testify against them in exchange for no jail sentence. I told them they forced me, that I had no choice."

"Had no choice?" Those three words resonated inside me and the simmering anger exploded. She reached for Kinsey, and I yelled out. "Don't you fucking touch her!"

My raised voice upset Kinsey, and she began to cry. Ryn reached out again, but I scooped Kinsey up into my arms.

"Roe…"

"You told them where to go for a quick score," I spat behind clenched teeth.

Her eyes were wide. "I didn't have a choice. Please, Roe."

"You had a choice, Ryn. You had a fucking choice to leave me out of your fucked-up life, but you just couldn't do it. You had to drag me down, hurt me again."

"I don't want to hurt you."

She wasn't understanding, because she was driven by the drugs. She *chose* to tell them about my apartment. She *chose* to help them break into my home.

"Get out!" I yelled.

"Please, Roe, just let me explain."

"Explain? *Explain?*" I seethed. "You brought those men to my house. To what? Were they going to rape me before they took off with all of my stuff? Or were they going to take me?" The sound of one of them crashing into the bathroom door, trying to get in, filled my ears. "Did you promise them a woman as well? How much stash did they give you in exchange? Or was it just the bruises from pushing you down and hitting you?"

"I didn't know they were going to do all that."

"But you knew they were going to rob me! You brought them to where your *daughter—your daughter*—lives and gave no shits about what happened to her. You are despicable, and I want you out."

"Roe, please." She had tears streaming down her face, but they weren't going to soften my anger. "I'm sorry, okay? I'm so sorry."

I glared at her. "Sorry won't fix it this time. Sorry won't fix what little trust that remained between us that your actions shattered into millions of tiny pieces."

"Everything all right?" Thane called out from the doorway, startling Ryn and making her jump.

"I should go," she said.

"Yes, you should. And don't come back," I hissed. "After what you did, I don't want to see you again."

"Roe, no. I don't have anyone," she pleaded.

"And whose fault is that? Now, get out."

She nodded, tears welling in her eyes. She gave one last look back. "I really am sorry. For everything."

As soon as she was gone, as soon as the door was closed, a sob left me and we fell into Thane's arms.

"Shh, calm down. It's okay," Thane said, pulling me against his chest.

"But it's not. It's not okay, and now she's seen you and she's just going to do it all over again." If I had any doubts before about adopting Kinsey and making her fully legally mine, they were gone. Kinsey was my daughter, and nobody was going to take her from me.

"It's okay. We'll be fine." He placed a kiss on top of my head, his arms securely holding us up.

The effect of his embrace hit both me and Kinsey.

Why was there always such peace in his arms? How was it he always made me feel loved and cared for? I felt secure in his warmth.

Thirty-Three

Thane

After Ryn's surprise arrival, it took Roe a while to calm down. By the time her mom arrived, she was back to celebration mode.

Kinsey had a great day, having no understanding what was going on, but she did take a hilarious and adorable face dive into her cake when that first taste of sugar hit.

Which was followed shortly by Oliver doing something similar. They were both covered in icing in seconds.

"This has been nice," James said as he stepped up next to me. "Thank you for inviting us."

I nodded. "It's been a great day."

"You two are getting quite cozy."

The words hit me hard, and not in a good way. I covered it up, because I refused to acknowledge my growing worry at the walls that Roe had built back up after our run-in with Liv. "And?"

"Lizzie thinks you'll make beautiful babies, and she can't wait. I think she's getting baby fever."

I quirked a brow at him. "Lizzie is? Are you sure it isn't you that wants more little Donovans?" I asked, a chuckle leaving me as I watched Kinsey stick her whole hand into her mouth.

He grinned. "It's a team effort."

"What kind of team? Baseball?" I asked.

"Not that many, ass. When we first started dating, Lizzie told me she wanted four kids, and time is flying. We're not getting any younger."

Bailey was sitting nearby, happily munching on a piece of cake and making faces at Kinsey and Oliver. They both giggled before returning to their sugary treats.

I wanted more times like this with our friends and their families. Again, that unease rolled in my stomach.

"Go for a girl. I bet Bailey would love a baby sister."

James started like he suddenly remembered something. "Lizzie reminded me that Roe's birthday is coming up, and we didn't know if there was anything planned for that."

Roe's birthday was soon? How did I not know? "It is?" The slice of pain this news brought me was swift and deep. I was beginning to see that when Roe put walls around herself, she fortified them until they were nearly impenetrable.

He nodded. "She's a Halloween baby."

"That explains some things."

"Like how she put a spell on you?" James said with a chuckle.

"Asshole."

"Pretty sure that's your name." He continued to taunt me.

"Then what's yours?"

He grinned at me. "That's between me and my wife."

A few hours later, we were carting a sugar-coma'ed one-year-old out of the zoo and back toward home. Roe said goodbye to her mom before she headed to the station, and we continued on to her apartment.

"Good day today."

Roe smiled. "It was. Kinsey got lots of presents. Yours may be the best. I *love* it. She's going to get so much use out of it."

"I'm really glad you like it, because shopping for a one-year-old is not easy." Kinsey was almost walking, and I'd found a toy where the wheels could flip, and it could change from a rocker to a riding or push toy.

"And I can't believe that dress you got her. It's beautiful. I don't know when she'll ever wear it."

"It's just a dress. Cloth. She can wear it whenever. Every girl needs to feel like a princess now and then."

Roe moved a fussy Kinsey into the bathroom, stripping her as the tub filled up. I leaned against the doorframe, watching as she patiently cared for the beautiful little girl who had taken over both our hearts.

I was still stunned at the amazing woman I called mine. The way she was with Kinsey told me she would be the most wonderful mother to my children as well. And fuck, if that idea didn't make me want to drag her to bed and make some.

"What sounds good for dinner, baby?" I asked just as Kinsey splashed the water, hitting Roe right in the face. It was hard to hold back my laugh, but Roe didn't seem to notice, her attention on Kinsey.

"I'm still so full of cake. I might just whip up some toast or something small."

"There's that tapas place down the street. I could get us something from there?"

"That could work."

"How about you and Kinsey come stay at my place tonight?" I twisted, trying to work the kink out of my muscles that had bothered me all day. "Your bed kills my back."

"I'd prefer if we stayed here; all of Kinsey's stuff is here. It just makes things easier."

That made a thought strike my brain, and I wondered if it were possible.

"You should go sleep at your place. It's fine. I don't want your back to hurt. We can just see you in the morning."

There it was again. That push.

The thinly veiled, passive-aggressive, very unlike Roe words that only solidified my growing concern that she was pushing me away.

I needed to do something to open her back up, to gain the ground I'd for some reason lost.

~

The next morning my back felt better, but my heart did not. I hated the distance that separated us both physically and emotionally. After having some coffee and before heading over to Roe's, I pulled out my phone.

If I was going to pull off my idea, I needed help from the one woman who was always there for me.

"Hi, Mom," I said.

"Is everything all right?"

I shook my head. We always talked on Sunday nights, so I was certain a midday call set off all sorts of internal alarms.

"I'm fine. How are things there?"

"Good. Trying to get your brother's schedule together so he'll come home for Thanksgiving. Maybe you can talk to him."

"I bet if I sweeten the pot with first-class tickets, you'll have all the information you need in an hour."

"You shouldn't spoil him like that. But if you two could get a flight together, that would be great."

"About that."

"You're not coming?" she asked, picking up on my subtle cue.

"I'm not sure if my girlfriend can travel for the holiday, so I may stay here with her."

"Girlfriend? Thane Alexander Carthwright, are you holding out of me? When did this happen?"

My face was starting to hurt from the ear-to-ear grin at her reaction. Roe was special. The meet-the-parents kind of special. But I knew with Kinsey that a long weekend in North Carolina was probably not in the cards, but maybe Christmas.

"Her name is Roe. She works for the same company I do, and she's a spitfire. You'll love her."

"Sounds like it. Why don't you bring her down with you?"

Ah, the complicated part.

"That's mostly why I'm calling you. I need some help setting up a baby's room."

"You got her pregnant?" she asked in a high-pitched shrill.

Of course, she would jump to that.

"No, she has a baby, and I want to set up one of my extra bedrooms for her so they can stay the night with me. Her apartment is tiny."

There was silence for a moment before a calmer version came back on the line. "You're dating a woman who has a child? That's… Thane, are you sure about her?"

"More sure than anything."

"But a baby? What if she's using you for your money?" she asked. Having known my last girlfriend, I had a feeling she was thinking I might be with another Liv.

"That's not what's going on. Trust me, it was hard enough just getting a date out of her, and that involved rescuing her from an assault on her home by some drug dealers."

"Drug dealers? Thane, what in the world have you gotten yourself mixed up in?"

"A great relationship with a selfless woman who took in a baby that wasn't even hers and lost a lot to save her from her drug-addict mother."

There was silence. "Oh, Thane."

She knew all about my birth mother, and knew how fucked-up that made me in some regards. No matter how hard she tried, she couldn't free me of my issues.

"She's beautiful and sexy and smart. Has the constitution of a warrior, and a wicked determination if you piss her off."

"Which you have firsthand knowledge of, I'm sure," she said with a knowing laugh.

"She poured a cup of coffee all over me after I was an ass."

There was a chuckle on the other line. "I like her already. So, maybe if the baby can travel. If not, you have to bring them down at Christmas, and definitely in the summer."

"I will. Now, what do I need to outfit a one-year-old's room?"

An hour later and a list three pages long, I had a plan in place and a full online shopping cart.

As I hovered over the Buy Now button, I looked at the price tag and reality settled in.

I was about to spend a couple grand on baby stuff for a woman I'd been officially dating for a month. It was a big gamble for a new relationship, but I wanted it.

The vision of picking Kinsey up from a crib in her own room in *our* home hit me square in the chest.

It was a future I never would have envisioned, but it had become the one I dreamed about.

The problem was convincing Roe that I was a good bet.

Thirty-Four

Thane

I had the day all planned out. It started with family fun pool time at my building's indoor pool. Roe still had failed to even hint that it was her birthday, so I planned a fun day with her and then an evening out, just the two of us. Linda was going to stay at Roe's with Kinsey.

Until then, I was getting hard looking at Roe in her bathing suit.

If you could call it that.

"What the fuck are you wearing?" I had barely been able to control myself before, but Roe standing in front of me in quite possibly the sexiest scrap of clothing I had ever seen had me throwing my hands up in defeat.

It didn't fit the norm for Roe's wardrobe. Red, low-cut top that accentuated her breasts, with red strips that crisscrossed her body twice before ending at very low bottoms.

She bit down on her lip as she gave me that minx-like smile that drove me wild. "You like? I bought it just for you."

An audible groan left me, and I palmed my cock. "You're not playing fair."

"How so?"

"Cut the coy act. You know how so."

She shimmied where she was standing, shaking those sinful hips.

I shook my head. "You are such a tease."

She leaned over to pick up Kinsey, and I about lost it. If I'd seen it while we were still upstairs, Kinsey would have gotten a show.

She held out the round baby pool float while my gaze was locked on Kinsey slapping her little hands on Roe's squished breasts.

"Get in before you scare someone with that thing," she said with a wink.

We were alone, the pool area was completely empty, but it didn't stop me from taking another glance around. "You're lucky there are cameras in here," I hissed.

She giggled in response before stepping up and grabbing my hard shaft through my swim trunks. "False threat." She leaned in closer and nipped at my pec, the highest her tiny frame could reach. "You'd love to give whomever is watching a show."

Fuck, I love her. If I could just get the words out.

"Is that a challenge? You know how I feel about challenges."

"Oh, I know, baby. Can you do something for me first?" she asked in a sweet whisper, batting her eyelashes at me.

I was completely hypnotized by her and by her hand that was working up to the tip. She gave it a squeeze before slipping her fingers into my waistband.

My breath was labored, and all blood had rushed to my dick. "Anything."

She grazed the tip, making me groan before trailing her hand up to my chest, right at my heart.

"Get in the pool," she said with a push, and I fell off balance.

My eyes went wide as I stared at her before I hit the water

with a splash. When I broke the surface and drew in a sharp breath, she was standing there laughing.

And so was Kinsey.

"You're in trouble," I said with a glare. She had distracted me, backing me up without me noticing.

"Ah-ah, I've got a baby in my arms," she said as she moved over to the steps.

I took hold of Kinsey's float and walked over to where they were entering. Kinsey was instantly kicking her little legs as soon as they hit the water. I held the float steady while she deposited Kinsey into it. Once she was settled, I wrapped my arms around Roe and held her close. She kept one hand on the float while her other hand wrapped around my neck.

"Hey, handsome."

"Were you ever going to tell me today is your birthday?"

Her eyes widened. "How did you know?"

"A little birdie told me. Happy birthday, beautiful."

She gave me a sweet, shy smile, seeming embarrassed. "Thank you."

"This is just the start of Roe day."

"The start, huh?"

I nodded. "I have a lot in store for my favorite birthday girl."

I had every intention of showering Roe with the love I felt, even if I wasn't able to give her the words. With that in mind, I was taking my girl out for a night on the town. It was only the second date alone we'd had in the month and a half we'd been together.

I had to do the math over again, because that short time couldn't be right. However, it was.

But first, I was going to start with her presents.

Once we were out of the pool and back upstairs with a swim-tired Kinsey. I grabbed a pillow from my bed, laying her down on my couch and wedging her in before covering her with a blanket. Roe appeared bemused by my actions. But her tiny smile and the sparkle that I could see in her eyes gave me hope.

"I've got something for you," I said casually as I stood and picked up the packages from the kitchen counter and slid the wrapped gifts across to Roe where she stood at the dining table.

"What's this?"

"Presents for my birthday girl. It's your day, and I plan to spoil you rotten."

"Spoil me, huh?"

I nodded, watching as she fought with the paper.

She pulled the box from the paper and blinked at it before opening it to verify the contents, as if she had to inspect that it was real. "You bought me a new phone?"

"Yours is cracked, and I'm honestly shocked it still works."

I'd watched Kinsey more than once slap the phone from her hand, sending it to the floor.

"Thank you, Thane!" She walked around the counter and threw her arms around me, peppering my cheek with kisses.

I didn't want to let her go as I enjoyed basking in her unreserved affection. "There's more."

She pulled back, a twinkle of excitement in her eye. "More?" She grinned and dove into the bag. Out came a small wrapped package, and her eyes widened as she looked at the bracelets inside.

She glanced at me, then back to the stack, pulling one up and reading the edge.

"Kinsey," she whispered and smiled. The rest were more generic sayings, but ones that reminded me of her—beautiful, strong, love. And then the one that meant the most to me—you are my everything.

Tears filled her eyes as her thumb ran along the words on the last one. Her eyes met mine, and I reached out to brush a fallen tear from her cheek.

I wanted to say it. It was the perfect time. Just as I was about to, my phone went off and a groan left me.

After hitting ignore on the unknown number, I pulled another small package out.

"What's this?"

"From Kinsey."

She rolled her eyes and smiled before ripping the paper open. More bracelets to help regrow her stolen collection. A mix of gems, wire-like, crystal flowers—a dozen varieties so that hopefully she would find something she liked.

"They're so beautiful."

"Kinsey has great taste. She knows what her momma likes." I took her hand in mine and kissed each one of her fingers. "Happy birthday, Roe."

I love you.

She took my face in her hands and pressed her lips to mine. "Thank you for a wonderful birthday and all my beautiful presents."

"You're more than welcome. And now that I know today is your birthday, I'll be better prepared for next year."

"Next year, huh? Think you'll be stuck with me that long?"

"Roe, I'm planning to keep you. I'm not stuck with you. And I want forever. You're never getting rid of me."

The light in her faded, her eyes glistening before she turned from me. They weren't just words, and I needed her to understand that.

Thirty-Five

Roe

I stared down at my pretty new phone with its perfect screen and bit my lip. Kinsey had already tried to slap it down, but Thane included a ring that attached to the sturdy case that would help keep it in my hand and from breaking if it did hit the floor.

"Next week I'm not going to be your assistant," I said as we drove to work.

"Good."

"Good?"

"You make terrible coffee," he said with a grin.

I rolled my eyes. "I just get your coffee. I don't make it."

"And yet somehow I didn't have a problem before you. Interesting. Maybe you're poisoning my morning brew."

"And rob myself of all the mind-blowing orgasms?"

His face scrunched up. "Are you kidding, and which item are you kidding about?"

I shook my head. "I'm serious. You've given me more orgasms than all guys before you combined."

"How many guys are we talking about?"

"Not nearly as many women as you have under your belt."

I looked out the window, watching as the city crawled by. There was a knot in my stomach, a bothersome pain that tugged at my heart. It'd been there ever since we bumped into his ex, Liv.

He'd never mentioned her since, and as far as I could tell, she'd never called.

But what if she had?

Thane threaded his fingers with mine and pulled my hand to his lips, kissing the back of it. "Something is bothering you."

I swallowed hard. There was a lot bothering me, but the biggest was the fear of next week. "What happens when the punishment is over?" I asked, trying for levity.

He shook his head. "It's not a punishment."

"Still, what happens?"

His brow furrowed. "What do you mean? You go back to Marketing and I stalk the fuck out of you, sending you dirty texts enticing you to go to 'lunch' with me."

That seemed to be the correct response, because the knot loosened. It wasn't gone, but I didn't feel nauseous.

"That doesn't sound too bad. I'll be happy not to have to answer your phone anymore." That was the complete truth, and it made him chuckle.

"And when the workday is over, we'll have dinner together and I'll have my way with you when Kinsey is in bed."

"That could work."

"What were you thinking would happen?" he asked as we pulled into the parking garage.

I shook my head, not wanting to expose my doubts about our relationship lasting past the week.

"It's nothing."

The car came to a stop in his spot and a sigh left him. "It's something, but I'll let you have this one. Know this, though—just because you won't be outside my door anymore doesn't mean you'll be out of my mind. You're not someone I'm just going to forget because you're not in my constant line of sight."

"It's stupid, I know," I said as I exited the car.

He came around and pulled me to him.

"I'm going to miss you, too," he said with a sigh as he held me close. "I hate it, but I can't hog you. It was temporary, and now it's time to go back to your real job and not having me piss you off."

"It's been a while since you pissed me off."

"That's because I know where all of your sweet spots are." He pressed his lips to a spot right behind my ear. "Like here." His thumb brushed against my nipple, making me gasp. "And here." He lightly bit down on my neck, and I bowed into him. "So many spots I love to enjoy."

It was Thane's turn to tease and leave me wanting, a sly smirk on his lips as he stepped away. With a tug of my hand, he pulled me toward the elevator.

"Come on, before I pick a random car to bend you over."

"You wouldn't."

"I would."

"Liar. You'd just love to have me think so to see me blush."

"It may have crossed my mind."

He wrapped his arm around me as we headed up. One week left beside him, and then what? For weeks I knew my emotions were all over the place, but the most prominent was the sense of dread I already keenly felt.

Thirty-Six

Thane

The week sped by. It was unnerving to imagine life without her so close all day every day. To celebrate, I ordered lunch and made certain Roe took an hour lunch on her calendar, claiming it was business.

Our last day working together had to be special. I could tell she was down, and it worried me. Reassuring her was going to become a part of my daily routine, but she was worth it.

"What all did you order?" she asked as she opened the door fully, allowing the delivery person room to bring the insulated bag in.

"You mentioned craving some chicken parmesan last night, so I ordered us an Italian spread."

Salad, four entrees, and three desserts—we had enough food for a few more meals.

Moving to the bar, I pulled out two glasses. They weren't right for the wine I'd had delivered, but they would have to do. After pouring the red liquid, I handed her a glass, then held mine up.

"To us. I'll miss having you close, but I'll love hearing all about your day every night."

As we ate, I vowed that every week we would have lunch just like this at least once. I was going to miss her so much, which was absurd because she would literally be on the other side of the building. A thirty-second walk at most.

"I'll miss annoying the fuck out of you by not answering the phone by the second ring," she said with a wistful sigh.

I threw my head back in laughter. "I'll probably miss that as well. Imagine my phone being answered in a timely manner."

"Unheard of."

"Seriously, though, you have done a fantastic job, and I'm so happy I bullied you into working for me. If not, I'm not sure we would have ever interacted."

She set her hand on mine. "Best punishment ever."

Another chuckle left me, and I leaned forward to capture her lips. A moan slipped from my chest when her tongue brushed against mine, and I pulled her closer.

"Our food is going to get cold," she said in an attempt to focus my mind back on the meal. Unfortunately all thoughts and focus had shifted.

"Let it."

"The dessert will melt." She tried again.

I trailed my lips down her jaw before pressing them against her neck. "I was thinking of another type of dessert, and we could save those for later."

"Oh, really? What were you thinking?"

I stood and took her hand, leading her around to my desk. She quirked a brow at me as I bent down and lifted her by her ass, placing her on my desk as I pushed her skirt up. She drew in a shuddered breath as I stepped between her thighs. That reaction ripped through me and I crashed my lips to hers.

I roamed my hands all over her, taking in each subtle curve before slipping under her shirt to grip her breasts.

"Fuck," she hissed as she pulled back. Her lips were

parted, and her grip on my arm tightened as I tugged at her piercings.

"What was that? Fuck what?" I asked in a mocking tone as I moved one hand between us, a moan leaving me when my fingers brushed against her damp thong. "Fuck it."

I sat down in my chair and pulled it close before slipping my arms under her legs.

"Wha—"

I cut her off as I yanked her thong off and dove between her thighs. Immediately my mouth covered her pussy as I began eating like a starving man. And I was. If I had my way, I would be between her thighs always.

Every sigh from her lips spurred me on. I reached out and gripped her breast with one hand, my fingers pulling at her piercing as I flicked her clit.

"Hey, Thane." I heard James say right before the door opened.

Shit.

Roe startled up into a seated position, but I kept her right where she was.

"Ah, I see you're eating. I'll come back."

The door clicked closed and I locked eyes with Roe, her hands shielding her face.

"You forgot to lock the door," I said with a lick as I looked up at her from between her thighs.

"I forgot to lock the door," she whimpered.

There was no way I was letting the opportunity slip by. Fuckers needed to knock.

I stood and Roe tried to get up, but I pressed her back down against the desk.

"Where are you going?" I growled as I pulled my belt from its buckle.

Her lips parted in surprise and she glanced over to the door, then back to me. "Thane—"

"It's your fault," I said as I lowered my zipper and pulled my cock out. "So now you have to pay the price."

I ran the head of my cock against her pussy before positioning and slamming in. A low groan left me, and I reveled in the way her eyes rolled back.

My hips retreated, pulling from her, a sigh of longing leaving her before I slammed back in. The musical pitch of her lewd gasp excited me as much as the realization that anyone could see us if they wanted to.

I set up a pace, watching as she stretched around me. It was moments like this that I was going to miss. The dirty little fantasies I was able to live out.

"Anyone could walk in," I said, leaning down, my eyes locked with hers. "They could see me inside you, filling you." I wrapped my hand around her neck, pressing at the right points just like she loved. A slight pressure. "Watch my cock stretch you wide open, begging me for more."

"Harder," she whimpered.

She didn't say which she wanted harder, so I slammed my hips against hers in a hard, fast rhythm while my hands squeezed her ass. I kept up the hard, punishing rhythm, loving the whimpered moans that slipped from her lips.

"You better come before that door opens again," I whispered against her lips, loving the way she clamped down on my cock. She was taking me so good and when her breath hitched, I knew she was about to break. "Fuck, yes, baby."

She screamed into my shoulder as she shook, her teeth clamping down to stifle the sound. It was more than I could handle. Every muscle tensed and I moved my mouth to her neck, mimicking her move and biting down as I slammed my hips as far as I could, grinding in deep as I came.

"You're a naughty boy," she said between pants.

"We should do this once a week from now on." I smiled

down at her, loving the pink of her cheeks and her swollen lips. Always the most beautiful creature I'd ever beheld, and she was all mine.

~

Monday was the first day we went in separate directions as we left the elevator.

And I hated every fucking foot that separated us.

Some of that was subdued by the blonde sitting outside my office beaming at me.

Thank the heavens—Crystal was back.

Nothing against the woman who held my heart, but she was a constant distraction I didn't need. She was a fantastic fill-in, but the platonic relationship I had with Crystal was better suited for the workplace.

I gave Crystal a last squeeze and pulled back. "I'm so happy you're back."

"By that hug, it's been a disaster, huh?"

I chuckled and shook my head. "Actually, no, it wasn't."

"Way to make a girl feel wanted."

I walked into my office and she followed, shutting the door behind her. "It's not that, it's just… Well, I did something."

"If you're referring to the way you steamrolled your authority to get a girl from Marketing to take over, I know."

"You do?" I asked. I knew the rumor mill had been going around about us, but I didn't realize Crystal was still in the loop.

She rolled her eyes. "Thane, the amount of gossip that has reached me is insane. The walls aren't soundproof, you know."

I squeezed my eyes shut. Crap, I hadn't thought about that. No, all I'd had on my mind was getting inside her.

I shook my head. "Don't let her know that. Roe takes no shit, but she's not immune to embarrassment and she'll blame me."

"And you aren't to blame?" Crystal asked, popping a knowing brow.

"Technically, she is."

"That's right, blame the woman. We're used to that."

"She's the one who spilled coffee on me. I can't be held accountable for all that happened after that." By my grin, Crystal knew I was full of shit. It was all my fault, but I still liked to tease Roe that it was hers.

"Did she immediately fall into your arms? The jealousy is high around here. I know you haven't noticed it, but at least one has it out for her."

"For Roe? Why?"

"My first question. Answer it."

I heaved a sigh. "She probably called me every name under the sun for two weeks. Insubordinate, inappropriate, and if it wasn't for the unusual arrangement, I would have fired her."

"If it was anyone but her."

Yeah, she caught me there. Roe had me from the first day she stomped into my office like a hellcat.

"Right. And falling into my arms?" I shook my head. "I had to pretty much beg and trick her to even go to lunch with me. Dinner was a completely different battle."

"Cut the crap. What did you say to piss her off so badly?"

Again, I squeezed my eyes tightly. If Crystal was a violent person, I knew a punch would be headed my way, but instead, I knew what was about to come out of my mouth would earn me a stern look of disappointment.

"I may have said some bullshit about you choosing your baby over me."

Crystal didn't know about my abandonment issues, so I was taken aback by her next words.

She stepped forward and took my hands in hers. "I'm sorry."

"You're sorry?" I stared at her like she had two heads, completely confused.

"I know change is difficult for you, that having someone to count on is tantamount to your stability."

"What are you talking about?"

She sighed. "I've been working with you for over five years now. We've gotten to know a lot about each other in that time. That's just what happens in this type of relationship. And what I know isn't fact, but a feeling I've long held."

"And that is?"

"You've dated many women. *Many*. But only once, maybe twice. I think there was once a whole three weeks you went out with a woman. Then bam, onto the next. Most just thought you were a manwhore, but I knew, because I know you in a way few do."

"There was nothing there, that was all," I said, but she shook her head.

"No, there was a reason. You were leaving them before you developed any feelings. You left them before they could leave you. You have abandonment issues, and while I was only leaving temporarily, you felt like I was leaving you and you lashed out."

I swallowed hard as every word hit me hard in the chest. The feelings I held for Roe I denied, but it didn't change the truth. "There was a spark with her, and I clung to that like I've never clung to anything before."

"And you wanted more, then more and more, in ways you never did before."

I scrunched my brow at her. It was almost like she'd been watching over me the entire time.

"Who is feeding you all this gossip?" I asked, wondering if I needed to soundproof my walls.

She laughed. "It's not just gossip. There was something inside Marketing Girl that made you willing to do anything to keep her close. No woman has ever done that to you."

"I think she was meant to be mine," I admitted. We were a perfect match, from the things we shared in common to the things that separated us. Roe was good for me, and I knew I was good for her.

"That's wonderful."

"But…" That nagging feeling settled in my stomach again. "I'm not sure she feels the same."

"Do you love her?"

"Yes," I whispered. How could I openly admit that to Crystal and nobody else? Probably because she was the first to ask.

"Then make her see how perfect you are for each other."

I pulled at my neck. "It's not that simple. There are other factors. We have similar issues, and it's been hard getting her to let me in. She's guarded because she has a child."

Crystal leaned back and folded her arms in front of her, her gaze narrowed on me. "Oh, I see now."

"See what?"

"Why she was so angry with you. Still, she must care for you if you're together. Give her time. Just be there for her, let her see the kind and reliable man I know you to be."

"I missed your advice."

She let out a loud laugh at that. "You never listened to it before, so why now?"

It was true. She'd given me advice about women for years and I'd ignored it. Probably because it was about women I wasn't interest in. "Back to work."

"Aye, aye, Captain," she said before turning toward the door. She stopped and looked back to me. "Oh, one last question."

I lifted my head back up. "Yes?"

"Does this mean I can throw your little black book away?"

I beamed at her. "Shred it."

She smiled back. "You got it, boss."

Thirty-Seven

Roe

The week was over before I knew it, and it was kind of sad and unsettling to be closing out my work outside Thane's door. I'd already removed any personal items and distributed them back at my desk. I was happy, ecstatic to be returning to the job I loved, but I was sad to be leaving the man I'd fallen deeply for.

When I arrived at my desk on Monday after leaving Thane at the elevator, I just stood there and stared at it. It felt odd to sit at my desk again. My little cube seemed foreign, and I found myself lost and confused.

What was I supposed to be doing? Working on?

For two months I'd sat outside Thane's door. I'd become his confidant and his sanity. There was a brightness I was missing. The marketing department seemed dark and cold. The whole world seemed off kilter. In fact, by the time it was almost noon, I had neither seen nor heard from Thane.

He was probably bringing Crystal up to speed and thought I'd be diving deep back into the Worthington campaign. That was what I should have been doing, but instead I was staring at a screen and missing my boyfriend's warmth.

I missed our banter and his random kisses and the way he could pin me to a wall.

It felt like all the joy had been sucked out of me.

I wondered if he felt it too.

All attempts to focus were shot, but I kept trying. I owed Donte a lot of work on my part, and I wasn't going to let him down.

When I didn't hear from Thane by the end of my day, I decided to head over to his office and let him know I was leaving. I nearly stopped in my tracks at the beautiful blonde guarding the gateway to his office. Was that Crystal?

She was gorgeous and put together. The woman didn't look like she'd just had a baby. I could barely brush my hair most days, but hers was in perfectly curled waves framing her face. When she looked up from her computer, I was struck by a beautifully blinding smile that nearly knocked me over.

"Can I help you?" she asked.

"Um, is Thane available?"

"No, I'm sorry, he's on a call. Is there something I can help you with?"

I shook my head. "No, I'm sorry to bother you."

There was a crash behind the door followed by stomping feet and then the door flew open.

When our eyes locked, the darkness I'd felt all day was blown away, replaced by the warmth of his gaze.

"Hi," I said tentatively.

He said nothing, but closed the distance between us in a few long strides. The breath left me when his arms pulled me tightly to him and his lips crashed to mine.

It was exactly what I needed, and I melted into his arms.

"Fuck, I miss you," he said when he pulled back.

"Missed me? It's only been eight hours," I said, trying to hold back the stinging in my eyes.

He brushed his thumb against my bottom lip. "And that is too many without you."

I smiled at him. "Missed you, too." I stretched up to press my lips to his, then relaxed back down when I felt his grip around me tighten.

"Dinner delivered tonight? I should be out of here by six."

I nodded. "Sounds good."

"Are you okay?" he asked, his brow furrowed.

I leaned into him, my face buried in his chest as I breathed in his familiar scent. "Yeah, today was just… different."

He placed a kiss to the top of my head and his hand swept up and down my back. "I know what you mean. I'm sorry I've been so busy today."

"It's okay. Really," I said as I looked up at him. Getting Crystal caught up on a Monday with an upcoming takeover spelled chaos. I knew his schedule and how busy he was. "I completely understand. I'm just off from the change."

He pressed his lips to my forehead, and a sigh left me. "I'll be home as soon as I can. Give Kinsey a kiss for me and I'll see you soon."

I tightened my grip around his waist and held him fast. "What about my kiss?"

"I just gave you one."

I shook my head. "That was a hello kiss. I need a goodbye one."

"Nope, not getting one of those."

"Why not?"

He leaned closer, his lips brushing lightly against mine. "Because I'm going to give you a see-you-soon kiss instead."

Before our lips touched, we were stopped by a squeal from behind Thane. "Aww, you two are so adorable."

I blinked at Crystal, having completely forgotten she was sitting a few feet away, watching us. Heat rose in my cheeks and I stepped away from Thane. Each inch created a deeper and deeper emptiness that threatened to swallow me up. He cupped my face and kissed me before I walked away.

If the day was any indication, I would be seeing less and less of Thane. The doubt crept in again. Maybe that was on purpose? Maybe he was trying to distance himself? I didn't have the answers I needed, only the curling anxiety of uncertainty that festered deep inside me.

Thirty-Eight

Thane

After a few days, an unease had settled deep in my bones. Something wasn't right. That growing fear was morphing into a reality, a bad dream I wanted to wake from.

I felt a disconnect from Roe, and it bothered me. Maybe it was simply the fact that she wasn't right outside my door anymore. I hoped that was it, because I didn't like the pit that was forming in my stomach.

Thane: I miss you

I texted her. I did miss her. More than I thought possible. For fuck's sake, she was in the same building. I could go to her whenever I wanted.

But that wasn't the problem. The problem was I'd go there and never leave because of the stupid pain in my chest.

I needed her validation, was desperate for it because I'd felt her start to drift away for weeks, and it was accentuated with the physical space that separated us.

It was something I couldn't take, couldn't handle.

Seconds ticked into minutes, and I was choking on the silence.

Finally, it buzzed.

Roe: Miss you, too.

They were the words I was hoping for, but it did nothing to quell the feelings rolling through me. Yet with the takeover happening in a few weeks, I was drowning in responsibility that was pulling my attention away from her.

I'd also been fielding calls all day, not all work related. My secret project for the second bedroom was really starting to come together. The paint and wallpaper were up, and the furniture and toys were arriving. I planned on staying up for however long it took to make the room perfect so that I could show them on Friday.

Soon, there would be a perfect little space for Kinsey to call her own.

It was the first step to what I hoped would one day be permanent. I wanted to be together with them in my daily life.

There was one last thing I wanted, and I needed Jace's help. It was odd going through my call list and realizing I hadn't talked to him in a month.

"Hello?" he answered after the third ring.

"Hey," I said.

There was a pause. "What the fuck, man? You've completely fallen off the face of the earth."

"Sorry, I've been occupied."

"You mean you've been whipped."

"No, occupied. How's it going?"

"It's been boring. I've had to dive into second-string friends cause all you dipshits are settling down."

"Such is life."

He scoffed at that. "Not my life."

"One day," I said, ribbing him, knowing it would set him off. Jace was one of those self-proclaimed bachelors for life, but I had a feeling one day he'd meet his match just as James and I had.

"Nah, man. I'm still going to be rocking the single scene in my fifties."

I rolled my eyes at him being his usual dickhead self. It would be sweet justice for him to find a girl to knock him on his ass.

"Listen, does your brother still do woodworking?" I asked.

"Yeah, he's got a shop out on Long Island. Whatcha need?"

I looked at the photo of the crib against the wall and the blank space above it. "I want a custom name to hang on the wall."

"He's making bank on shit like that. I'll shoot you his number."

"Thanks."

"Are you going to ask me what I caught recently?" he asked.

I shook my head. "Herpes?"

"Ass."

"You always catch ass."

"You're a fucker," he grumbled.

I chuckled at that. "Have fun fishing."

"Say hi to James for me."

"Will do."

"Bunch of fucking pussy-whipped assholes," he yelled.

"Yup, and we love it."

"All right, I just caught the eye of a hottie across the restaurant."

"Because your stupid ass was yelling. Have fun."

"Always." Right before he hung up, I heard his first line and shook my head.

A few minutes later my phone buzzed.

Jace: Here ya go, fucker 631-555-0187

Kent, Jace's brother, was backed up with orders for a month. Jace was right, he was making bank, so I sweetened it, offering him ten times what he normally charged if he could deliver it tomorrow.

Money talks, and a rose gold script piece of wood was being specially made as the afternoon continued on.

Thirty-Nine

Roe

At noon, my alarm went off as it always did, and I popped a pill. It wasn't until I swallowed that I noticed something was off.

I stared down at the pill pack.

I'd just popped the last pill. The last sugar pill.

And no period.

Dread surged through me at the implication. I'd never gotten so far and not had my period rear its ugly head.

Was I pregnant?

Oh, no. Even thinking the word made every hair on my skin bristle.

There was only one way to find out, and since I'd already taken my lunch break, I was stuck waiting until four thirty. The mere idea that I could be pregnant stifled all concentration, leaving me unable to focus. Donte was waiting on my idea, but I sat there and stared at my computer, unable to come up with a single word.

I watched the cursor blink. Harder and harder. One harsh

blink after the other, and nothing came to me, leaving my mind free to run wild with the possibility of being pregnant.

What would Thane think?

Everything inside me stopped as the answer was crystal clear—he would do what was right.

If I told him, he'd stay.

I suddenly felt trapped by an invisible force, cornered with no way out, and it had me clawing at the walls.

Could I even tell him? I wasn't sure with how unsteady things were between us. All I knew was that he'd do the honorable thing and sacrifice himself to me because that was the kind of guy he was. Not because he wanted Kinsey or me, but because of a baby that was his. Just like he did with his ex.

That was the last thing I wanted. I needed him to be with me because he loved me. I refused to be an obligation, or a placeholder like I was with Pete—not worth the effort of a real relationship.

It was my fear and insecurity talking, but the more I thought about it, the more my chest tightened and my anxiety grew. Over and over the men in my life had left me, many times without a reason or knowing what I did wrong.

The last thing I wanted was a relationship with no real substance, held together by honorable intentions.

It clicked then—life had taught me that men left, and that I wasn't good enough for anyone. I had to let him go before he woke up and left me. But first, I needed to find out if I was pregnant or if it was just stress.

It was the most agonizing four hours of my life. The pit in my stomach consumed me, and I didn't pause when the time came. I just left.

My hands were shaking, and I couldn't stop my leg from bouncing the entire half-hour train ride back to Lenox Hill. After picking Kinsey up, I rushed toward home, stopping at a drug store on the way. The clerk took one look at me, then Kinsey, then the package, and after my card went through, I glared at her as I ripped the bag out of her hand.

Judgmental bitch.

Kinsey was upset the whole walk home, and I wasn't sure I'd ever related to one of her moods so much.

As soon as we were home, I put her on the floor and ran into the bathroom. She was still crying as she crawled down the hall toward me. I had to be quick.

I ripped open the package and when I set the completed test down on the counter, she was inside the bathroom. After cleaning up, I picked her up and wiped a tear that slid down my cheek.

I held her close and bounced her in an attempt to soothe us both. She rubbed her snotty face on my shirt, and I could hardly care.

After a few minutes had passed, I moved over to the counter and looked down.

I blew out a breath and nearly cried when only one pink line showed up. Relief flooded me, and I sat down on the edge of the tub, completely drained.

The whole scare highlighted one thing—I needed to let Thane go.

I stood and moved toward the kitchen, my eyes stinging, tears filling my vision.

He wasn't meant for me, despite how much I loved him, and it would just hurt more when he woke up to that fact. The relief I felt at not being pregnant was quickly followed by the disturbing thought of him not being in my life. My chest clenched and I had trouble drawing in a deep breath at the thought of him with someone else.

How much worse would it be in a month? Six months? When he finally got tired of me and woke up, how much more in love with him would I be?

I would be a mess. I'd never in my life felt so deeply for any man, and the thought of that ending gutted me. The realization of what I needed to do hit me so hard that my knees went weak and I dropped down onto the couch.

In the background of my mind I could hear Kinsey, but aside from that was a reverberating emptiness that opened up inside me. It was an out-of-body like experience. I could feel nothing but the blackness of pain slowly creeping in.

There was no way to know how long I stayed in that paralyzed state when my phone notification going off brought me back.

Thane: What do you want for dinner, baby?

I stared at the screen, blinking before I processed the words.

Roe: I've got it covered.

What was I going to do? I knew what I needed to do, but could I actually break up with him?

Thane: You sure? I'll get you whatever you want.

The truth was I didn't want anything. I had no appetite.

Roe: Yup, I've got what I want. You should just get yourself something.

Thane: What is going on lately?

I bit down on my bottom lip as my fingers hovered over the screen. The emotions rolled inside me and I tried to get a handle on what I wanted to say, but one hand seemed to be fighting with the other.

Tears flowed freely from my eyes as I typed out the words that broke my heart. But he was never meant for me.

Roe: I don't think we should see each other anymore.

Forty

Thane

I nearly rear-ended a car when her text came through my speakers.

What the fuck?

Somehow I managed to park at my building without further incident while my chest was fucking bleeding out. I didn't bother going home. I just started walking to her apartment, because I refused to believe her message. There was no way we were over.

That text contained words nobody ever wanted to hear, especially not from someone that you loved with all your heart.

I was shaking on the walk to her apartment. I didn't respond to her text. I couldn't. There was something I missed, a word she forgot to type. Maybe she didn't think we should eat out anymore? We had just been talking about food.

I prayed that was it, but I knew that it wasn't. Her walls, her trust issues—I'd failed to get through them.

The air between us had felt stiff and awkward for weeks, ever since we ran into Liv. Something about that day shifted our relationship, but what happened this week for her to end things so suddenly?

With each step I wracked my brain, replaying every conversation over and over in an attempt to pick out where I fucked up.

Finally, I was standing at her door, slamming my fist against the wood.

There was silence before the lock spun and there she was.

Her expression was lifeless and lost. Still, I could see the evidence that she'd been crying.

I pushed past her into the living space and turned, noticing Kinsey wasn't in the room. "Tell me that text didn't say you wanted to break up with me."

She swallowed and looked away from me. "We don't belong together."

I stared at her in stunned silence, trying to process the words that came out of her mouth because I knew I didn't hear her right. There was no way she was saying we were through.

She was my perfect match. The light in my day and the beating of my heart. A heart that was cracking, because it was true—she didn't want to be with me anymore.

She didn't want me.

"What the hell are you talking about?" I asked.

She swallowed hard, and that lost look in her eyes hardened into resolve. "Guys like you don't normally date girls like me."

"Girls like you? What does that mean?"

"I have a baby. I may not have given birth to her, but that doesn't change the fact that I am her mother. And this isn't temporary. I am her legal guardian. I'm all she's ever known."

"And?" It wasn't like it was something new, and I'd never treated it as temporary.

"And I'm a package deal. Nights without her don't happen often."

Is that what this was about? Date nights? "I understand that."

"Do you?"

My jaw clenched as I stared at her. "Are you trying to fight with me? I'm not getting what you're trying for here."

She wrapped her arms around her torso. It wasn't a standoffish gesture, but more of a protective one, leaving me even more confused about how shit went sideways.

"What I'm getting at is that she will come before my job. She will come before you. And I know how you feel about that."

"How do you know?" I asked. I couldn't keep the anger out of my tone. "Have I ever given you any indication that I wouldn't want you because of her?"

"Yes!"

"When?" I asked. I needed to know where the fuck she got such a ridiculous idea.

"When you bitched about Crystal taking time off to bond with her newborn instead of working. About her putting her baby before you."

I shook my head. We'd talked about that day. She knew my issues. "That's not it."

"Then what is it?"

"I was an asshole to say that, and it was said in frustration because Crystal keeps me sane. She's worked for me for years, and we are a well-oiled machine. But you know, you fucking know, that's not how I feel."

"What happens now that she's back and has to leave early because the baby is sick, or calls off because the baby needs her, or has to always leave on time every day to get to the daycare before they close?"

I stared at her, at a loss where the sudden anger was coming from. "Roe..."

"Does she no longer have value? Will you get rid of her

because she can't be there for you every moment of every day?" She was practically screaming at me and all I could do was stare at her. I wanted to pull her to me, to comfort her, but her body language suggested that would be a bad idea.

"Where is all this coming from?" I asked, keeping my tone low and even in an attempt to calm her.

"Because Kinsey is getting attached to you! So am I. And I can't bear it when you decide you should be my sole focus and I can't do that and you leave me."

Her bottom lip trembled, tears filling her eyes as she looked away. I reached out and cupped her face, bringing her back to face me.

"Who said I was going to leave you?" Because I was never going to leave her.

"Nobody."

"Then why would you think that?"

"Because we don't make sense, and when you see that or when you get tired of me always putting Kinsey first, you'll be done with us."

I gently cupped her jaw with both hands and pulled her closer. "And why do you get to decide how I may or may not react? What I feel for you is more than just a skim coating of emotional attachment. It's not going to crack and fall away at the first stress."

Tears filled her eyes. "You deserve more than me and all that I come with."

I shook my head. "No. You've let shitheads like your ex warp your mind over years and years."

"And you haven't? Our pasts are impeding the present, but you're overlooking the obvious. You were so mad at Crystal for staying home with her baby when you yourself know what it's like to be abandoned by your mother. What you say now doesn't match with the words and actions from when I first took over."

"Crystal has worked for me for five years and when she extended her maternity leave, I was afraid she wasn't coming back and that fucked me up. Because I have this fucked-up fear that makes me lash out." I pulled at my hair. "I was afraid she was going to abandon me just like you're doing now. It fucks me up and I've never been able to shake the fear that I would never be important enough for *you* to stay."

The silence between us hung in the air as prevalent as a third person. An observer to heartbreak watching over us.

"I was honest with you about my baggage," I said after a few minutes.

"But my baggage makes this so much worse."

"How so?"

"Because no matter what, I will always have to make Kinsey my priority. No matter how much I love you, her needs come first, and…" she trailed off, her lower lip trembling, tears filling her eyes. "I don't think you can handle that."

"No," I growled. "You will not pin this on me. I want you. All I want is you. I don't want anyone else."

"Please don't make this harder."

"Why does it have to be hard? Why does it have to be done at all? Tell me!"

She shook her head and back away. "This is best for both of us."

"Like hell it is!" I yelled. No. Fuck, no. "Why do you get to decide what's best for me? Especially when that decision will fucking slice me open and tear my heart from my chest. Why do you get to decide that?"

She was silent, her gaze glued to the floor. "You should go."

I lifted her chin to look at me, our eyes locking. "No. Not until you tell me why."

"Because we just won't work," she said as a tear slipped down her cheek.

Lies. It was all fucking lies. I knew it. She knew it.

But we were at an impasse, and her decision was final.

She was dumping me for no fucking good reason.

"I won't accept it, Roe. You're scared right now, and you have the right to be so I'll give you some space, but know this—I'm not going away. I will always be there for you for whatever you need. I'm not done with you, and I never will be."

And with that, I walked past her and out the door. I had to get away from her before things became worse, before she convinced herself that she could never love me.

Forty-One

Roe

The sound of the door slamming jolted my system. It felt like that one act cracked open my chest and had me bleeding out. I wanted to go after him, to tell him I loved him and beg his forgiveness, but my feet were firmly planted.

My bottom lip trembled as I looked around the room. There were scattered reminders of Thane everywhere. He'd become so integrated into our lives. How did I not notice that? Was it because he fell so easily, fit in so nicely with us?

I pulled a bag out and scrambled around picking up anything and everything that was his. I needed it all gone. All reminders of him needed to disappear so that I could breathe again because I was choking on my despair.

Despair borne of a situation that I created. That I instigated. Because I knew he'd be better off with someone like Liv, someone more like him.

Someone who could love him more...

A sob broke out and I fell down to the floor, clutching his NYU shirt in my hands.

My chest felt like it was breaking open and caving in on itself at the same time.

"Roe?" Mom called as she walked in. "Baby, what's wrong?" She sat down in front of me, her hand on my back. I'd forgotten that I asked her to come over, knowing I would need the only person in my life I could truly count on.

"I broke up with Thane."

"Oh, sweetie." She pulled me to her, and I cried on her shoulder. "What happened?"

"I had to let him go. He's better off without us."

"Wait, *you* broke up with *him* because you think he'd be better off?"

I nodded.

"Roe, baby, I don't agree with you. Any man who treats a woman and her child like they're the most precious things in the world isn't wanting anything but to be loved in return."

I shook my head. "He doesn't love me, so it's—"

"How do you know? Did he say he doesn't?"

"No."

"What did he say when you broke up with him?"

I stood up and worked my way around the room picking up anything I came across that was his. "What does it matter, Mom? He's gone."

"Roe Alexandra Pierce, you're the one who's going to listen to me right now the same way I listen to you when talking about Ryn."

I hadn't heard my mom's terse voice or seen her scowl directed at me in years. "That man is not only head over heels for you, but Kinsey, too. That's a commitment to you."

"It was a way to control me."

She looked at me in shock. "Control you how? How in the blue hell is wanting to be with you, doing all that he has done for you, a controlling move?"

I collapsed down even more. "I don't know."

"You just convinced yourself of it. Decided that was what it was to give yourself an out."

"And I took it," I ground out. "He's free of us to find someone better suited for him."

"And why do you get to say it isn't you?" she asked. It was a question close to what Thane had asked and I still didn't have an answer.

My mom may have been right. Thane may have been right. But I had to follow my gut. I may not have been looking into a crystal ball, but I also had to do what I believed was best for my daughter and me.

Forty-Two

Thane

My chest felt like it was splitting in two. I felt nauseous as I tried to process what the fuck had just happened.

She broke up with me.

Without provocation and without a valid reason. There was nothing I could do to stop her, no changing her mind. She was firm in her decision, leaving me broken and confused.

I should have told her "I love you," but I had a feeling she would have just pushed me out even harder.

My world wasn't right. Everything was off kilter.

I moved to the liquor cabinet and pulled out the first bottle I could find. Anything to numb the waves of agony that were surging inside me.

For months she had been my life, and she severed it as if it meant nothing.

"I love you, Roe," I whispered as I swallowed back the tears threatening to explode.

I was going to figure out how to get her back, how to get her to believe in me and us, but until then I was on a personal mission to see the bottom of every bottle I had stored away.

In my haze I sent off texts begging with her, pleading with her to undo it, to unsay it. A venting of the turmoil inside me. She never responded, and eventually my battery died. I didn't even bother plugging it in, because there was no reason.

My reason shoved a knife in my heart and left me bleeding on the floor as she walked away.

The sun had set and I stumbled around, the soft glow of the city my only light source. I flipped on the light in the kitchen and grabbed another bottle, tossing the now empty one in the trash.

She didn't even let me say goodbye to Kinsey.

The hole in my chest ripped even wider, and I gulped down the burning liquid that was in the bottle.

I didn't want to remember. It was all a bad fucking dream, and I was going to wake up and she would be curled into my side.

I held onto the wall for support, my vision locked on the door in front of me. With a few steps I stood in the doorway and flipped on the light.

The once white walls were still white except for one. A bright bouquet of watercolor flowers reached down from the ceiling, coating the wall in a beautiful pattern. Something Kinsey could grow into.

What was weeks ago an empty space was filled with furniture and toys.

Anything a growing girl would need.

Mom helped me with a list of all that I needed, and I picked everything out—a convertible crib, a dresser, armoire, a night stand, and a comfortable chair that rocked and swiveled.

Above the crib in perfect rose gold script wooden letters was her name—Kinsey.

It was all so perfect and all so ruined. It felt wrong, but why? Why was my love so wrong?

I did it so we could be together more, so that Kinsey would be comfortable in my home. So that maybe one day I could convince Roe they should stay. But she didn't even let me show it to her. For weeks I'd kept my plans a secret and everything was perfect... until it was all gone.

I took another long pull from the bottle, then wiped the back of my hand across my lips.

All I wanted was her. It was a visceral need. Like she was the air that kept me breathing. How did I ever function before her?

The answer was simple—I didn't. I existed, but I wasn't living. With Roe, the world slowed down and the simple act of watching a movie with her brought me more joy than anything in years.

How was I going to go on without her?

I was a fucking disaster. That was the only way to describe it. The weekend was spent wallowing in my own misery, drowning in booze until the liquor cabinet was empty.

It took everything I had left in me to take a damn shower and get dressed on Monday morning.

The elevator pinged, and I winced against the sound. I let my feet carry me to my office on autopilot. There were some whispers on my path and more when I reached the door, but I ignored them. My foot tapped something on the floor, and I looked down to find a bag leaning against my door. On top sat my purple NYU T-shirt.

"Fuck," I whimpered, feeling my chest rip open again.

It hadn't even been forty-eight hours and she'd cleaned all traces of me from her apartment. Almost like if there was nothing left of mine, she could forget all about me.

But I knew that couldn't be true because the ghost of her haunted my home.

I still didn't understand why she'd pushed me away, why she'd broken up with me and torn my heart apart.

"Thane?" Crystal's voice floated into my thoughts, pulling my attention away from the bag.

I turned toward the sound, and she gasped when she saw me.

"Oh, Thane."

"What did I do wrong?" was all I said as I swallowed back tears. I wasn't the kind of man prone to tears. In fact, the last time I could even recall crying was in the elevator with my mom when I was five. But something about my situation with Roe made fighting them almost impossible.

It was the same feeling as then—complete helplessness and abandonment from the one I loved.

Crystal ushered me into my office away from the prying eyes and ears.

I didn't tell Crystal everything. It somehow felt like telling on Roe because Roe was a private person, and I never wanted to hurt her in any way.

"Are you going to give up? Because you look like you have."

I shook my head. "I had to let go, get fucked up to dull the pain." I met Crystal's eyes that were filled with such sympathy. "I love her so much, but I just don't know what to do."

"Well, you know where she is right now..."

I straightened at that. I did know exactly where she was, but what was I going to say to get her to listen? I had no game plan.

But I needed to see her.

The whole morning was a waste. I was a wreck trying to think of anything, any sound reasoning that she might listen to.

Around noon an email with her name popped into my inbox and I practically fell over myself to read it. The emotion quickly died out. It was just a leftover from when she worked with me. An inquiry that took a long time to get back to her.

Were there more emails out there she was waiting to hear back from? More information that hadn't yet made its way back?

I was up from my chair and out the door on a path to the marketing department before I could even grasp a single idea on how I was going to spin it from "who else are you waiting to hear from" to "I love you, please come back to me."

When I drew closer, I watched her slip into a cube and after taking a sip from a coffee cup, set it down on her desktop. She looked beautiful, even if her eyes were puffy and red.

"Roe."

She froze at the sound of her name and looked up. Our eyes locked, and I could see my pain mirrored in her. She shook her head, her body trembling like she was stifling tears. With another shake of her head, she turned and slipped out of her cube and headed down the hall away from me.

"Roe," I called, trying to get her to stop.

She turned on me, her hands up, but she wouldn't meet my eyes. "No. Just go back to your office."

"I just want to talk."

"Well, I don't."

"Please," I begged. I just needed her to stop locking me out.

"We're done, Thane. Please, just leave me alone."

The way she backed up, the tears welling in her eyes, told me the truth—she didn't want to break up. She did it for some misguided fear that ran rampant through her mind, festering until it became a truth in her own head.

How was I supposed to combat that? Convince her that we should be together?

Roe was her own worst enemy when it came to her heart.

I needed help, guidance, just fucking *anything* to set my world right again.

I stormed into James's office, surprised to find Lizzie there.

"Thane?" he asked, his eyes wide as he took in my appearance.

"James, Lizzie, you need to help me. What did I do wrong?" I asked as I paced in front of them. The agitation, the anger, the despair needed an outlet.

He shook his head. "I can't help you there."

"But you know, don't you? Tell me!"

"Calm down."

"I can't! Not until I have her back. I can't fucking stand this." I thrust my hands into my hair. "She's not talking to me, and I… How do I get her back? How do I get her to see I'm not going anywhere? That she can trust me?"

That she can love me.

James cleared his throat, gaining my attention.

"James," Lizzie said, giving James a warning look.

He looked to his wife. "They're both my friends, Lizzie, I'm not going to let the two idiots suffer."

"Tell me," I begged.

It was Lizzie who spoke up. "Her feelings for you scare her. She can see that you care, but she thinks you'll get tired of playing house—"

"I didn't—"

She held up her hand. "I know, but those are her words." Lizzie sighed and before I could speak, she let out the hard truth I needed. "The saying is if you love something, set it free. If it comes back, it was meant to be. She set you free, so you better come back with force. Prove to her you're not going anywhere."

"I made a room for Kinsey," I admitted. "A room for her to grow into, but I didn't get to show her."

That made Lizzie smile. "That can't hurt. She's scared of her feelings, scared you'll leave her."

"I never want to do that. But if she won't talk to me, how do I fix this? I need her."

They looked to each other, then back to me. "The fix is different for every relationship. It hasn't always been rainbows and sunshine in our relationship, but we got through it. You will, too, you just have to figure out how to get through her thick skull first," James said.

I blew out a hard breath. "She thinks I'd be better off without her, but she's so wrong. I was better with her than I'd ever been before."

"Tell her that," Lizzie said. "Tell her everything."

"She won't let me near her. How do I get her to see me? It's not like I can kidnap Kinsey..." I trailed off, the idea hitting me like lightning.

"No. That is an absolute no! You can't do that," Lizzie said, her eyes wide.

I looked between them, the answer suddenly clear. "I have to go." I turned, not even waiting for a response, and was gone.

"Oh, shit," I heard just before the door closed.

It was a longshot and would take careful planning and some help from Linda and convincing of Stacia, the woman who ran the daycare center.

It was a harebrained idea that could go horribly wrong, but I needed something drastic if I was going to get her to understand how much I needed her. And I definitely needed her. Always.

That was never going to change.

Forty-Three

Roe

It'd been three days since Thane had tracked me down in the office, and thankfully he hadn't tried again. I'd kept to myself, not wanting to talk to anyone about anything.

Which was why having an all-afternoon pow-wow with Donte drained me before I even walked into the conference room.

"Hey, are you okay?" Donte asked, waving his hand in front of my face.

I blinked at him, his deep brown eyes staring at me, his brow furrowed.

"I'm sorry, where were we?" My concentration had been shit. I was lucky I'd been able to accomplish what I had the past few days. I desperately needed to stop spacing out.

He heaved a sigh and sat back. "Have you slept at all this week?"

The puffiness of my red eyes was a dead giveaway there. "Not really."

"Eaten?"

I shrugged. "Maybe yesterday."

"How's Kinsey?"

His rapid-fire questions almost made me dizzy.

"She's fine."

"How's Thane?"

My lips pursed, and I blinked some tears away.

"Okay, there's the cause. Did you two break up?"

I nodded.

"Was he just in it because you were acting as his assistant? Does he just like to bang women who work for him, then throw them away? Do I need to get a tarp and a shovel?"

I shook my head, unable to even crack a smile at his tarp and shovel comment. "I broke up with him."

He froze and stared at me. "Why?"

"Because I love him."

Donte leaned back and narrowed his eyes. "What kind of fool answer is that?"

"I couldn't take it if he left me."

"So your logic was to leave him first? That's crazy talk." His eyes were wide, and he threw his arms in the air in apparent exasperation. I'd be exasperated with me too.

"I didn't have a choice," I tried to stress, but it was closer to a whisper with little strength behind it.

"Of course you did. Not reacting like an idiot is a pretty big choice."

"You don't understand."

He held his hands up. "Oh, no, I've never had my heart broken. No clue what that feels like."

I huffed at him. "He deserves better than me and my baggage."

"Listen, Roe, and I'm saying this from a place of love. I saw the two of you together more than once. Hell, everyone in the office saw you two together and some even heard."

Heard? Oh, fuck, no. *Please say he doesn't mean what I think he means.*

"That man looks at you like you are the moon and the stars. Why do you think he'd leave you?"

"Because they all leave me. Every man who has ever been in my life has left me, and I couldn't let it happen again. Not when I feel so much." A tear slipped out and I wiped it away.

Donte's lips pressed into a straight line. "Were you happy with him?"

I nodded. "So happy. I've never had a man take care of me like that."

"Then why would you throw him away?"

It was becoming impossible to convince anyone why when the only reason I knew was that he could do better than me.

~

By Friday, I was a zombie. I could count the number of hours I'd slept in the week since I broke things off with Thane, and they barely hit the double digits. Food? My stomach was in knots and my heart hurt so much that I couldn't fathom actually eating. Personal hygiene was just enough that I could go into work every day and do my job. Although I seriously contemplated taking some personal time, I also didn't want to feed into the rumors circulating rapidly through the office.

Thank God it was quitting time and I could grab my daughter and just go home, only I was in for a rude awakening when I arrived at the daycare.

"Kinsey isn't here, Roe," Stacia said in surprise when I arrived to pick up Kinsey, her eyes wide in horror.

The blood in my veins turned to ice. "What do you mean she isn't here?" Did Ryn come and take her? Where was she?

"That man, Thane, came to pick her up. He said you got delayed."

I blinked at her. "Th-Thane picked her up?"

Stacia nodded. "Oh, my God, Roe, I'm so sorry."

I shook my head. There was no way Thane would hurt Kinsey, but still, my mind was in overdrive. Why did he pick her up? What was he up to?

"I told him I might be late. He probably just assumed I was and picked her up just in case," I told her. Because even now, I trusted Thane with Kinsey.

That didn't mean I wasn't about to kick his ass.

"Is that true?" she asked. I nodded, and she blew out a breath. "Thank God. I was so afraid."

"Everything is fine, Stacia. Just a miscommunication," I assured her. "We'll see you on Monday morning."

"Okay, we look forward to it. Have a good weekend."

"You, too." I waved at her and headed back out the door.

My jaw clenched as I made my way down the street, pulling up my phone and dialing Thane. It rang, again and again, before his voicemail picked up.

I redialed, and it rang again.

"Answer the phone!" I screamed in frustration as I picked up the pace. The daycare was only a few blocks from my place, but it felt like miles. My heart hammered in my chest, stressed with anxiety.

Roe: Where is she?

I texted him in hopes he would respond that way, and he did almost immediately. Which meant he didn't answer the phone on purpose.

Thane: With me.

Roe: Where?

Thane: Home.

Considering he didn't have a key to my house, that meant his house. With each step, my anger grew. He knew how much I loved her, how much I protected her, so why did he go and do something so stupid?

Forty-Four

Thane

I answered the pounding on my door to a tornado of fury blowing past me.

"Are you out of your fucking mind?" she growled as she whipped through in search of Kinsey.

It was possible, but I didn't care. She was in my home, a home I was desperate to have her in full time. I knew I was about to get my ass reamed, but I didn't fucking care.

"We need to talk," I said as I followed her into the living room.

"The hell we do." She ran to Kinsey, who was happily playing on the floor.

"She's fine," I assured her.

Roe turned to me, her eyes alight with anger and unshed tears. "Why? What the hell were you thinking?"

"I was thinking there was only one way I was going to get you alone."

She shook her head and packed up the few toys and snacks into Kinsey's diaper bag. "We have nothing to talk about." She was vibrating with anger, her fury emitting into the space between us as her head snapped toward me. "Why would you do that to me? Why would you scare me like that?"

I knelt down next to her. "That wasn't my intent."

"Just because it wasn't your intent doesn't mean it was right."

"You're right, but I've been miserable this last week."

She paused, her jaw clenching. "Good." Her bottom lip trembled, and I knew she didn't mean it.

"Will you let me tell you why I did it? Picking her up today?"

Kinsey squirmed out of her grip and crawled her way over to me, then stood. Roe watched carefully as Kinsey's little hands patted my cheeks.

"Dada," she cooed at me. I froze, the small word striking my heart, and looked over to Roe, who stared wide-eyed at us.

Her gaze flickered to mine. "I didn't teach her that."

I wasn't sure I would ever have the desire for children again after I lost my son, but the second I laid eyes on Kinsey in Roe's arms that night, I'd begun to change. My chest clenched, knowing the perfect little toddler in front of me thought I was her father.

And I loved it.

Visions of Roe beside me, beautiful mixes of us all around us, made me long for something I had convinced myself I didn't want.

I was so in love with Roe. Not just her, but Kinsey as well.

I *wanted* to be Kinsey's father, and the father to an entire brood of Thane and Roe Carthwright babies.

"That's why," I whispered as I pulled Kinsey into my arms and pressed my lips to her forehead.

Roe was frozen as she stared at us. My gaze met hers.

"What I did today was drastic, and I'm so sorry I made you worry, but it was the only way I could get you to see me."

"You could have found another way," she ground out.

"Could I? Would you have seen me?" I asked. The anger in her features faltered. "You had every scrap of me packed up and gone within hours of breaking my damn heart. For what?"

"To save myself. To save Kinsey."

At least I finally had an honest answer. We were a fucking mess of abandonment issues.

"I'm going to say this now, and I will repeat it until I get it through that thick skull and the wall around your heart. Are you listening?"

She nodded.

I made certain our eyes were locked when I said the next words.

"I love you, Roe."

Her eyes widened and watered, then she began shaking her head.

"I love you so much."

"No."

"I love Kinsey and I want you both to be mine."

"Stop," she begged, her bottom lip trembling. "You made it clear."

"What clear?"

"You said she was mine."

"And she is."

She shook her head. "The way you said it. Those words. In the park. I wanted you to claim us in front of that bitch, but you didn't."

I knew then what she was talking about because they had weighed me down more than once. "I hated those words as soon as they came out. They didn't feel right then. And they don't feel right now. Kinsey is mine in the same way you're mine. All I want is to love you and take care of you."

"I don't need you to take care of me! I don't need a sugar daddy."

Sugar daddy? I was going to have to circle back around to that one after I got her straightened out.

"I want to take care of your heart, your body. I want to heal your soul. To restore your inability to trust by proving that your faith in me isn't misplaced. You've done so much for so many people over the years. You selflessly opened your home and heart to a tiny baby, despite knowing it would cost you. I want to help you. I want to be your partner in crime. Be your strength when you feel weak. I want you to rely on me."

Tears flowed down her cheeks.

"I love you, Roe. Not just for now. Not until someone else comes along, because there is nobody else for me. There is only you, and I want only you. I love you, and all I ask is for your love in return."

Her head swung from side to side, her face scrunched up. "I'm not good enough for you."

"It's me who isn't good enough for you."

"You should be with Liv."

"Why the fuck would I do that?" I asked with more of an edge to my voice than I intended.

"Because she's the right fit for you, not me. You could pick up right where you left off."

I ground my teeth for a moment to try and calm down. "Where the fuck did you ever get the idea that I wanted to be with Liv?"

"Because you said it! You were all wistful and sad and you were thinking about how things could have been with her!"

My stomach dropped. "Oh, God." I shook my head, finally understanding my pile of grave mistakes that day. "No, baby, no, that's not it at all."

"What the hell else could it have been?"

I set Kinsey back down on the floor and scooted closer to Roe. Reaching out, I then brushed her tears away.

"First—I don't want Liv. At all. We fought non-stop and I stayed with her to do the right thing for our child. She's a spoiled, gold-digging rich bitch, and I want nothing to do with her."

"Then why were you all friendly and agreeing to talk soon and all that?"

"Because we do have history, shared trauma, but that's it. What I was thinking about involved my son. I was thinking about how if I'd had him you would have opened up to me a lot sooner. That he and Kinsey could grow up as siblings." I took hold of her hand. "I was wistful about what *our* life would have been like if I hadn't lost him. It had nothing to do with Liv."

Roe seemed to consider it for a moment before asking, "Did she ever call?"

I nodded. It happened earlier in the week. "She did. She wanted to meet and I told her no, that there was no reason to ever seen her again, and to delete my phone number."

"Really?" she asked, her jaw clenching.

"Really."

"But..."

"Why do you keep trying to make something out of nothing?"

"Because I don't want to get hurt again."

"What about what you're doing to me? Do I deserve this because of the assholes in your past? Why is it so terrible that I want to take care of you because I want to? I want to be with you because you are the sunshine in my life. I've never been happier than these past few months. I love you, Roe, so much. I love Kinsey, more than I thought possible. Part of that is because I see how much you love her."

The tears kicked up again and streamed down her face as she crumpled, her hands bracing against the floor. I rubbed her back in an effort to help her calm down.

I hated seeing her so broken, but it was the only way to put us back together. I had to make her face her fears before reinforcing my support.

"That bracelet I got you for your birthday was from the heart—you are my everything."

She sat back up and rubbed her face. Kinsey cooed, her little forehead knitted as she looked at her mother. Kinsey made another uneasy transition to standing before Roe scooped her up into her arms.

"I need to show you something," I said, then stood.

She looked to my outstretched hand, trepidation in her eyes as she slipped a shaking hand into mine. After helping her up, I kept hold of her hand and pulled her to the spare bedroom.

I gestured to the door.

"Open it."

Her brow scrunched as she looked at me. "What is it?"

"Something I worked hard on for weeks and was ready to show you when you broke up with me."

The moment the door swung open Roe's eyes went wide and her mouth dropped open.

"Thane?"

"Do you like it?" I asked. The awe in her wide eyes and parted lips gave me hope.

"It's so beautiful," she whispered as she stepped in, her head whipping around as she took it all in.

"Kinsey deserves the best."

She turned back to me. "What does this mean?"

"It means I want you both in my life. Originally, this was the first step."

"What first step?"

"Of getting you to trust that I was in it for the long haul. That I was thinking about our future together." I pushed a lock of hair behind her ear. "No regerts, remember? I'm the bad tattoo you can't get rid of."

"You can't buy us back."

"Oh for fuck's sake," I hissed. I ran my hands through my hair, gripping the larger strands and pulling to vent my frustration. "Woman, I love you, but your stubbornness to accept my love drives me insane. I don't want to buy your emotions. Any gifts I give are because I want to, because all I want is for you to be happy and safe, so if a fucking bracelet makes you happy, guess what? I'm going to fucking buy it because nothing makes me happier than to see you smile."

There was no response and her continued silence was unnerving, so I just plowed ahead.

"Move in with me. Share your life with me. All of it. The good, the bad, and the beautiful. Because that's all I want. To go to bed with you next to me. To have Kinsey stop me mid-stroke with her cries. To wake on a Sunday morning to make pancakes. I want to be Kinsey's dad—on paper and always."

"You don't really want her to stop you mid-stroke," she said. The break in resistance and the small shard of the firecracker I loved coming out sparked hope.

"Not really, but if it means you're both with me, I'll suffer blue balls again and again."

"Both?" she asked, her tone a bit dubious sounding.

"You said it before—you're a package deal. Best of all, I get a 'two for the price of one' deal."

"What kind of deal is that?"

"Love. I get to experience two different kinds of love, with two different, incredible women. I don't just love you, Roe. I love Kinsey as well. Like she is my own. I want you both."

Tears filled her eyes and she set Kinsey down on the floor. She stepped around the room taking a hard look at everything.

I stayed where I was, watching her as I gave her some space. She stopped in front of the crib and stared at the sign of Kinsey's name I'd gotten made.

"It's so beautiful," she said.

I couldn't see her expression, but when she reached up and swiped at her face, I knew she was crying.

Kinsey made a high-pitched squeal as she crawled over to the chair where a stuffed bear sat. Using the edge to stand, she pulled herself up, then reached out for the bear. Once it was in her chubby fist she turned and called out for Roe.

"That's an adorable teddy, baby boo." She swallowed hard, then knelt down on the floor in front of her. "What do you think of this room?"

Kinsey fell down onto her butt and shook the bear at her and she squealed and made some other baby noises.

"Uh-huh. You think?" Roe asked like she could understand. It was adorable.

Some more gibberish, then Kinsey looked to me. "Dada." She held up her bear for me to see.

Roe swallowed hard as she also glanced my way. "I'm scared."

My muscles relaxed a bit, and I moved down to the floor with them. "Of what?"

"Of you, of the pain, of being disappointed again. I don't know how to stop it. The negative thoughts are always there, swirling in the back of my mind."

Reaching out, I took her hand in mine, and this time she didn't pull back.

"I don't know the future. Nobody does. What I do know is that I've never felt this way before and that I never want to hurt you."

"Most people don't *want* to hurt another person."

"I can tell you what I want for my future. I want you beside me every night. I want to take you to meet my family. I want to be Kinsey's dad, on paper, not just emotionally. I want to one day give Kinsey a sibling or siblings. I want you in my life forever. I'm not above begging at this point—please, let me love you."

Her face scrunched up again, and she turned toward me as she reached out. I was confused for a moment before her lips crashed against mine.

All the cold and despair that had seeped in flashed out in an explosion of heat and fire that raced through my veins.

She pulled back, her hands cupping my face as her forehead pressed against mine.

"I love you so much it scares me."

My heart slammed in my chest, and there was nothing stopping me from wrapping my arms around her and pulling her tightly to me.

She loves me. Thank fuck, she loves me.

My heart was no longer pounding. The unease inside me subsided as I held her in my arms. After the best few minutes I'd had in a week, Roe's voice permeated the silence.

"I'll move in on one condition."

"Name it. Anything." I nearly stumbled over the words I tried to get them out so fast.

"That I get to decorate it and make it feel like a home, and not a show place. I want it to be warm and inviting like this room, not cold and sterile like out there."

I pulled the wallet from my back pocket and dislodged a card from its slot. Holding it between two fingers, I presented it to her.

"This will help. Go wild."

She shook her head and covered the card with her hand. "How about we start off with some shopping together?"

I leaned forward and pressed my lips to hers. "I love family outings."

I was still trying to believe that she loved me, that the last few minutes hadn't been some elaborate dream I'd summoned. It was all real. I knew it by the tingle of her lips against mine, the hard beat of my heart that matched hers, and the hard dick that was desperate to show her just how much I would love her for the rest of our days.

Finally, things were on the right path again, with my loves beside me. It felt like I could breathe again.

Roe

Days later my apartment was full of cardboard and a mile-long to-do list. I agreed to move in, and Thane was determined to "lock it down," as he said. With my past irrationality, I didn't blame him. The pain I caused us both was damaging, and no amount of apologizing could put it right. I had to show him how much I loved him and wanted to be with him, just as he had shown me.

Since it was Thanksgiving week, the office pretty much shut down so he suggested we both take the week off. That way I could get moved in and we could celebrate Thanksgiving with my mom at his… *our* place.

By Sunday, he'd already set up a moving company for Tuesday. It didn't give me a lot of packing time, but my apartment wasn't so big that it would really take a lot of time. I'd already packed up my clothes and all my accessories along with Kinsey's, so the bedroom was pretty much done.

However, it was now Tuesday and things were a mess.

I stared at the stack of boxes, then looked to Kinsey. "Are we really doing this?"

She stared up at me and pumped her arms and legs. "Dada," she cooed.

Why did hearing her say that have to hit me so hard? If I hadn't already been on the floor the first time she said it, I would have been. The way she searched him out was a big factor in getting back together with him and agreeing to move in with him. I could see how much he adored and cherished her. I'd seen it before, but my insecurities had kept me from accepting it.

Being with Thane was overwhelming. My feelings for him were stronger than anything I'd ever felt, which was why I was so scared. That fear hadn't left me, but maybe one day it would. For now, I covered what was left with love and happiness.

A sigh left me, and I nodded in agreement. "Dada."

"Did I hear my name?" Thane said from the doorway.

As always, I was blown away by how handsome he was. My still-lingering self-doubt tried to whisper that he was too good looking for me, but I quieted it. Or rather the blinding smile directed at me stifled it.

He wanted me. He wanted *us*. And didn't Lizzie tell me to find a man who wanted us both? Thane had more than proved that he did. As my mom said when she saw the room he created, "Nobody spends thousands of dollars to make a home for a baby if he isn't madly in love."

She was right. I'd allowed all my fears and insecurities to sabotage our relationship. It was something I regretted, but Thane told me not to, that it was just a stepping stone to our forever. I knew that was just him trying to push out the negativity, and it worked.

"Kinsey was just reminding me why I was standing in a sea of cardboard."

He looked down at her all serious, and her eyes popped wide at his expression. "Good girl," he said, his lips turning back up into a brilliant smile, which Kinsey returned.

I taped up the box of kitchen utensils and labeled it with a marker before setting the heavy square on top of another.

Thane's hands landed on my hips when I turned back around, and he pulled me tightly to him.

"Hi."

"Good shower?"

He nodded and I leaned in, taking a deep pull of his spicy, citrus scent. A moan left me, and I wrapped my arms around his neck and pulled him down. I released an unsteady breath a second before his lips pressed against mine.

I deepened the kiss, wanting it to never end, but he pulled back, making me whimper. He chuckled at my discomfort.

"We have a task today, remember? The movers will be here at two and you still have a lot to do."

"Whose fault is that?" I asked, giving him a swat on the chest and a scowl as I stepped out of his arms.

"No clue. Being lazy?"

I turned to him, that shit-eating grin on his face, and threw a towel at him. "Lazy, my ass. Every time I tried to pack, you started groping me."

"You could have resisted."

I rolled my eyes. "Like that would have worked. As you said, you know my weak spots, and you exploited them."

He shrugged. "Happy fucks."

A sigh left me, and I couldn't keep the smile from my face at his lunacy.

"What furniture do you want to take?" he asked as he picked up a pad of paper and a marker.

I looked around the room, taking in what little I had. With a small apartment came little furniture.

"The bed, dresser, and nightstand from my bedroom. We can set up a guest room in the third bedroom." They were mine growing up, and I didn't want to get rid of them.

He nodded. "Good idea. I've got a desk in there and some odds and ends, but they can go in the library."

I let out a small chuckle and shook my head. "You call it a library." It was an empty flex room on the other side of the kitchen.

He shrugged. "That's what it said on the floor plan. Okay, what else?"

I bit down on my bottom lip. There wasn't much more. We were buying a new sofa together, so there was no need for mine. It was well worn, anyway. The coffee table had come from my parents, so it was definitely going. There was my small kitchen table that maybe could be used somewhere, and it was small, so why not? Last was my bookcase by the front door. It was a piece I bought with Pete, and there was nothing special about it, so it could definitely stand to be replaced with something bigger and better.

"The lamp?" I pursed my lips before moving to the built-in hutch, a box in tow. "I don't remember—are there bookshelves in the 'library'?"

"We can definitely put some in."

"Built-ins."

He nodded, then flipped the page, probably to make a note. "They'll look great."

I stared at the cabinet before me. It was filled with odds and ends, and I didn't know where to start first.

"Are you purging anything?" Thane asked as he folded one of the boxes and taped it up.

A sigh left me. "Besides some of Kinsey's stuff, I don't know. There isn't really time to."

"Are you freaking out over there?" he asked, noting my stare down with the shelf in front of me.

I glanced over my shoulder back at him. "A little." He closed the space between us and wrapped his arms around me, and I melted into him. "How can you calm me with just a touch?"

He chuckled and pressed a kiss to my temple. "Magic. Now, what has you stumped?"

I looked back at the mish-mash of items. "Do I go through it now or later?"

"Let's just make it easy and say later. Just get it all in boxes and you can go through it at home."

Home. I loved the way he said it with ease. It was going to be our home for our family.

I nodded and leaned my head back against his shoulder. "Hey."

"Hmm?"

"Have I told you today that I love you?"

His arms tightened and his voice was strained. "No."

"I love you," I whispered.

A shuddered breath left him. "I love you. So much. And if I haven't told you today, I'm so fucking happy you're moving in with me."

"Are you sure it's not too soon?"

"Nope. Not a single doubt. I want you full time. So does my cock."

I rolled my eyes and smiled. "Always with the cock."

He was giving me no wiggle room, and with his answer I realized that it didn't bother me, because in the end, that was all I'd ever wanted. To be with him. To share our lives. To never leave him.

And we were taking the biggest step toward all of that being made into more than just dreams and words. It was a reality.

We tag-teamed boxing up everything with entertaining Kinsey, and after two hours the movers arrived. Four men had everything out in just over an hour and a half like it was nothing.

I walked around the empty apartment checking for any last-minute or overlooked items, noting how much larger the space looked when it was empty. It was a small place, but it had worked. It was the home I brought Kinsey into, the home where I learned how to be a mother, and the home where I opened up my heart to someone.

As much as those memories meant to me, it was just an apartment, one that I'd only lived in for just over a year.

"Ready?" Thane asked, carrying Kinsey in his arms. She had her head against his chest and her chubby hand gripped his shirt. The sight made my heart soar.

He was the partner and father we deserved. The one who chose us both. The arrogant man with a heart just as fragile as mine.

We headed toward the entry and walked through. I gave the room one last look before I closed the door and said goodbye to my past, ready to step into my future with Thane beside me.

Forty-Six

Thane

Three months later…

My home was no longer my own.

And I loved it.

The changes Roe had made to the place were all simple and cosmetic, but they warmed everything up. From colorful rugs to curtains, a new sofa that was comfortable, not like the modern one I had before.

I gave her free reign and as hard as it was to see some things go, when the new stuff came in, I realized that she was right. All of my furniture had been sleek and modern, and while there was nothing wrong with the style and it looked nice, it wasn't very comfortable or warm.

I was stuck staring at my computer, my nerves kicking into high gear, causing me to read the same paragraph over and over. We'd made it through three major holidays and Valentine's Day with flying colors. My parents came to New York for the Christmas holiday and finally got to meet Roe and Kinsey.

Just like me, they fell in love with both of them. Linda, Roe's mom, came over as well, along with my little brother, Wyatt. It was wonderful to have everyone in our home for the holiday creating family memories in a place that had no memories before Roe.

It was just a place I lived in. Now, I truly lived in it.

Yes, Kinsey had stopped me mid-stroke more than once, but having Roe in my bed was completely worth it. Kinsey made up for it with her cuteness, and every day our connection grew.

The warm feeling that always took over when I thought of my girls was doused with my overactive nerves again.

"Get it together, Carthwright," I grumbled to myself.

A knock on my office door was a welcome break from my inability to focus.

"Come in," I called out.

Crystal smiled as she walked in. "Lunch is here," she said, holding up a bag.

My stomach gave a rumble at that and I stood, walking over the table where she was pulling containers out.

"I didn't realize how hungry I was until you walked in."

She chuckled. "You never do."

While she opened containers, I pulled out some plates and silverware I kept in a nearby cabinet. It made sharing easier, and I just liked using actual utensils and not plastic.

On Fridays, Crystal and I always ordered in and ate lunch together. It started when she was first hired on as a get-to-know-you type of gesture, and for the most part, continued on. Oftentimes, these days Roe joined us. The day's meal was from a nearby tapas restaurant.

"What's the plan for the weekend?" Crystal asked as she began piling food onto her plate. There was a knowing tone to her voice, but I refused to verify her suspicion so that I didn't jinx myself.

"Dinner with James and some other friends, along with Roe's mom."

"Her mom, too, huh?"

I narrowed my gaze at her. "Housewarming dinner."

"Sure," she said with a grin.

"Don't say a damn word."

"I didn't say anything."

"You were going to."

She shrugged. "Maybe."

"Well, don't."

"You're leaving at three today, right?"

I nodded. "Correct."

Crystal was good and didn't press for more, but I knew when the armed courier arrived earlier in the week that she knew exactly what was going on.

Near the end of lunch my phone went off with a text.

Jace the Idiot: Yo, what time is this thing tonight?

Thane: Drinks at seven, dinner at eight.

I couldn't help but chuckle at the contact name.

"What's so funny?" Crystal asked.

I turned the phone toward her and showed her the name, which made her laugh. "Let me guess—Roe?"

Roe's first meeting with Jace went as spectacularly bad as I thought it would. Jace said all the wrong things and baited Roe who just trounced him, just as she always did with me. Her wit was still something that amazed me, and even more so when directed at someone else.

After that night, Roe altered his name in my phone, and I'd never changed it because it was fitting.

Even with their bad first meeting, it turned out it apparently wasn't as awful as I believed it to be. Jace was impressed by Roe, and Roe, while annoyed by Jace, had fun with her verbal smack-down.

A few hours later there was a knock on my door, and I looked up at the most beautiful woman in the world.

"Ready?" Roe asked as she sauntered over to me.

"I will be by the time you're in front of me if you keep walking like that."

She giggled and rolled her eyes as always, then pulled on the collar of her scoop-neck shirt, exposing her gorgeous cleavage.

"Really? I want a fucking hand job on the way home for that shit."

She stood in front of me, her minx-like grin in place as she leaned over. As her lips pressed against mine, a low moan crawled out when she cupped my now straining dick.

"Fuck, woman."

"Rest of the day is ruined, might as well go home," she whispered against my lips before swiping her tongue across them.

A chuckle left me. "You're killing me."

She straightened and held out her hand. "Come on."

Roe continued to tease me and so when we got home, I pinned her to the fucking window with my cock. It helped release my tension and nerves.

Afterward I hit the shower while she went to pick up Kinsey. When she returned, I took Kinsey into the kitchen for a snack while Roe showered and I worked on prepping for dinner.

Only James knew what tonight was really about. All but Jace had visited since Roe moved in, so calling it a housewarming party was a bit false. When Roe pushed back, I explained that I just wanted a get together with our friends now that we'd made it a home.

"How's it going in here?" Roe asked as I pulled out a large wooden tray from the cabinet for the charcuterie we were putting together. She was running a towel through her wet hair, and a groan left me.

"You make me want to repeat an hour ago looking like that."

She bit down on her bottom lip and smiled. "You know I like to tease."

Oh, how I knew that. "Yes, but we have four and a half people coming over for dinner in an hour and a half."

She wrapped her arms around my waist and placed a kiss to the side of my arm. "Okay, I'll behave until they're gone."

Sex happened a lot more since she moved in, and I was not complaining one bit. I found it was a way we bonded, a way that we both needed to keep our abandonment insecurities at bay. It was odd to say that sex made us a stronger couple, but it was true. I believed living together helped as well.

A few minutes before six, Roe was finishing off the charcuterie in the dinning room while I cut up potatoes in the kitchen when the doorbell went off. Out of the corner of my eye, I caught a waddling Kinsey stomp past the kitchen door with Roe right behind her. Roe gave me a wink and blew me a kiss as she went by.

"Well, hello, my pumpkin!" I heard Linda say.

I rinsed off my hands and walked out to greet her. She had Kinsey in her arms admiring her dress when I reached her. "Welcome," I said, leaning down to kiss her cheek. Kinsey made a sound and I turned my head and kissed her as well, earning a peal of giggles.

"Evening, Thane. It all smells wonderful."

"Thanks." I had an herb-crusted beef filet roasting and some garlic cream sauce simmering. There were about to be potatoes roasting as well. There was still a lot more to go and now that Linda was there, Roe could help me again.

"Wine, Mom?" Roe asked as they walked into the dining and living room.

"I would love some."

Roe appeared back in the doorway. "Where are we?"

I glanced around. "I need you to finish up the salad, then start in on your asparagus magic and sauté the green beans."

"Okay, Captain."

I couldn't help but stare at her wearing an apron to help keep her dress clean. Visions of her wearing only it danced across my mind, and I let out a low groan.

"Stop it."

She blinked at me. "Stop what?"

"Looking so damn sexy all the time."

She giggled and stretched up to kiss my cheek. "Just like with your hotness, it can't be helped."

A little while later, the doorbell rang again and Linda answered it for us. James and Lizzie's voices bounced off the walls followed by a screech from Kinsey and an echoed one by Oliver. There would be another high-pitched sound, but Bailey was on vacation with her grandparents.

They'd barely made it through the door when another familiar voice sounded. By the intro to Linda I knew it was Jace, and on cue he appeared in front of the kitchen door.

"The party can start, *I* have arrived!"

"You mean it can end now that you're here," Roe said.

"I can't even get in the damn door and you're already on me. Just admit it, baby, you want me over this sack of dung," he said, staring at me with a grin.

Not two minutes and he was baiting her. She just grinned beside me, ready to strike back.

"I'd rather eat shit than be with you. Besides, his ass is hotter."

He slapped his hand over his heart. "You sting me, babe. That hurt. Do you know how much time I put into this ass to get it so fine?"

I jumped as Roe's hand slapped my ass, then grabbed it. "Hey, I am not a plaything in your bickering."

They both ignored me.

"You couldn't get an ass this fine if you worked on it ten hours a day. Some men are just made that way."

"What way is that?"

"Perfect."

I leaned over and kissed the top of her head as I covered the potatoes in oil and herbs. "The night starts out again with Roe on top."

"Yeah, I'd like Roe on top of me. Think I could borrow her some time?"

My eyes turned to slits as I turned to him. "Shut the fuck up and go get a drink."

He was wearing a shit-eating grin and looked between us and the group in the living room.

"So," Jace rubbed his hands together. "Are we playing strip poker tonight?"

"No!" Both James and I shouted at the same time.

Roe and I quickly finished up what we were doing so that we could join our guests. It was almost like a dance as we moved around each other, stealing kisses as we went. We had become excellent kitchen dance partners.

Finally able to take a break, we joined everyone. When we entered, Kinsey squealed and toddled over to me.

"Dada!"

"Yeah, baby boo?" I leaned over and picked her up. I looked around the room to find more than one set of eyes on me. "What?"

"Dude, she called you Dada," Jace said

"And I am."

"It's sweet," Lizzie said, daring Jace to say one bad thing about it.

It didn't matter if he did, because I was her dada in my heart and now everyone knew.

"She's your sister's kid, right?" Jace asked, looking to Roe. He didn't know much about how Kinsey came to be with Roe.

Roe nodded. "But I'm her legal guardian."

"And her mother," I added.

"Whatever happened to your sister?" Lizzie asked.

We hadn't seen Ryn since Kinsey's birthday, but when we

received more information about the case, we came to find out why.

"She got caught high by her parole officer, and now she's serving time," Roe said. "That was part of her parole. To stay off drugs."

"Well, maybe this will make her straighten out," James said, groaning at his wife when she elbowed him.

I saw how Roe's expression dropped, and I reached out for her hand. Losing Kinsey to Ryn was one of her greatest fears.

"Stop," I whispered in her ear.

She drew in a breath and straightened, then turned to me. "Thank you," she said as she lightly pressed her lips to mine.

I squeezed her hand. If things went the way I hoped, we could start the process of adopting Kinsey. At least we knew where Ryn was. I just worried how susceptive she would be to giving up her parental rights.

A little while later, we were all sitting at the table, including the kids—Kinsey in a high chair and Oliver on James's lap.

A year ago, the room we were in held none of the life it did now. Dark and grey and empty compared to the warmth to share with friends and family. I would have met Jace for drinks, then gone home, worked half of the weekend, rinsed and repeated. I couldn't imagine how my life could change with the simple act of spilled coffee.

My nerves kicked into overdrive as dinner ended. Even though we hadn't been together long, there was no doubt in my mind or heart that it was right.

We were right.

There was lots of chatter going on and I tapped my fork on the edge of my glass to get everyone's attention.

I stood, pushing my chair back, and caught James's eye. He gave me a subtle thumbs up, which helped to calm me a little.

"I wanted to thank you all for coming over tonight and christening our home as a place for friends as well as family. The night has been great, but I keep thinking there is one thing that could make it even better."

"Skinny dipping? Weed?" Jace said, making the whole table laugh.

"Somebody smack him," Roe said, to which Lizzie obliged.

With a hard swallow, I pulled the small box from my pocket and adjusted to kneeling on one knee beside Roe.

Her eyes popped wide, and her lips parted as I opened the box and exposed the diamond ring within.

"Thane?"

"Roe, from the moment you didn't so accidentally spill coffee on me," I began, earning a few chuckles from our guests. "I have been completely taken by you. At first I didn't understand why, but I learned—it's because you were meant to be my everything. We're a perfect match and I can't express the depth of my love for you. I want to blast away the rest of our fears and insecurities and bind us together forever, because I have no life without you. You, me, and Kinsey against the world. I know it hasn't been long, but I know we are right together. Will you please marry me, become my wife, and stay with me forever?"

Her bottom lip trembled, and her brow furrowed as she fought tears. "Yes!" she cried out before throwing her arms around my shoulders and pulling me close. "Yes. Yes. Yes. Forever, yes."

Epilogue

Thane

Two and a half years later…

I pushed the door open, barely making it through before Kinsey was sliding down my torso and hitting the ground. Immediately she was off, running to her room.

She was getting almost too big to carry, but it wasn't something we did often anymore. After daycare, she just liked the connection of being held after hours apart, but as soon as we were home, all bets were off.

I smiled at her before heading to the kitchen. Out of the refrigerator I pulled a small container of grapes and one of broccoli. The kid's love for broccoli amazed me. I then pulled a pack of crackers from the pantry and set them on her little play table. After filling two glasses with water, I set the one with a lid down on her table, then took the other with me to the master bedroom to check on Roe.

The lights were off and the door was open a crack. There were a few slivers of light coming from the edge of the blackout curtains that lit up the room enough to navigate and to find her eyes on me.

"Hey, baby," I said as I sat on the edge of the bed, placing the water next to her on the nightstand. My eyes adjusted to the dim light, and I brushed the hair from her face. "How are you feeling?"

"Tired," she said, unable to lift her head up. It'd been days of this, and I worried that something was really wrong. She'd been feeling off for weeks and had waved off my requests that she call the doctor, but the last few days had beaten her down too much.

"Mommy," Kinsey said as she ran in. She jumped onto the bed, but wasn't tall enough to make it. Little grunts made me chuckle at her attempts to pull herself up.

I took hold of her waist and hoisted her up onto the bed. "Tanks, Daddy," she said in her high-pitched voice before crawling across and into Roe's arms.

"Hi, baby boo, did you have a good day?"

"Yes!" she squealed. "Can go to da park?"

Roe's brow furrowed. "Mommy doesn't feel well, but Daddy might be able to take you for a little while."

Kinsey set her big round eyes on me, and I knew I was going to say yes. I couldn't deny my girls anything.

And they were my girls, in every sense. Roe and I were married a year and a half ago at my family's lake house in North Carolina, and shortly after we initiated the adoption of Kinsey. Both of us.

For the last three months, she had been officially ours—a Carthwright—and nobody could take her away. Mackinsey Ryn Carthwright.

"Your snack is on the table. Give me a few minutes to talk to Mommy and we'll go, okay?" Thankfully, St. Catherine's Park was just across the street. I didn't want to be far in case Roe needed me.

"Okay!" she cheerfully squealed before wiggling out of Roe's arms and sliding off the edge of the bed.

I looked back to Roe. "Did you talk to the doctor?"

She nodded and pointed to a piece of paper on the nightstand.

My hands shook as I reached out, my heart hammering to find out what horror had taken over my love.

I read the results.

Then read them again.

My eyes met hers. "Well, I guess that explains a lot."

She burst out laughing and turned into the pillow. I leaned over and climbed onto the bed, caging her beneath me.

I moved my hand between us and rested it on her abdomen. "Why, Mrs. Carthwright, I do believe you have officially made all of my dreams come true."

"Takes two to tango."

"If you are up to it, I plan to tango all night long in celebration. But how?"

She turned onto her back and locked eyes with me. "My noon alarm wasn't doing such a good job reminding me a while back."

A while back? "How far along?"

"About ten weeks."

Right around the time of the adoption. We were so busy between the adoption and all the paperwork that went with it. We visited Ryn where she was still in jail. I was ready for a fight, but Ryn simply locked eyes with her sister and said, *"You have given her a life I'll never be able to. I've messed up a lot of things in my life, but giving you my daughter is the one good thing I can do for her."*

Signing over her rights was a peace offering and belated wedding present for all that she'd put Roe through. She wasn't going to fight it, and in the end, they hugged with tears in their eyes before we left.

Memorial Day weekend it was official, and we had a party to celebrate the adoption—a huge celebration with friends and family. Kinsey had no clue what it was all about, but she got presents, so to her it was like an early Christmas.

Getting pregnant was in our future, but we'd decided to make it past the wedding and the adoption before trying.

"Guess that whole trying thing is out," I said as I leaned down and ghosted my lips against her neck, pressing them against her skin every few inches.

"Practice really does make perfect."

"I *love* practice."

She bit down on her bottom lip and smiled at me. "Me too. We can always practice for number two."

A groan left me, and I ground my hips against hers. "You're getting me worked up."

"I like it when you're worked up."

"But you forget I'm about to take our daughter to the park. I'm going to look like a massive perv going down there with a hard-on." I loved how her expression melted every time I called Kinsey "our daughter." "And you're tired."

"I think you could perk me up a little bit."

I growled against her neck and bit down on her most sensitive spot, earning a gasp from my beautiful wife below me. She bowed against me, her hands gripping my suit jacket hard.

"Such a tempting little siren. You know we can't right now, and you're just egging me on because you're a teasing little minx who loves to see me suffer."

"Only sexually."

I pulled myself away from her and palmed my cock through my slacks as I stood. "This is your fault."

"And I love it," she said, running her tongue across her lips as she reached out for me.

I stepped forward and groaned when her tiny hand gripped

my shaft. "It's warm out. You should strip into something cooler."

"You just want to touch my cock and get me even more insane for you."

"Admit it—you love that I want you so much."

I leaned down and pressed my lips to her forehead, then down to place a light kiss to her lips. Anything more, and Kinsey was going to walk in to my being balls deep in her mother.

And I really didn't want a repeat of that. At least last time we were clothed.

"I do," I said. Before things heated up even more, I stepped into the walk-in closet, giving me some space to try to calm down.

I pulled off my suit and changed into some shorts and a T-shirt. It was enough time that I was down to half-mast when I walked back into the bedroom, only to find my wife masturbating. One of her pierced nipples was exposed and her eyes were heavy and dark. It took everything in me to keep from pouncing on her right then.

"Fuck," I hissed. "You're going to kill me."

I pulled the blanket from her body to find her panties pushed to the side, two fingers slipping in and out of her slit.

I focused on the sounds outside the room and found Kinsey happily singing, the tunes of one of her videos in the background. Probably focused on her snack.

A moan hit my ear and snapped my attention to the woman writhing on my bed. She was close. I could tell by the uncontrollable roll of her hips. I smacked her hand away before grabbing her thighs and pressing them against the bed.

"She-devil," I whispered before biting the soft flesh of the inside of her thigh. I ran my tongue across her opening, taking my first taste in days of her sweet musk. A groan left me and I licked deeper, then flicked her clit with the tip of my tongue, making her jump before starting over again.

I'd barely begun when her hands gripped my hair, holding me against her as she moved across my face.

Not today.

I tightened my grip on her hips and held her still, going in for the final blow.

"Fuck!" she hissed when I took her clit between my teeth. Another low whimper, thighs clamped around my head, her body shaking almost unable to contain the pleasure that rocked her.

She shattered, and I slowly lapped at her until she calmed down.

With a last kiss, I slipped her panties back in place and stood. I knew my eyes were dark with lust. All I wanted to do was bury myself between her thighs and find release.

"Daddy! We go!" Kinsey called from the doorway, then ran back out.

Roe looked pleasantly sated as she smiled at me. I loved that look, but right then I hated it because I needed a release I wasn't going to get.

"You owe me. I'm talking balls-deep, throat-fucking blow job."

Her eyes flashed in excitement. "Whatever my husband wishes."

I glared at her. "Your husband wishes not to go to the park at full fucking attention. If I go to jail, you're going to tell the judge why I'm in this state."

"Yes, my love," she said sweetly.

I moved to the bathroom to wipe my face off before returning to the bedroom. Roe was almost asleep again, and I bent down and pressed my lips to her forehead.

"I love you."

"Luf you," she managed to whisper, though almost incoherent.

"We'll be back," I said and found her completely gone to the world.

On the elevator ride down I tried to will my dick to calm down, but I knew that was going to be a problem, because what I felt couldn't be cured by cold water thoughts and baseball.

No, not today. My wife was pregnant, and we were going to expand our family.

"Ready, Daddy?" Kinsey asked.

"Yes, baby boo," I said with a smile. It was the absolute truth I felt in my soul.

I was ready to spend the rest of my life happy in the arms of my family.

A last note from Roe…

On March first, Malcolm Alexander Carthwright was born. It was Thane's idea to name our son after my father.

I no longer had one foot out the door. No, both feet were snuggled under Thane's leg. He kept them nice and warm, just like my heart.

I used to believe that I wasn't destined for true love. It was just in fairy tales and romance novels, but Thane proved that real life could offer a deeper love than any story. That love was more powerful than all my self-doubts and trust issues.

Our story was just beginning, with the first pieces in place, and I couldn't wait to spend the rest of my life surrounded by the ones I loved.

The End

Acknowledgements

To Danielle for helping me wrangle the arrogant ass.

To my boo, Massy, for always believing in me and all of her "You know I love you…" nuggets of wisdom. You are my rock.

Soundtrack

Come & Go—Juice WRLD

Savage Love—Jawsh 685

X—Jonas Brothers (feat. KAROL G)

Break My Heart—Dua Lipa

Blinding Lights—The Weekend

What A Man Gotta Do—Jonas Brothers

Capital Letters—Hailee Steinfeld & BloodPop

Before You Go—Lewis Capaldi

Bang!—AJR

Raising Hell—Kesha (feat. Big Freedia)

Trampoline—SHAED

Senorita—Shawn Mendes & Camila Cabello

About the Author

K.I. Lynn is the *USA Today* Bestselling Author from The Bend Anthology and the Amazon Bestsellers, *Breach* and *Becoming Mrs Lockwood*. She spent her life in the arts, everything from music to painting and ceramics, then to writing. Characters have always run around in her head, acting out their stories, but it wasn't until later in life she would put them to pen. It would turn out to be the one thing she was really passionate about.

Since she began posting stories online, she's garnered acclaim for her diverse stories and hard hitting writing style. Two stories and characters are never the same, her brain moving through different ideas faster than she can write them down as it also plots its quest for world domination…or cheese. Whichever is easier to obtain… Usually it's cheese.

Website—www.kilynnauthor.com

Facebook—www.facebook.com/kilynn.breach

Twitter—twitter.com/KI_Lynn_

Instagram—www.instagram.com/k.i.lynn

Get my Newsletter—http://bit.ly/1U9NSoC

More books from K.I. LYNN!

Wicked Rule

I am the ruler.

The old guards are changing, and the new blood is taking over. My role? I am the new king of the de Loughrey family. The new ruler.

But my place isn't set in stone, and my grandfather delivers an ultimatum—get married and produce an heir, or lose the empire.

I don't do relationships. I don't do love.

I do business and money.

But I would do my waitress.

It's a business contract, an act of deception, one that involves time, an "I do," and a lot of money.

There's only one problem—her clause in our contract.

No sex.

But I'm the wicked one, and I'll have her beneath me no matter what.

Find out more here—books2read.com/WickedRule

Ruthless Rule

They call me the ruthless ruler…and they're not wrong.

In the boardroom and the bedroom I take no prisoners and when I'm done, it's all stop.

There's something about my father's new assistant and a chance encounter brings us closer than I ever expected. Once isn't enough, but for the first time in my life, I'm shot down.

Me.

A de Loughrey.

So I sweeten it with money. An indecent proposal that gives both of what we need.

When I learn her secrets I find the impossible bloom inside me.

I'm the ruthless ruler, but she has me by the heart.

Business is business, and when it's done, I don't know what will happen to the heart she holds.

I've met my ruthless match.

Find out more here—books2read.com/RuthlessRule

That Night

I got pregnant on New Year's Eve.

That night was hands down the best night of my life. A magical night with the man of my dreams.

The aftermath changed everything.

After weeks of silence from him and a positive pregnancy test, it was safe to say I was in full out panic mode.

Until I walked into a conference room only to find Mr. Man-of-my-dreams-father-of-my-unborn-child at the head of the table.

Turns out the VP of finance isn't an old boring guy with white hair.

Two different cities.

A baby on the way.

An intense attraction.

And he's technically my boss.

Life just got even more complicated.

Find out more here—books2read.com/ThatNightKILynn

Domenico

The mafia never lets you go.

I thought I was safe, free, but I never expected to find myself locked in a cage.

I'm in his territory. His prison.

The beast.

A fate worse than death awaits me if I can't get away, so when the opportunity of salvation presents itself I grab it, even if I'm unsure if I can trust the hand I'm holding.

The only way out is through, exposing secrets and spilling blood.

Things aren't how they appear. Nobody is what they seem.

Forever and All The Afters

He promised me forever.

Then he boarded a plane for a college a thousand miles away and never returned. A decade later there's a ring on my finger with a new promise from a new love.

Just as my life falls into place, pretty as the pages of a magazine, my world is knocked over. The moment he touches me everything around me begins to crack, exposing all the lies I've told myself.

Every glance reminds me. Every touch ignites.

Things aren't how they used to be.

Love isn't easy.

Find out more here—books2read.com/ForeverAndAllTheAfters

Welcome to the Cameo Hotel

I get what I want.

When I walked through the door of the Cameo Hotel I didn't expect such a beauty to be working the front desk.

The effect she has on me is intense, and I make her life a living hell because of it.

I love her spirit, her internal defiance when completing the most inane task I assign her. My two week stay has turned into unending, just to be near her.

She's under my every command if she wants to keep me happy.

There's one last thing I want.

Her.

Find out more here—

books2read.com/WelcomeToTheCameoHotel

Becoming Mrs. Lockwood

Every girl has dreams of meeting Prince Charming, or at least I know I did.

A fairy tale-like meeting of love at first site.

Real life and fairy tales are very different.

I'm just a small town Indiana girl that had a chance encounter with one of Hollywood's golden boys. You may think you know where this story goes—not even close.

Life is different. Marriage is hard. It's even worse when you're strangers.

Find out more here—books2read.com/BecomingMrsLockwood

Six

I had a one-night stand. It wasn't my first, but it would be my last.

A gun to the head.

A trained killer.

A deadly conspiracy.

Kidnapped and on the run, my life and death is in the hands of a sadist captor who happens to be my one-night stand. Armed with countless weapons, money, and new identities, the man I call Six drags me around the world.

The manhunt is on and Six is the next target. Can we find out who is killing off the Cleaners before they find us?

Two down, seven to go.

When it's all over he'll finish the job that dropped him into my life, and end it.

Stockholm Syndrome meets bucket list, and the question of what would you do to live before you died. The questions aren't always answered in black and white. Gray becomes the norm as my morals are tested.

Death is a tragedy, and I'll do anything to stay alive.

Are you ready for the last ride of your life? Six has a gun to your head—what would you do?

This isn't a love story.

It's a death story.

Find out more here—
books2read.com/Six-KILynn
Check out the Trailer—youtu.be/fzpON3PadIA

Breach Book 1

His body was sin, his cock was sin, and I was a sinner.

To keep myself safe I hide in the world and let life move around me.

My new partner, Nathan, isn't safe. Far from it.

The darkness coils around him, hidden by a shield created by a blinding smile. But those who live in shadows see past the façade we create.

Even in darkness, there is light. A spark that ignites, then explodes.

Every filthy word from his mouth, every possessive touch—I crave them, need them. Violent and passionate and everything I need to fill the void inside me, but one thing is missing.

He can never love me.

More than my heart is on the line, and I don't know if I'll survive our breach.

The Executive

Business is king, and I have an empire to topple.

Ivy is my new assistant and a threat to me. She's my undoing. If ever I was to believe in a cosmic connection, it was the moment I met her.

For years I've had one goal—revenge. As CEO, I have crafted a strategic plan for business, but never a life beyond.

With one touch from her, the veil is lifted. Things are different, and every moment I'm near her, my world begins to change.

A wall of propriety keeps me from her. I need her as my pawn in this war, beside me in battle. Sharing the secrets of my enemies, and her desires in my bed. Her body to claim as mine.

Getting what I want has consequences.

Collateral damage is real.

In the game of crushing kings of men, I never planned on my heart being a sacrifice.

Find out more here—books2read.com/TheExecutive

Cocksure

Co-written with Olivia Kelley

A life altering lie, ten years, and one wild night later, the game has changed.

Niko

My life is great. I love my job, have awesome friends, and a great family.

Women love me, even if they know it's just for a night.

I always thought love at first sight was bullshit. Then she came storming into my life. She tore through my every rule, rocked my world, and knocked me on my ass.

There's only one problem…she lied.+

Turns out my best friend's little sister isn't so little anymore.

Everly

I stole a night with my fantasy. Lied to him.

After ten years of not seeing each other, Niko doesn't even recognize me.

So I take what I want from him, what I need from him. Without worry. Without consequence.

What I didn't count on was the lingering need for him.

Once the truth is out, the game changes. There are consequences.

I should have known nothing in my life is ever simple.

My brother is going to kill his best friend and I have nine months to figure out what I want.

Find out more here—
books2read.com/Cocksure-Lynn-Kelley

Need Book 1

Co-written with N. Isabelle Blanco

I was Kira's from the first moment I saw her. Maybe it was love at first sight, but I was only ten.

She became my best friend.

My crush.

The girl I can't live without.

But I have to.

She was almost mine, but my father took away my chance.

Now she lives across the hall from me. Instead of the title of girlfriend, she's now my stepsister.

But that doesn't stop how I feel, how I want her. Thankfully, I'm off to college two hundred miles away, but even that doesn't help.

She's under my skin, all around me, and I watch her morph from a sexy teenager to an irresistible woman.

I can't take it anymore, I need her.

Is it possible to ever be happy without the one person you *need*?

"I'm Brayden, baby. The man you've been dreaming about your whole life. And I'm about to fucking show you why."

Part 1 of a 3 part series.

Find out more here—books2read.com/NeedSeries

CPSIA information can be obtained
at www.ICGtesting.com
Printed in the USA
LVHW020152290921
698984LV00001B/19

9 781948 284318